LISA DIETRICH

In the Silence of DARKNESS

In the Silence of Darkness
Copyright © 2025 Lisa Dietrich
All rights reserved.

ISBN: (ebook) 978-1-964636-51-1
(print) 978-1-964636-53-5

Inkspell Publishing
207 Moonglow Circle #101
Murrells Inlet, SC 29576

Edited By Toni Kelley
Cover art By Emily's World By Design

DEDICATION

For Jen

LISA DIETRICH

Xma k'o wi naqi la' lo k'olik.
Xa kachamanik,
Katz'ininik,
Chi q'equ'm,
Chi aq'ab'.

Whatever might be is simply not there: only murmurs, ripples in the dark, in the night.

Popol Vuh: Translated from K'iche' by
Dennis Tedlock

LISA DIETRICH

PROLOGUE

I am in a dense shadowy tangle of trees; the air is thick with an eerie silence that seems to swallow all sound. Standing at the entrance of a cave, its mouth resembling a gaping maw, I feel an ancient energy emanating from the dark interior. I know I am supposed to enter, but I am afraid.

A low growl rumbles behind me, and I turn to find a jaguar emerging from the shadows. Its coat is black as midnight, but in the dim light, I can see rosettes shifting beneath the surface like hidden stars wheeling across the night sky. What strikes me most are its eyes—amber-gold and unnervingly human, filled with an intelligence that makes my heart race for reasons that have nothing to do with fear.

The jaguar circles me slowly, its muscled body moving with fluid grace. Each time it passes, it draws closer, until I can feel the heat radiating from its body. Its tail brushes against my leg, sending shivers up my spine. There's something almost protective in the way it positions itself between me and the darkness.

I hesitate at the threshold, and a Vision Serpent appears before us, its scales glistening with a supernatural glow. The jaguar tenses beside me, a warning growl vibrating through its chest. But the serpent's eyes lock onto mine, and I feel my consciousness shift. The jaguar presses against my leg, as if urging me to stay, but I find myself walking into the cave.

The jaguar follows, its presence both reassuring and unsettling—like a half-remembered dream trying to tell me something important. Time and space become distorted. The walls pulse with life, echoing with distant whispers that grow louder as I venture deeper. And then I see her.

Nayla stands at the edge of an underground lake, her eyes vacant, her skin pallid as if drained of life. Our father stands beside her, his hand resting on her shoulder. His presence is both comforting and distressing. Our father is dead. Why is he standing next to Nayla?

"There can be no rebirth without death." The words, coming from nowhere and everywhere, reverberate inside the chamber.

The water surface ripples ominously and a white snake emerges. It wraps around Nayla's legs and slithers up her torso. The jaguar snarls, its fur bristling as it crouches beside me. For a moment, its form seems to waver, like heat rising from sun-baked stone, almost taking on a human shape.

An owl flies through the dark, landing on my father's outstretched arm. My father disappears, transforming into Hun-Came, the Maya god of death, his malevolent smile taunting me. The jaguar springs forward but passes through Hun-Came like smoke.

"Run! Run, Nayla!" I scream.

Nayla turns her empty eyes toward me. "There can be no rebirth without death."

I watch in horror as the snake crawls into my sister's mouth and the skin melts from her bones.

The jaguar's roar splits the darkness—something ancient and wild that makes my blood sing with recognition. As the shadows consume us, those amber eyes are the last thing I see.

CHAPTER ONE

The average person lives 28,000 days. That's roughly 4,000 weeks. My twin sister? She lived each day as if the universe might cut her time short, as if she knew something the rest of us didn't. Brave, brash, utterly fearless—she was everything I wasn't. Nayla was always dragging me into situations I would prefer to avoid—like flying in a very small plane 500 feet above the endless green sprawl of the Guatemalan jungle.

I squinted against the harsh light as I stared out of the window. Below me, the jungle stretched in every direction, an unbroken expanse of emerald with winding rivers snaking through it like veins. There was nothing but wild, untamed nature as far as I could see.

"It won't be much longer," Raúl, the pilot, shouted over the loud drone of the engines, his voice crackling over the headset.

I nodded absently, my eyes fixed on the endless canopy below, searching for the archaeological site. I wasn't here for the beauty of the landscape.

Nayla and I called ourselves "almost" twins. We were twins, but we did not share a birthday. I was born at 11:54

p.m. Nayla was born the next morning at 12:19 a.m. Our mother liked to say we were two sides of the same coin. Our father called me his hija de la luna—daughter of the moon. Nayla was his hija del sol—daughter of the sun. There was never any doubt who generated the light and who reflected it in my relationship with my sister.

Our father had died when we were young, murdered in Guatemala. He had been a lawyer and Indigenous rights activist fighting against injustice. For Nayla and me, his absence became a presence, the ghost that haunted our childhood. Nayla embraced our father's Guatemalan legacy like a second skin, wrapping herself in his stories, his traditions, his dreams by studying to become an archaeologist and an expert on the ancient Maya. Me? I ran from it, staying as far away as I could from Guatemala as I built a fortress of facts and logic to control the messiness and chaos of life in law school.

As I glanced out the window of the plane, a sudden memory surfaced, unbidden. Nayla and I, barely six years old, crouched in our backyard, digging furiously with plastic shovels.

"We're gonna find buried treasure, Niki!" Nayla had exclaimed, her green eyes shining with excitement.

I remember pausing, frowning at the deepening hole. "But what if we dig too deep and fall into the underworld?"

Nayla had laughed, tossing her ponytail. "Then we'll fight the Lords of Death and become heroes!"

I smiled wryly at the memory. At twenty-five years old, Nayla was still digging for treasure.

"Over there." Raúl pointed out the window, his finger tracing a distant shape.

I followed his gesture and saw it: a stone pyramid, ancient and weathered, rising above the trees like a forgotten relic. Scattered around it were splashes of blue, orange, and red—the tents and tarps of the archaeological team, dotting the jungle floor like confetti in the green abyss.

Raúl dipped the nose of the plane, aiming for a narrow

strip of red dirt, wedged between the towering walls of jungle. It didn't look like much of a runway, more like a thread of earth barely wide enough for us. My stomach lurched as we banked sharply, the small plane shuddering with the shift.

I gripped the armrests tighter, my knuckles white.

"No te preocupes," Raúl's voice crackled through my headset again. "It'll be a soft landing."

I forced a tight smile, though my stomach disagreed. He chuckled, clearly enjoying himself.

As we approached the landing strip, something caught my eye on the horizon. A ridge of darkness, shimmering like smoke, undulated just above the treetops. I blinked, leaning closer to the window. Was it a fire? No—there were no flames, no smoke rising into the air. It wasn't smoke at all. It was...something else.

I inhaled deeply, willing myself to keep calm as I watched the canopy below ripple, as if something massive moved beneath the surface. The trees shifted unnaturally, like the jungle itself was alive. I pressed my forehead against the cool glass, heart racing as a shadow rolled over the treetops, moving fast, swallowing the jungle in its path.

I glanced at Raúl, but he was focused on the landing, completely unaware of the strange phenomenon. Lately, I'd been seeing things out of the corner of my eye—shadows that moved with intent and shapes that seemed almost alive. I dismissed them as stress-induced hallucinations, but I was beginning to worry that they might be something more.

I turned back to the window, my breath catching in my throat. The shadow was gaining on us, closing the distance between the jungle and our plane. It was like a wave—dark, roiling, and alive—rising from the depths of the forest. It swept toward us with terrifying speed, and I braced myself for impact.

The plane shuddered violently.

"Turbulence!" Raúl shouted over the roar of the engines, gripping the controls as we descended.

Muscles tense, I twisted in my seat to look behind us, just in time to see the shadow crash against some invisible barrier surrounding the archaeological site. It was as if the air itself was a shield, holding back the darkness. The wave of shadow slammed into the barrier, cresting and curling like a wave breaking on a shore, before collapsing in on itself. It pooled in swirling, dark patches among the trees, then slowly seeped away, vanishing as if it had never been there at all.

The plane bounced as we touched down on the dirt landing strip and a flash of movement caught my eye. Hidden within the dense canopy, a figure emerged briefly— like a mirage materializing from the jungle's depths. A man, black hair, his skin the color of burnished bronze, stared at us. There was something vaguely familiar about him. For a heartbeat, our eyes met. His eyes were an impossible shade of gold. I blinked. When I looked again, he had vanished.

"There can be no rebirth without death."

The voice echoed in my mind, an eerie, whispered memory. The same phrase that I'd been hearing in my dreams for weeks. Nayla's voice. An icy chill crawled down my spine despite the heat pressing in around me. I closed my eyes, trying to shake the feeling, but the dread lingered, gnawing at my insides.

What the hell had Nayla gotten us into this time?

CHAPTER TWO

The propellers whirred to a stop, and Raúl turned to me with a grin. "See? Soft landing, just like I promised."

I unbuckled my seatbelt with shaky hands, managing a weak smile in return. My legs felt wobbly as I stepped out of the plane and into the thick heat of the jungle. The humid air wrapped around me like a suffocating blanket as I breathed in the scent of damp earth and greenery.

In the distance, I could hear happy shouting. A group of people were hurrying toward us from the direction of the excavation site. I scanned the faces as they approached, my heart quickening. But the one face I desperately wanted to see—Nayla's—wasn't among them.

"Nayla, I'm here. Where are you?"

Our connection had always been more than just sibling intuition. Even as kids, we had a way of communicating beyond words, a bond that stretched farther than most twins ever knew. We didn't need to speak aloud to understand each other's thoughts. But now, as I reached out mentally, there was only silence.

The group gathered around the plane, glancing at me curiously as they began unloading the supplies Raúl had brought. Their eyes flickered between me and the cargo, but I stood apart, feeling a gnawing emptiness. The humid air clung to me, each breath feeling like inhaling steam. The jungle loomed on all sides, thick and tangled, as if the trees and vines had conspired to trap everything within.

"Ny? Where are you?"

I willed my thoughts out into the thick air, hoping she'd somehow hear me. The back of my skull suddenly prickled and I whipped around, half-expecting to see my sister. Instead, my gaze caught a shadow flitting between the trees. For a moment, I glimpsed those impossible gold eyes again, widening with surprise as they met mine.

"Hello."

Startled, I turned around to see an older man with sun-weathered skin and graying hair approach. His brow furrowed as he took in my appearance, his gaze lingering a beat too long. I recognized the look—people who had never seen Nayla and I together always did that double-take, the same expression of confusion mixed with recognition. My sister and I had the same features, the same build, but while I inherited our mother's pale skin and our father's dark hair and eyes, Nayla had our father's olive complexion and our mother's striking green eyes.

He extended his hand, a polite smile tugging at the corner of his lips. "I'm Dr. Kelling." His tone was friendly, but his eyes searched mine as if expecting me to explain myself.

I shook his hand awkwardly. "I'm Nayla's sister Nikita. Most people call me Niki." I noticed the way Kelling"s jaw tightened at the mention of my relationship with Nayla. I looked over the collection of people unloading the plane. "Where is she?"

The muscle in Kelling"s jaw jumped. He hesitated, weighing his words carefully. "She's left the site."

"Left?" My voice rose. My gaze darted toward the excavation site—an exposed, fragile thing in the heart of this untamable place. The trenches looked like open wounds in the earth, and I felt a chill, as if the jungle were eager to close them up again, to bury everything that had been uncovered. "What do you mean left? Where did she go?"

Dr. Kelling sighed heavily. "Apparently, she decided that she needed to visit some of the local villages to gather information."

"Are you saying that my sister's out there in the jungle?" A knot of anxiety twisted tighter in my chest. Nayla always chased after the unknown with reckless abandon, but this time it felt different. I shot a fearful look at the menacing wall of undergrowth and trees that looked ready to swallow everything in their path.

"Hey, Kip."

With a look of relief, Dr. Kelling abruptly broke off our conversation. I turned to see a tall, broad-shouldered man, his blonde, sun-bleached hair tied back in a ponytail, jogging toward us. Under a battered broad-brimmed hat, he wore a blue bandana around his head. A silver and turquoise ear stud glinted in the sunlight, giving him a roguish, pirate-like appearance. His eyes, a startling shade of blue, raked over me before turning back to Dr. Kelling.

"Everything's unloaded and Raúl's asking if you have anything for the return trip."

Kelling nodded. "Yes, I do." He turned once again to face me with a brief nod. "Niki, this is Jake Starmer. One of the grad students. He works with Nayla. Jake, Niki is Nayla's sister. Perhaps you can help answer her questions while I take care of this."

Jake flashed a row of perfect teeth my way. "I knew it! The minute I saw you, I knew you were related to Nayla. You look just like her."

Normally, I might have smiled back at his flirty tone, but my mind was already spinning with the possibilities of my missing sister. My forehead creased with worry. "Where's Nayla?" I asked, cutting straight to the point.

He shrugged. "We don't know. She didn't exactly leave an itinerary. She just kind of took off."

I sighed heavily and looked down at the ground as I rubbed my temples. I could feel the tension headache building already. I'd been trying to convince myself for weeks that Nayla was fine, and that my concern was the result of anxiety and an overactive imagination. It seemed that Nayla was just being her usual impetuous self which didn't mean that she hadn't found trouble, but it didn't sound too dire. "That sounds like my sister. When is she expected back?"

Jake's easy smile faltered slightly. "We thought she'd be back today, but she hasn't shown up yet."

My head snapped up. "What?"

"I'm sure it's nothing to be worried about." Jake's tone was relaxed, but I caught a flicker of concern in his eyes. "You know how she is—always getting caught up in something."

"Exactly," I muttered, more to myself than him. *That's what I was afraid of.*

The sound of a ringing bell interrupted us. Jake's easy smile returned. "Lunch time. You can come up to the Dining Hall and meet the rest of the crew. Who knows? Maybe Nayla will be back by the time we're finished eating."

I hoped so. While no one at the excavation site seemed concerned, I couldn't shake the feeling that something was wrong.

I followed Jake along the narrow path leading to the excavation site, a patch of scarred earth carved out of the jungle. The trees had been pushed back just enough to make space for tents and equipment among the ruins. Blue tarps, their color a startling contrast to the green foliage and red dirt around them, were strung between the trees, offering makeshift shelter for the open trenches and exposed fragments of ancient stone walls.

The smell of freshly turned earth dominated the air around the site, mingling with the scent of canvas and plastic tarps baking under the relentless midday sun. Though the walk wasn't far, the heat and humidity caused my shirt to cling to my damp skin. I wiped the perspiration from my brow with the back of my hand. "Toto, we're not in Southern California anymore," I mumbled under my breath.

"Are you studying archaeology also?" Jake asked.

"No." I shook my head. "That's Nayla's specialty. I just finished law school."

"A lawyer, huh?" He gave me an appraising look, before the roguish grin returned. "Imagine that. Two brainy and beautiful women in the same family."

I rolled my eyes, but I couldn't hide the small smile that rose unbidden to my lips. In her letters, Nayla always referred to the other grad students with nicknames. With his roguish good looks, bandana, and smooth talk, Nayla's nickname for him was perfect: Captain Jack. He would be a shoo-in for the next *Pirates of the Caribbean* movie.

We stopped in front of an open-air structure sporting support posts and a low-slung thatch roof stretched over two plywood tables. "Here we are," Jake said with a grand sweep of his arm. "Welcome to the Dining Hall of Choja q'eq. Finest dining this side of the jungle."

He ducked under the roof, I followed. A short, older woman stood by a wood-burning stove, expertly cooking corn tortillas on the comal. Her hands rhythmically patting masa, while a pot of beans simmered on the burner.

Jake sniffed the air, switching easily from English to Spanish. "Buenas tardes, Doña Juana. It smells great, as always." He draped an arm over my shoulders. "This is Niki, Nayla's sister. She's joining us for lunch today."

Doña Juana glanced over her shoulder, her expression as steady and serious as her hands. She regarded me with those sharp black eyes. "Nayla is not here," she said flatly, her tone heavy with something unspoken.

I forced a weak smile. "So, I've been told."

"Hmph." She turned back to the comal.

"Doña Juana doesn't talk much, but she cooks like a dream," Jake said in Spanish, loud enough for her to hear.

11

His voice held that teasing tone again, the one that was impossible to pin down as either sincere or simply charming.

Another "hmph" from Doña Juana, though I saw her cheeks lift in the faintest hint of a smile at the corners. She patted another tortilla into shape, dropping it onto the hot pan with practiced precision.

I gently pushed Jake's arm off my shoulder. "You are quite the charmer, aren't you?"

He grinned and dropped his arm, easily code switching back to English once again. "Can't hurt, right? Come on, I'll introduce you to the crew."

A group of Guatemalan men sat at one of the tables "Caballeros, this is Niki," Jake said in Spanish with the wide smile of a television game show host. "Niki, meet our local talent."

I nodded and smiled. The men tipped their hats. We exchanged "mucho gustos."

Next, Jake led me to a table where a group of graduate students were gathered, their half-eaten plates of beans, rice, and tortillas spread before them.

"Everyone, this is Niki. Nayla's sister," Jake announced as he plopped down on the bench next to a wiry guy wearing a backward baseball cap. "You guys can introduce yourselves."

The only woman at the table slid over to create a space for me. "I'm Alma Soto." She smiled warmly; her lively brown eyes gleaming. "Nayla and I share a tent. She's told me a lot about you."

"Nice to meet you," I said as I sat beside her.

The guy in the backward cap grinned, pushing an empty plate toward me. "Enrique Ramirez. I gotta say, it's kinda freaky how much you look like Nayla."

"It goes with the territory. We are twins," I explained, sliding the plate closer.

"Ohhh, right. That makes sense." Enrique laughed, slapped his hand theatrically against his forehead. "Why didn't I think of that?"

David, a thin, pale guy, with thinning hair, and deeply etched frown lines, rolled his eyes and passed me the stack of tortillas. "David Lundquist," he said flatly.

Next to him, a bearded man with a scholarly air and wireless glasses paused his chewing just long enough to stare dispassionately at me and mutter, "Roman Wernecke," before returning to eat his food.

"Nice to meet you all," I said, mentally matching their faces with my sister's nicknames to each of them. Alma with her long braid was easy, my sister called her Rapunzel. Knowing my sister's penchant for snark, I pegged David as "Mr. Sunshine" and Enrique as "El Cerote." Roman with his beard, glasses and air of detached analysis was definitely "Freud," leaving Dr. Kelling as "Cacique," ruler of this archaeological kingdom.

A slight awkwardness hung in the air as I spooned some beans and rice into my tortilla. The silence stretched until Alma asked, "So, did anyone find anything exciting today?"

Jake swallowed a bite and wiped his mouth with the back of his hand. "Unless you count scorpions, not much."

David's dry voice cut in. "That's what you get for digging in Nayla's trench." His eyes shifted toward me. "Did your sister tell you about discovering the jade pectoral that has "cursed" our excavation?"

"No…" I said cautiously, setting my tortilla down.

Alma sighed, clearly annoyed. "Don't be ridiculous," she muttered, shooting David a look before turning back to me. "The excavation is not cursed. We've just had a string of unlucky coincidences, that's all."

Enrique grinned. "Well, you have to admit, they didn't start until after Nayla found the pectoral."

My gaze shifted between the grad students. "A pectoral? What is that?"

Alma turned to face me, pointedly ignoring the others. "A pectoral is kind of like a medallion or jewelry that the ancient Maya would wear on their chests. Nayla found a very unusual blue jade one with one of the skeletons she was excavating."

"Did she think it was cursed?"

David raised an eyebrow, his tone biting. "You'll have to ask Nayla. Oh wait—you can't because she took off on some wild goose chase."

Alma's smile faded as she gave David a sharp look. "Cut it out. Nayla left to do some research in the local villages. She is not on some wild goose chase."

"Do any of you know where she might be? Or when she's planning on returning?" I asked, my eyes drifting around the table.

"If she comes back." Enrique leaned in, his voice dropping conspiratorially. "Li Xul might have turned the ancient Mayan spirits loose on her." He laughed aloud at his own joke.

Jake rolled his eyes. "Stop scaring Niki. Nayla's fine. She's just kicking back in a village somewhere."

"Li Xul?" I asked, my throat tightening as I remembered the shadow wave and the golden-eyed man.

Enrique snorted. "The local shaman," he explained. "According to Li Xul we've pissed off the spirits that rule this area. He's telling everyone that the Lords of Death are coming for us—and anyone who associates with us. He's been causing us a shit-load of problems."

"What kind of problems?" I asked, a knot forming in my stomach.

"Petty theft, broken tools, excavation sites mysteriously collapsing at night, and problems with the local villages," David said, jerking his head toward the second table where six men sat eating in wary silence. "Kelling"s big on 'community archaeology," he continued, his voice laced with sarcasm. "But it's tough to 'empower local communities' when there is some local hack telling them that the Lords of Death are going to kill them if they help us."

"We've made a few goodwill visits to some of the

villages, but when we do find people willing to work at the site, they don't stay long. Kelling tried to meet with Li Xul to smooth things over, but the guy never showed." Enrique jerked his head in the direction of the men sitting at the other table. "Fortunately, there's a small Christian settlement not too far from us. Pastor Miguel's flock are willing enough to work at the site. For pay, of course."

"It's all a big power play. Li Xul doesn't want us undermining his control of the area by paying people or teaching them about their own history," David sneered.

I could feel my pulse quicken. "I don't understand. What does Li Xul have to do with the artifact that Nayla found?"

"Nothing. Nayla was interested in finding out more about the pectoral," Alma said, giving David a reproving look. "She wanted to interview people who live in the area. She thought they might have some insight into its significance."

"That's your opinion." David's face tightened. "She wasn't just interested in finding out about her big discovery. She was obsessed. It was all she talked about. She wanted to meet with Li Xul and find out what he knew about it."

A chill ran down my spine. "Is that where she went? To find this shaman?"

Alma commented, giving David another look. "We don't know where she went."

Her words made my stomach heave. My heart began to race as I gestured wildly toward the dense line of trees surrounding the dig site. "So, you're telling me that my sister is out there somewhere," I said, my voice rising, "and no one knows where she went or when she's coming back?"

Roman finally broke his silence, looking up from his plate with an indifferent shrug. "Yep. That pretty much sums it up."

Alma reached over and gently touched my arm. "Don't worry. I'm sure Nayla is fine."

Jake's easy-going charm vanished. "If you're worried about your sister, maybe you should start by looking at who she's been spending time with," he said loudly, jerking his thumb in the direction of the second table.

I twisted in my seat and looked over my shoulder.

The man I'd seen earlier stared back at me as he walked toward the table where the local men sat. He wore jeans and a T-shirt, a leather cord with a pendant of a predator's tooth—jaguar, perhaps—hung from his neck. His strange-colored eyes—gold with flecks of green—met mine, unwavering. A shiver traced a cold line down my spine, and the air seemed to thicken between us. I couldn't shake the feeling that I knew him from somewhere.

I quickly turned back to Jake. "Who is he?"

"His name is Zen Cazares. He's a cultural anthropologist," Alma answered before Jake could respond.

Roman and David snorted derisively.

My gaze flicked between them. "What?"

David rolled his eyes. "Let's just say his knowledge about archaeology is basic, to put it mildly."

Jake was more hostile. "It's bullshit, is what it is. I busted my ass to get here, and he gets the red- carpet treatment from Kelling because he's an anthropologist from some Ivy League university."

Alma shot Jake a sharp glance. "Not everything is a competition, Jake." She turned toward me.

"You're right." Jake's smooth smile returned. "There's no competition." His eyes fixed on me. "But if you're worried about Nayla, you should definitely ask him what he knows."

Alma sent a withering look his way. "Stop it, Jake. Just because they left camp on the same day doesn't mean anything."

"Hey, that's exactly what I'm saying. Zen disappeared the same day Nayla did." Jake's voice was light, but there was an edge to it. "He came back. She didn't."

Alma's tone was mild. "Don't be ridiculous."

Enrique flicked a quick glance Zen's way. "I don't know, Alma. You gotta admit, Jake's got a point."

Alma's eyes narrowed. "You two are impossible. Zen went to visit his grandmother. It was just a coincidence they left the same day."

Jake raised an eyebrow. "How do you know? We only have his word for it. No one's checked his alibi."

"Alibi?" Alma slammed her hands on the table, making everyone jump. "Really? Are we doing this now? We don't even know that Nayla is missing."

I stole another glance at Zen. He watched us, his movements calm, controlled, like he hadn't heard a single word of the escalating argument around him. His composure felt deliberate—like a challenge.

Alma huffed, grabbed her wide-brimmed hat, and stood abruptly. "I'm going to the lab." Her eyes flicked to me. "Niki, do you want to see the artifact that Nayla found? I can show it to you."

I hesitated, torn. Alma clearly wanted to talk, but my gaze lingered on Zen, who still hadn't acknowledged me or the others. His silence was unsettling, as if he knew something I didn't—and wasn't planning to share it.

In the end, I followed Alma. Zen wasn't going anywhere. I'd deal with him later.

LISA DIETRICH

CHAPTER THREE

The tropical sun shone fiercely overhead. I squinted at Alma's hat enviously as we threaded our way among the trenches and tarps.

"Look, don't pay attention to Jake and the others. They're just jealous."

"Jealous?"

"Yes, jealous."

"Why?"

Alma shrugged and gave me a picaresque grin. "We don't have a lot of entertainment options out here. No cell phones. The only place that has electricity is the field lab, and Dr. Kelling practically lives there, so we tend to find other ways to amuse ourselves. Nayla and the boys well— when Zen arrived things became more complicated."

"Ah." I cleared my throat. I could only imagine what Nayla was doing for fun.

"Nayla was spending most of her time with Jake," Alma continued. "When Zen showed up a few weeks ago, Nayla...well... You can probably figure out why Jake and the boys are unhappy. Jake means well. We don't know much about Zen, but I don't think he's dangerous. Though, it doesn't help that Zen is a loner. He hasn't made much of an effort to hang out with the rest of us—except for Nayla." Her lips curled into a wry smile.

She stopped in front of a closed canvas tent, secured with sturdy ropes and poles. Unzipping the tent flap, she stepped inside. The drone of an engine or machinery hummed from somewhere inside the enclosure.

I could feel a surprising draft of cool air as I stepped into the makeshift laboratory, thanks to what looked like portable air conditioning units humming in the corners. I stared around me, wide-eyed. The plywood tables were covered in an assortment of objects, a laptop, pieces of pottery, microscopes, and what looked like a 3D scanner and sophisticated camera equipment. The walls of the tent were lined with metal shelving units; each filled with clear plastic boxes containing more artifacts. I noticed some boxes had little packets inside them, each with its own handwritten label attached. It felt like a strange mix of high-tech lab and Indiana Jones movie set.

Dr. Kelling and Raúl were hunched over a table, their eyes fixed on a computer screen. I caught sight of the image they were examining—something that sent a shiver racing down my spine. It was a close-up of an artifact, its details sharp and unnerving. The familiar jagged lines of a skull with an owl mask grinned malevolently from the screen.

My breath hitched. Hun-Came.

Hun-Came, the god of death, darkness, and disaster. The god of childbirth and new beginnings. The name alone brought back frightening childhood memories of the stories our father used to tell us about the god who ruled over the Maya underworld. His cold cruel smile stared at me like a warning from beyond.

There can be no rebirth without death.

Nayla's voice echoed inside my head. My stomach lurched, and I grabbed the edge of a table to steady myself.

"Niki?" Alma's voice was muffled, like she was speaking through water.

The world around me began to blur, but the image of Hun-Came stayed sharp, his eyes boring into mine as I swayed on my feet.

"Are you okay?" Alma's voice wavered.

I wasn't. Closing my eyes, I tried to gather myself, inhaling slowly before forcing a weak smile. "I'm fine. Thanks." Shifting my gaze to Kelling and the image on the screen, I asked, "Is that the artifact my sister found?"

Kelling"s glare was sharp, his voice simmering with barely controlled anger. He stepped aside, revealing an empty plastic container. "I wouldn't call it 'found.'"

Alma gasped, her eyes widening as she stared at the empty box.

Kelling"s expression hardened, his voice icy. "As you can see, the artifact is missing."

My chest tightened. "You mean someone took it?"

"It would appear so." He speared me with a glare. "Your sister and the artifact both seem to have gone missing."

His cold gaze locked on me, before shifting toward Alma. "Alma, please ask Roman to come to the lab so he can inventory the artifacts and cross-check with the Finds Index. Raúl's agreed to delay his departure so that we can ensure everything is labeled and repacked before he leaves."

"I'll get him," Alma said, throwing me a quick look before slipping out. "And I'm happy to help with the inventory if you like."

Dr. Kelling nodded. "Good idea."

The canvas closed behind her, leaving an awkward silence in the tent.

I stared at the rotating 3D image of Hun-Came on the computer screen. The artifact slowly turned, its blue-green stone shimmering with an otherworldly light, becoming almost translucent at the edges. As I watched, Hun-Came's grinning skull changed into a gruesome image—a dead body laid upon a platform, its chest flayed open, the bones and viscera clearly visible. A tree sprouted from the body's exposed heart, a baby floating in the empty space above it.

Nayla's words echoed in my mind: *There can be no rebirth without death.*

"Dr. Kelling, my sister didn't steal it." Even as the words left my mouth, doubt niggled at the back of my brain. I knew my sister. Nayla would never steal, even though she had been known to occasionally "borrow" items without permission.

"Well, someone did. And Nayla's the only one who can't answer for it." Kelling"s lips thinned and formed an angry slash across his face.

I squared my shoulders. "I know my sister wouldn't have taken anything without a good reason. If Nayla has it, she'll bring it back."

"I appreciate your faith in your sister, but I'd like you to leave. We have a great deal of work to do," Kelling said, his words clipped with tightly controlled anger.

I stared at Hun-Came a moment longer, before turning on my heel and exiting the tent.

After the cool air of the Field Lab, the heat and humidity hit me like a solid wall, pressing down with the weight of the sun. "Nayla, what were you thinking?" I muttered under my breath.

"I don't think she can hear you," a cool, calm voice said.

Zen Cazares leaned causally against one of the tent poles, his cat-like eyes following my every move.

"Where is she?" I demanded.

He shrugged. "That's the question, isn't it?"

I narrowed my eyes at him, noting the hard muscles under his shirt, the dagger-like canine pendant at the base of his throat. "You left the same day my sister disappeared. If you know where she is, you need to tell me!"

He fixed me with a long look, his strange-colored eyes gleaming. "I thought this might be a good time to search Nayla's tent. You're welcome to join me." He stretched languidly and stood.

"You can't just break into someone's tent...that's criminal trespass," I shot back, but Zen was already ahead, his voice casual as though we were discussing dinner plans.

"Come or stay, it's your choice."

After a moment's consideration, I followed him. We wound our way through the excavation site, skirting open trenches and ducking under tarps until we reached a row of small khaki-colored tents. Zen stopped in front of one.

"This is Nayla's tent. You should be the one to search through it."

"Me?" I spluttered. "It was your idea."

He gazed at me, one eyebrow raised. "I don't think she'd want me pawing through her personal things. Besides, she's your sister. It will look better if you do the searching."

I had to admit; he had a point. "Fine," I huffed.

I fumbled with the zipper, the soft hissing sound louder than my heartbeat, very much aware of Zen's presence behind me.

"There are two cots in here," I called over my shoulder.

"Nayla's cot is the one on the left."

The back of my neck tingled. Zen knew which cot belonged to my sister? "Of course, he does," I muttered under my breath. I shouldn't have been surprised. Nayla had a thing for exotic wildlife and there was something not quite human about Zen Cazares.

There was a low rumble of laughter from behind me.

"What are you laughing at?" I snapped.

"You."

"Well, stop it!"

As I stepped into the tent, the air instantly felt different—heavier, closer. The canvas flap fell back into place behind me with a soft thud, plunging the space into a dim twilight. My skin prickled with sweat, the air inside too thick to breathe properly. I unzipped the window coverings to let in more light and air.

"What am I supposed to be looking for?" I called over my shoulder, my pulse thudding in my ears.

"Anything that seems out of place or that might tell us where Nayla went."

I surveyed the inside of my sister's tent. Two narrow cots, each draped with mosquito netting lined the side walls. A blue cooler sat between them like a coffee table, topped with lanterns and books. Nayla's clothes hung from a makeshift laundry line strung above her cot. Against the back of the tent was a jumble of bags and supplies.

I turned around and pulled the front of the tent open. "You need to help me. I don't know what I'm looking for."

I held the canvas open, waiting. Zen hesitated for a moment then slipped inside, his hip brushing against mine. My pulse jumped and I found it hard to catch my breath. I wasn't sure if it was caused by the stifling heat or Zen's proximity.

His eyes scanned the tent's contents, taking everything in before squatting to look under Nayla's cot. "Her daypack is still here," he said. "It doesn't look like she took many clothes with her, if any."

I cleared my throat. "You don't think she was planning on staying away for more than a day?"

He pulled a notebook from under her cot and stood, rifling through the pages. "That'd be my guess, assuming she left willingly."

"What do you mean by that?" I asked, my pulse quickening.

He looked up, his gaze intense. "You know your sister better than I do. Would she go into the jungle alone? Would she go without leaving an itinerary or telling people where and who she was going with?"

The weight of his words settled over me. "The others said she went to do research at a village," I said in a small voice.

"Maybe she did, but she didn't tell Alma where she was going or leave a note. Is that something she would normally do?"

My sister might be reckless, but she wasn't foolish. I shook my head slowly, a knot forming in my stomach. "No... no, she wouldn't."

Zen nodded grimly. "Then we need to consider all possibilities."

I swallowed hard, my mind racing with dark scenarios. I felt weak, my knees folded beneath me, and I suddenly found myself sitting on the ground.

Zen looked at me, concern etched on his face. "It's hot in here. You need water." He set the books and lanterns on the ground next to me, lifting the lid of the cooler. There was no ice, but it was stocked with bottles of water. He handed one to me. "Drink this."

The water was warm, but I gulped it down anyway. "Thanks." My stomach felt queasy, but it wasn't from the heat.

"Who's in there?" a male voice called from outside the tent. I flinched, shooting a guilty look at Zen.

The front of the tent opened. "Hope everyone's decent," Jake chirped as he peered inside.

Jake didn't even try to hide his suspicion as he peered into the tent, his razor-sharp gaze flicking toward Zen, before turning to face me with a friendly smile. "Ah, I thought I heard your voice. You are just the person I was looking for. What are you doing in here?"

"I..I was hoping to see if Nayla left any notes about where she was going," I stuttered guiltily.

Jake didn't appear to notice my discomfort. "Great minds think alike," he said tapping his temple with his finger and offering me another quick grin. "I was hoping we could put our heads together to figure out where Nayla might have gone."

At my eager expression, his smile widened. "Why don't we chat out here. I'd come in, but you know what they say— three's a crowd." He held open the canvas entrance of the tent, his gaze flicking briefly to Zen once again.

I glanced at Zen who stood unnervingly still, his face a mask of calm that made the hair on my arms prickle. I took another gulp of the warm water, the plastic aftertaste lingering as I got to my feet.

"Um, sure." I guzzled the rest of the water and set the empty bottle on top of the cooler.

I stepped outside the tent, Zen following behind me.

Jake zipped the tent closed, tossing a look of smug satisfaction at Zen. "There. Snug as a bug. Now Alma won't have to worry about any pesky visitors showing up uninvited."

Zen regarded him with a predatory gleam in his eyes but said nothing.

"Now that that's taken care of," Jake turned to face me, "I'd be happy to give you a tour of our facilities. I can show you where Nayla was working. Maybe we'll find something helpful."

"Sure." I raised my hand to shield my eyes from the intense afternoon sun.

"But first, you need a hat," Jake said. "Luckily, I know where to find one." He plucked the battered broad-brim hat from his head and plunked it onto mine. "There you go." He stepped back to study me. "It suits you."

I adjusted the hat. "I doubt it," I replied a wry smile tugging at the corners of my mouth.

"No really. It looks good."

"Thanks."

"Kelling"'s asked Roman to review the inventory and repack the artifacts for shipment before Raúl takes off," Zen commented, eyeing Jake appraisingly.

Jake looked over at him, his expression startled. He quickly turned to face me, his smooth smile back in place. "I'd better help with that. How about we delay our tour by a couple of hours."

"Um, sure."

"Enjoy your tour," Zen said with a nod in my direction, before sauntering off.

As soon as Zen was out of sight Jake asked, "Look, I've got to go and help, but I was wondering—how long are you planning to stay?"

"I'm not going anywhere until I see my sister," I said

with a defiant lift of my chin.

He nodded. "I was hoping you'd say that." Jake reached for my hand, his blue eyes looking deeply into mine, his expression becoming serious. "I didn't want to say anything in front of Cazares, but I don't trust that guy. You shouldn't either."

"Zen? Why?"

"What I told you earlier today is true. Your sister and Zen Cazares left the archaeological dig on the same day. Two days later, he returned. Your sister didn't." His eyes bored into mine. "You should watch yourself around him. I wouldn't want anything bad to happen to you."

I swallowed past the lump in my throat and licked my lips, a tight knot of worry rooting deep inside me. "Do you think something's happened to Nayla?"

"I don't know. I hope not, but I am getting worried about her."

"Me, too. Did Nayla say anything to you about where she was going?"

He shook his head.

"But David said she went to see that shaman, Li Xul."

"We think that's where she went. David didn't exaggerate when he said she was obsessed with the jade pectoral she'd found." He paused. "You know what she's like. She was like a dog with a bone about the Hun-Came jade. I think that's why we all assumed she hiked to a nearby village to try and find a way to contact Li Xul."

"By herself? That doesn't make sense. Why would she go into the jungle by herself?" A feeling of dread settled like a stone in my stomach.

Jake put his arm around me. "I don't mean to scare you. She could have arranged something with a few of the locals. She was kind of secretive that way. She's done this kind of thing before, which is why Kelling didn't call out the calvary when she went missing this time."

"She's gone missing before this?" I asked incredulously.

Jake nodded. "Yeah. She went with Doña Juana to her

village. Kelling told her he didn't want her leaving the site. Nayla ignored him and went anyway. She left a note on her cot. Kelling was furious when she showed up the next day."

I rubbed my temples. "That is irresponsible, reckless and...sounds just like my sister."

Jake's hand rested on my shoulder. "Nayla was always like that, wasn't she?"

The knot in my stomach tightened. Something about the way he said *'was'* made my skin crawl. I opened my mouth to correct him, but the words died on my lips. Deep down, I couldn't shake the feeling that something terrible had happened to my sister.

CHAPTER FOUR

The camp started to settle into a hushed stillness as the sun dipped lower, casting long shadows that stretched like fingers across the ground. The chorus of insects grew louder, their song punctuated by the distant cry of something unseen in the jungle. The sky above was fading from fiery orange to deep indigo, as the suffocating heat of the day gave way to a heavy, sticky coolness.

Earlier, when I'd told Alma I wanted to shower, she had given me a grin.

"I'm not sure shower is the right word, but I'll show you where to rinse off."

She wasn't exaggerating. The "shower" was a makeshift setup—a pallet floor constructed over a small stream surrounded by a privacy screen constructed from dried branches. A hose placed in the stream was used to fill the buckets with water.

"Fill up both buckets. You rinse with the first bucket, lather with the soap and shampoo, then rinse again with the second bucket," she explained, amused by my dismayed expression. "We're in a protected biosphere so the soap is natural and won't pollute the water. It doesn't really foam like normal soap, but it gets the job done. I usually wash my clothes after I'm done showering." She grinned. "Killing two birds with one bar of soap, so to speak."

I gave a resigned sigh as I surveyed the setup, trying to imagine Nayla using it every day. The "privacy flag," a red lace thong hanging from a hook on the doorframe, confirmed it: only Nayla would find this funny.

Alma chuckled when I gestured to the thong. "Of course, it's Nayla's."

I "showered" as best as I could listening as the sound of insects thickened, growing louder as the shadows lengthened and light slowly bled from the darkening sky above. I wrapped my wet clothes in the towel and tucked the bundle under my arm before hurrying back to my sister's tent.

Inside the tent, Alma was lying on her cot, reading. She looked up when I entered.

"How was the shower?" she asked, the corners of her mouth turning up into a teasing smile.

I carefully zipped the tent closed, before glancing at her. "Wet." I held up the soggy towel wrapped around my clothes. "I took your advice and did my laundry while I was there."

"Smart move." She eyed me up and down. "You're wearing Nayla's clothes."

I shrugged. "I wasn't planning on staying. I didn't bring a change of clothes."

Alma closed her book. "You weren't going to stay?"

"No. Camping is not really my thing. I just wanted to check on Nayla. Make sure she was okay."

"You were worried about her?"

I nodded.

"Why?" There was a flicker of something in her gaze—curiosity edged with something sharper, unreadable.

I wasn't sure how to answer. How much I was willing to share. Alma said nothing, waiting. Given that my twin sister was still missing, I opted for honesty. More or less. "She sent a letter inviting me. "I wasn't planning on coming out here, but then I had a dream. A nightmare really. I decided I'd better pay her a visit and check on her."

Alma's face softened in surprise. "You two really are twins."

I raised an eyebrow.

She laughed self-consciously. "I mean, you look alike, of course. It's just. Well, I haven't said anything to anyone else because I promised Nayla, but..." She paused. "Nayla was having nightmares, too. Sometimes she'd yell or shout in her sleep so loudly it would wake me."

A frisson of alarm spiraled along my spine. The vision that had been haunting my nights played like a horror film before my closed eyes.

"What kind of nightmares?" I asked, my voice shaking.

Alma shook her head. "I don't know. She didn't talk about them, but I know she wasn't sleeping much. You might want to ask Doña Juana."

"Doña Juana? Why?"

"She didn't say anything when she returned, but I know Nayla went with her to see her pastor."

A jolt of unease coursed through me. "Jake told me she went with Doña Juana but he didn't say anything about why."

"The nightmares were really getting to her," Alma said with a sympathetic smile. "I think she wanted to talk to Pastor Miguel about them."

My mind reeled. I couldn't imagine Nayla visiting a pastor to talk about her dreams. Something was very, very wrong.

Alma opened her book. "Are you okay if I read for a while longer?" she asked.

I nodded distracted by my thoughts about Nayla. "Sure."

I hung my wet things on the laundry line before climbing onto Nayla's cot. The sounds of the night-time jungle came to life around us, the increasingly loud buzzing and chirring of insects, the calls of the night birds punctuated by the howler monkeys' guttural roars as they rolled across the treetops echoing through layers of vegetation until it was impossible to tell how many were calling or from which direction.

Eventually, Alma closed her book and turned off the lantern. I could hear her breathing slow, but I lay rigid and tense, nerves frayed. Would I dream my nightmare—or Nayla's—tonight? Or were they one and the same?

Sleep finally claimed me, and the darkness became a river.

Nayla is standing in a river. Brown water swirls around her knees. She looks at me. "There can be no rebirth without death."

My chest tightens. "What the hell is that supposed to mean?" I ask angrily. "Why are you standing in water? Where are you?"

I watch in horror as a long black snake slithers between Nayla's legs, climbing up her thigh, wrapping itself around her torso while my sister stares at me her eyes calm and serene.

"There can be no rebirth without death."

"Nayla!" I scream her name. The serpent wraps itself around Nayla's neck. Her skin falls off in strips revealing patterned scales. Her tongue flicks in and out of her mouth as her body elongates and grows larger. Nayla is no longer my sister. She has become Vision Serpent, a giant undulating snake. His red eyes fixate on me and he rears skyward.

Panic roots me in place as he towers above me, blocking the sun. He rears back, then lunges, his mouth widening to consume me. In one horrified instant, I am swallowed, sliding down his gullet, feeling my bones fracture under the weight of his crushing coils. My body changing, transforming itself as I claw for breath, gasping and choking, trapped inside his dark belly.

My perspective shifts—I am inside him, and also above, watching as Vision Serpent slithers out of the muddy water.

I am going to die! I do not want to die! Help me!

A large dark jaguar leaps from the trees. In a swift motion, he slashes Vision Serpent open with its claws. Bright red blood gushes from the gaping wound onto the riverbank. The stench of putrefying half-digested food mixes with the sharp metallic odor of blood.

I watch as I spill out of Vision Serpent's belly and lie curled up like a fetus in a pool of slime and filth. My pale pelt is slick with blood and mucus. I lurch drunkenly as I try to stand on shaking legs, my paws scrambling for purchase. Fear shoots through me, I draw back my lips, exposing dagger-like canines and snarl a warning at the other wild cat.

The jaguar eyes me coolly, its golden eyes shining like flashlights, before once again melting into the jungle shadows.

I woke with a start, gasping for air, the nightmare still clawing at my mind. My heart thundered in my chest, a nauseous weight pressing downward. I needed air. My legs shook and my hands trembled as I fumbled my way out of the cot and slipped outside the tent.

The night air was dense and thick like velvet; a heavy yellow moon spilled its light from above silvering the trees and ancient stones as the stars pulsed in harmony with its lunar glow. I stood quietly breathing in the dark, moonlight on my skin, bare feet on the earth, until the lingering terror faded.

Once my initial panic receded, I realized that I had to go to the bathroom. Dread pooled in my belly at the thought of crossing the dark excavation site alone to the latrines. But I needed to go. I shook out my boots to dislodge any wayward insects, spiders or scorpions, and slipped my feet inside them, then cautiously made my way to the latrines.

One of the reasons I don't camp is that I happen to really like indoor plumbing. It doesn't have to be fancy. I'm satisfied with a functioning faucet, hot water, and soap. None of which existed at Choja q'eq. I sighed unhappily as I took care of business as quickly as possible, stepping outside and carefully latching the door closed to keep out any curious jungle critters.

A voice startled me. "Hey."

I choked back a yelp as Zen stepped out of the darkness.

"What the hell?" I hissed, clutching my chest. "What are you doing out here?"

He regarded me, his amber eyes shining strangely in the

faint moonlight. He tilted his head and studied me intently. "Nayla was right. You really are in denial."

I stared at him, heart still pounding from his sudden appearance. "What are you talking about? Denial? Denial about what?" My voice trembled slightly.

He exhaled slowly, then spoke, each word deliberate, unsettling. "You pulled me into your dream."

"You weren't in my dream."

He shrugged. "Whatever you say, Dream-walker."

A shiver ran down my spine, his words hanging in the air like a prophecy. I opened my mouth to respond, to demand an answer, but Zen was already fading back into the shadows, leaving me alone under the weight of the jungle's watchful silence.

CHAPTER FIVE

"It's called looting, and Kelling's got no choice but to boot her ass out of the program." David's words cut through the morning air, sharp with self-righteousness.

"Maybe it was just mislabeled." Alma's voice wavered between defense and doubt.

David's voice rose. "There's no way it was mislabeled. You know that as well as any of us. She took it."

"Yeah. I agree with David. Who else?" Enrique's formerly teasing tone had hardened. "Really, Alma, think about it. She's the obvious choice."

I approached the dining area, my footsteps silent on the packed earth. Jake caught sight of me first, our eyes meeting across the wooden tables.

"If Nayla did take the jade, I'm sure she had a good reason," he said, pitching his voice deliberately for my ears. His smile was all calculated charm. "Hey, Niki."

Alma and Enrique turned, guilt flickering across their faces like shadows. David didn't bother to acknowledge me.

I slid onto the bench beside Jake and faced the group across the table, stomach churning. "I take it the Hun-Came jade hasn't turned up?"

David's mouth tightened as he pushed his plate away and rose, muttering something under his breath. His eyes were winter-cold as he shot a look at Jake, then strode off, back rigid with indignation.

Enrique shifted, his characteristic ease nowhere to be found. "Uh, not yet," he murmured, offering an awkward shrug before gathering his things. "I'll...see you later." He hesitated, words dying on his lips, then shook his head and fled.

Only Alma stayed, twisting her fingers. "I'm sorry, Niki. We shouldn't have jumped to conclusions. It's not fair to Nayla."

I held her gaze, fighting to keep my voice steady. "I get that everyone's worried about the artifact. What I don't get is how you all seem more upset about the missing jade than my missing sister." The crack in my voice betrayed the fear and anger roiling beneath my forced composure.

Jake's arm settled around my shoulders, warm and heavy. "Hey, I know you're worried. Look, Kelling put out an APB on Nayla this morning. It's something, at least."

I turned to him sharply. "An All Points Bulletin? What does that even mean out here?"

"He's contacted the nearby towns, and asked local authorities and the military to search for her," Alma offered quietly. "The military have helicopters. They can cover a lot of area. They even use our landing strip sometimes. She'll turn up soon, you'll see. It's only been a few days." Her gaze flicked to Jake. "We should get to work."

Jake squeezed my shoulder. "Back to the coal mines," he teased, but his voice had lost its usual luster.

"Wait—have either of you seen Zen this morning?"

Jake's hand tensed on my shoulder, his grip tightening until it hurt. "Why are you asking about Zen?"

"Jake, that hurts," I said, shrugging away from him. His hand dropped as if burned.

"Sorry," he muttered, his face darkening. "It's just...I don't think you should be spending time with him. He's dangerous."

Alma rolled her eyes. "He's no more dangerous than you, Jake." She turned to me with a warm smile that didn't quite reach her eyes. "I'm sure Zen's around somewhere."

They left me alone with the weight of unspoken tensions. I pushed away my unease and focused on the plate of eggs and tortillas that Doña Juana set before me.

"Gracias, señora," I murmured, then gathered my courage. "Señora, can you tell me why my sister went with you to meet with your pastor?"

Doña Juana's fingers flashed in a swift sign of the cross, her expression hardening like cement. "She was seeking protection."

My stomach clenched. "Protection? From what?"

"From the Lord," she replied, voice dropping to a reverent whisper.

"But...why did she need protection?"

Doña Juana's eyes darkened, her whisper both fearful and defiant. "Evil was eating your sister's soul." Ice spread through my veins. I leaned closer, reaching out a hand to touch her sleeve. "What does that mean? Please, I don't understand."

She jerked back as if scalded, crossing herself again. Her eyes went distant, cold as temple stones. "Nayla refused to give up the dark so that she could be reborn into the light." Venom dripped from each word. "Your sister was a bruja."

I stared after her retreating form, my heart thundering against my ribs. The word hung in the humid air, thick and choking. Bruja. I'd heard enough whispered stories about witches to know the danger that label carried, especially here. It was the word they used to describe my father before he died—before they hunted him down and killed him.

But Doña Juana's words burrowed deep, each one another nail in my gut, feeding the dread that had grown inside me since the moment my sister disappeared. I pushed the plate of eggs and tortillas away from me, my stomach roiling with tension. I needed answers. I needed to find Zen

Cazares.

I skirted the edges of the bustling excavation area, the oppressive heat already baking the earth and pressing down on me. Kelling and Enrique were absorbed in their work in one trench, while Alma and Jake crouched nearby, brushing the exposed stone of what looked like an ancient wall. I turned, glancing at the pyramid on the opposite side of the site, and I hurried toward it.

By the time I reached the crumbling stone pyramid, my shirt was soaked through. I stopped and wiped the perspiration from my forehead with the back of my hand.

The stone pyramid rose before me, its weathered face a maze of vegetation, stunted trees, and broken stone. Roots and vines snaked through cracks in the structure, both holding it together and slowly tearing it apart. An apt metaphor for my life right now.

"I'm in the middle of the friggin' jungle. My sister's a witch and I'm a dream-walker," I muttered pressing my hand against the rough stone.

"Could be worse," a voice spoke from behind me.

I whirled around to find Zen standing there, his golden eyes gleaming with quiet amusement.

"What the hell is a dream-walker?" I demanded.

He studied me for a moment. "You really don't know, do you?"

"No." I crossed my arms, not caring if I sounded petulant. "I really don't know."

His gaze drifted up the pyramid. "Think you can make it to the top?"

I set my jaw. "Of course, I can."

"Good. Let's talk up there." He turned and began climbing, reaching back to offer a hand.

I pushed his hand away, planting my foot firmly on the next stone. "I don't need your help."

He shrugged, his mouth twitching in amusement. "Suit yourself."

I followed behind him, pressing my palm against the

ancient limestone, searching for a stable hand hold among the crumbling steps, testing each stone before putting weight on it. Sweat trickled between my shoulder blades and dripped from the tip of my nose as I climbed.

"Watch that block," Zen called from above me, his voice tight with concern. "It's loose." He balanced precariously on a ledge above me, watching my progress.

I shifted my weight and reached for a different handhold. "You know," I panted, "when I imagined climbing a Mayan pyramid, I pictured actual stairs." I pulled myself up using a tree root, yelping as a chunk of limestone disintegrated beneath my foot.

Zen's hand shot down, catching my wrist. "I got you." His grip was strong, steady. "And those 'actual stairs' collapsed about seven centuries ago." A small smile played at the corners of his mouth, despite the tension in his eyes.

"Almost there," Zen announced as we neared the summit. He hauled himself onto a wider platform, then turned to offer me his hand.

I grabbed it, letting him pull me up. Breathing hard from the climb, I took a moment to stand and admire the view. The jungle stretched endlessly in every direction, a rippling green ocean under the late morning sun. From this height, I could see other ruins peeking through the canopy, ancient stones reaching toward the sky like drowning men's hands.

As I studied the jungle below us, a dark shadow seemed to ripple through the trees. I shot a quick glance at Zen, his amber-colored eyes giving nothing away. When I looked back it was gone.

"This way. I want to show you something." Zen turned and carefully picked his way across the top of the pyramid to what had once been an opening to a chamber.

I followed him, my pulse ticking in my throat as much from anxiety as from the exertion of the climb.

The chamber was shallow; the opening provided enough light for me to see the black and red murals decorating the walls. My breath caught in my throat. It was as if an unknown artist had reached into my mind and brought my nightmares to life.

I walked slowly along the walls studying the gruesome images. In one scene, several figures with jaguar faces and human bodies danced across the room, holding plates and bowls filled with human remains—severed hands, femurs, skulls, and eyeballs clearly visible. In another scene, a headless figure lay on the ground, a snake wrapped around her legs and torso, its head, tongue flickering, as it emerged from her heart. A skeleton with bat wings hovered above the body. In one hand he held her severed head, long hair flowing behind her, in the other a bloody knife. Floating above it all, was the image of Hun-Came, his sunken eyes watching the gruesome scene with undisguised glee.

Heart pounding, blood thundering in my ears, I staggered backward and Zen caught me as I stumbled outside. When my heart stopped trying to escape my chest, I pushed away from him, angry and embarrassed. "What was that about? Are you having fun trying to scare me?"

He regarded me calmly. "It wasn't about anything, except helping you understand."

"Understand what!" My voice rose. "Climbing up a pile of stone ruins to look at some ancient Mayan paintings. How is *that* supposed to help me understand? How is *that* supposed to help me find my sister?" I glared at him.

"Niki, think about what you saw on the walls. The bright colors. Fresh paint. Those murals aren't ancient," he said quietly. "Someone painted them recently."

I glanced over at the chamber opening. He was right. The colors were too vibrant, the paintings too fresh to be hundreds of years old. Something I should have noticed right away.

His golden eyes seemed to catch the sunlight. "Someone painted those murals as a warning for you and Nayla."

"What are you talking about?" I asked, my voice catching.

"You're a dream-walker, Niki." The words lingered in

the air, heavy and strange, as if they were woven with some ancient meaning. "You travel between worlds when you dream. You don't just imagine things—you experience them. You cause other people to experience them also. And someone is very threatened by that."

"What are you talking about?" I asked uneasily.

"I'm talking about what the ancient Maya called *wahy*."

I felt a flicker of memory, Nayla telling me about the Maya belief that each person was born with two souls. One soul connected the person with the everyday world, the other was linked through dreams and sleep and connected the person with their deeper, limitless self.

"*Wahy*... that's like a soul, right?"

"Not exactly," he replied, watching me carefully. "Your *wahy*... is your shadow soul. A spirit companion. Some people, like you, have a very strong connection to their wahy. Their spirit companions are free to roam far from their bodies. People like you are not bound to the physical world or your physical body. You have the ability to travel between this world and the supernatural realm. You can enter other people's dreams, their subconscious minds. You can influence what they see, what they think, and what they feel."

I took a shaky breath, feeling something in his words resonate deep within me, before resolutely rejecting them. I squared my shoulders, lifting my chin defiantly. "You sound just like my sister. But I'm not into Mayan superstitions. My dreams are just dreams. Nothing more than my vivid imagination producing crazy images. Trust me, my spirit companion is not running around doing things while I am sleeping."

He held my gaze. "If you really believe that, why are you here?"

"I am here because I am worried about my sister!" I replied heatedly. "I love my sister, but all her talk about wandering souls, spirit animals and shapeshifters is nothing more than superstitious bullshit."

41

He was calm, his cat-like eyes followed me as I paced like a caged animal. "Is it?" he asked.

I speared him with a glare. "Yes!"

"Niki, you know the truth. You know it's not just superstition."

I heard him speak the words, but his mouth didn't move.

"I know it's a lot to take in, but you can't ignore who you are. You were born with this ability. You are Xolo Balam's daughter. It's in your blood. You need to accept who you are, or it will destroy you."

I stared at him, doubting what I saw with my own eyes, even as his words echoed inside my head. "I need to sit down," I said aloud, my voice shaking.

Zen's gaze softened. "There's some shade by the tree. We can sit there."

I wobbled over to a scraggly tree improbably sprouting among the pyramid's stones and sat. "I should have eaten breakfast."

Silently, Zen slipped his daypack from his shoulders. He pulled out a water bottle and a granola bar, handing them to me.

With trembling hands, I uncapped the water bottle and took a long, deep drink.

"How do you know my father's name? Did Nayla tell you?" I asked aloud.

"Yes. She also told me that you refuse to acknowledge your gift."

Once again, I heard his voice in my head, even though he hadn't spoken. I stared at him, eyes narrowed. *"How are you able to talk to me like this?"* I asked without speaking. *"I've only ever been able to do this with Nayla and my father."*

Zen's golden eyes caught the light, blazing bright as glass. *"Our spirit companions are linked through your dreams."* Zen reached out, placing a hand on my shoulder.

I angrily rolled my shoulder out from under his hand. "Bullshit!"

"Last night your spirit companion was set free. Your wahy is a jaguar. It is your co-essence, it is your protector, your strength," Zen continued, ignoring my outburst. "You need to learn to travel with it, to trust it. It will keep you safe."

As I stared into those amber-colored eyes, my gaze drifted to the pendant hanging around his neck. I felt a sudden spark of recognition. My cheeks flamed with embarrassment. Zen Cazares had been inhabiting my dreams for weeks. "You're the jaguar in my dreams!"

The corners of Zen's mouth turned upward. "*I knew we'd get there eventually.*"

LISA DIETRICH

CHAPTER SIX

I slumped at the table in the Dining Hall, the throbbing in my head keeping time with my racing heart. My mad scramble down the pyramid had left me dizzy, the world tilting at odd angles. *Not running from the truth*, I told myself, pressing my forehead against the cool wood. *Running from... him*. I closed my eyes, but that only made the spinning worse.

Dreams had always been both my refuge and my torment. As a child, night terrors plagued me—dark, writhing monsters that left me screaming into my pillow at three a.m. But with my mother's herbs and my father's help, I'd learned to control them, to bend the nightmares to my will like a lucid dreamer taming shadows. I hadn't had a single nightmare in years—not until Nayla went to Guatemala.

After her arrival, my nightmares returned with a vengeance, populated by the Maya gods and demons that haunted my father's stories. Hun-Came and his Lords of Death circled my sister like vultures, tearing her apart and feasting on her during their grotesque celebrations. Then the jaguar appeared, golden eyes blazing in the dark. I'd assumed my subconscious had conjured him as a shield against my fears about Nayla. Now, I wasn't sure what to think about my dreams—or about Zen Cazares.

The mere thought of him sent heat crawling up my neck and across my cheeks. Dream-walker. The word echoed in my mind, impossible yet undeniable. I couldn't ignore that he knew about my dreams, that he had somehow slipped into my head in a way that no one—except my father and Nayla—had ever managed before.

The harsh scrape of chair legs against packed earth jolted me upright. Jake settled into the seat across from me, his brow furrowed.

His eyes narrowed as they swept over my face, lingering on what I suspected was a telling flush. "I saw you at the pyramid with Cazares." His voice tightened around Zen's name like a noose. "He shouldn't have taken you up there. It's not safe."

"It was fine, Jake. We were careful." I pressed my fingertips against my temples, trying to massage away the persistent throbbing.

"You don't look fine." Worry and something darker threaded through his voice.

"It's just the heat getting to me." The words sounded hollow even to my own ears.

Without comment, Jake pushed back from the table and strode to the cooler and retrieved a Gatorade. He slid it across to me. "Warm and tastes like crap, but the electrolytes will help."

"Thanks," I murmured, twisting off the cap. The lukewarm liquid hit my tongue tasting like a combination of baby aspirin and salt, but I forced myself to take small sips.

Jake watched me drink, his fingers drumming an irregular rhythm against the plywood table as the silence between us grew.

Finally, he spoke. "Did he show you the graffiti?"

My stomach clenched at the memory of those grotesque drawings, their red lines like fresh wounds against the stone.

I nodded.

"What did he say about it?" His tone was carefully neutral, but the muscle working in his jaw betrayed him.

"He said it was a warning. For Nayla. For me."

Jake's eyes flashed as he leaned forward. "That's bullshit, Niki," he hissed. "Listen to me. Zen Cazares is dangerous. Stay away from him."

Anger flared in my chest, tangled with something else—fear? "I appreciate your concern, Jake, but I can take care of myself."

"The same way Nayla took care of herself?" The words sliced through the air between us.

I recoiled as if he'd struck me, shock and hurt warring beneath my ribs.

Jake's face crumpled. "God, Niki, I'm sorry." He reached for my hand. "I shouldn't have said that. It's just... I can't bear the thought of anything happening to you too."

"What do you mean? Do you know something? Did something happen to Nayla?"

"No," he said quickly. "I'm just concerned about you, that's all." His hand squeezed mine.

I pulled away, my mind reeling. "Like I said," I managed, my voice barely a whisper, "I can take care of myself."

Jake's blue eyes darkened with emotion. "Just be careful, Niki. That graffiti he showed you—It only appeared after Zen arrived."

My head snapped up. "What?"

"I didn't think he'd mention that." Jake stood, looking down at me, a sad smile playing at the corners of his mouth.

As he walked away, I slumped back, my mind racing like a trapped animal. The graffiti, my dreams, Zen's revelations about dream walking—it was all too much. And underneath it all, the constant worry about Nayla gnawed at my insides like acid. What had she gotten herself into? What had *I* gotten myself into?

With a heavy sigh, I finished the Gatorade and closed my eyes, trying to center myself, but all I could see was a pair of jaguar's eyes, watching me from the shadows.

"Help! Ayuda!" The panicked cry shattered the humid air. I jerked upright, my eyes flying open. Enrique leaped from a deep trench, arms windmilling frantically. Other heads popped up from various trenches like prairie dogs scenting danger. Jake sprinted past me. My heart hammering against my ribs, I watched Roman and David scramble from their trenches and race toward Enrique, Alma close behind. I pushed myself up on shaking legs and hurried after them.

When I reached the trench, my blood turned to ice water. Dr. Kelling was slumped against the earthen wall, his face the color of old ash. Two angry puncture marks stood out on his ankle like accusing eyes, the flesh already angry and swollen, purple spreading beneath his skin.

"Fer-de-lance," Enrique choked out, his voice raw. "I saw it slither away."

Jake cursed under his breath.

"David—find the satellite phone. Call for medevac. Alma, bring the first aid kit." Roman's voice cut through the panic, steady but tight as a drawn bow. "Enrique, Jake, help me lift him."

They moved with careful precision, maneuvering Dr. Kelling out of the trench and onto level ground. The professor's breathing came in shallow gasps that seemed to echo in the heavy air.

"Keep his heart above the bite," I said, surprised by the steadiness in my voice. "It'll slow the venom. He shouldn't lie down."

"She's right," Kelling wheezed, each word a struggle.

Roman nodded, sweat beading on his forehead. "Alright. Let's get you propped up."

Jake and Roman shifted Kelling so his back rested against a stone stela. His condition was deteriorating before our eyes—skin taking on a waxy sheen, breathing becoming more labored with each passing minute.

Roman knelt beside him, fear plain in his eyes. "We'll get you to the hospital, Kip. Don't worry."

Alma returned with the first aid kit, thrusting it at me like it might burst into flames. "David's on the phone with them," she panted, words tumbling over each other. "ETA thirty to forty-five minutes."

Roman turned to Enrique and two of the local men, his voice tight with urgency. "Enrique, you take Bembe and Felix and grab chairs from the lab. We can use them to carry him to the landing strip." He looked at me, eyes dark with worry. "Check to see if there is anything we can use in the kit. We have to slow the spread of the venom."

My hands trembled as I searched through the supplies, medical terms blurring before my eyes. "Here!" I thrust a pressure bandage at Jake. "We can use this! Tie it above the bite wound!"

"You're going to be okay," Alma soothed Kelling, who was looking worse by the minute, his skin taking on a grayish tinge as Jake fumbled with the pressure bandage.

"I have antivenom." Zen's voice cut through the chaos like a blade. Jake's head snapped up, fury flashing across his face.

Zen ignored him, kneeling beside Kelling with fluid grace. "It's not enough to cure you," he said softly as he prepared the injection, his hands steady and sure where everyone else's shook. "But it will buy you time."

**

We watched until the helicopter disappeared completely, swallowed by the dark line of clouds that had crept closer during our vigil. The engine's drone faded into the distance, leaving behind a silence that felt like a physical weight. The air was electric, charged with rising tensions.

"He's going to be okay," Enrique said, shading his eyes against the sun that stabbed through gaps in the gathering clouds. His voice held a desperate edge, as if saying it might make it true.

"San Benito Hospital has antivenom. I'm sure he'll be

fine," Roman added quickly, but his words rang hollow in the thick air.

"Realistically, he's got at best a 50/50 chance," Zen said, his clinical tone cutting through their fragile optimism like a scalpel.

Alma gasped, her hand flying to her throat. The sound seemed to break something in the group's careful composure.

"Shut up," Jake snarled, rounding on Zen. His fists clenched at his sides, knuckles white with strain. "You don't know what you're talking about."

Zen regarded him calmly. "I'm no expert, but I have had some training. His odds are 50/50."

I couldn't argue with Zen's assessment. I'd grown up in rattlesnake country, I'd seen people bitten by snakes. Dr. Kelling had looked more corpse than man when the medivac finally arrived. His skin had taken on a waxy, yellow-gray sheen, each breath a desperate battle. He hadn't even stirred when they'd loaded him into the helicopter, his body limp as a broken marionette.

Jake's eyes blazed with fury. "How convenient that you happen to have antivenom with you."

Zen laughed aloud. "What? You think I caught a snake and dropped it in one of the pits? So I could—do what? Use my antivenom?"

The muscle in Jake's jaw jumped. "No. I think you dropped a snake into the pit because you want to sabotage the dig."

Zen stared at Jake for a moment before speaking, enunciating each word slowly and clearly. "You are an idiot."

Alma reached out and touched Jake lightly on the arm, her voice soothing. "Jake."

"Okay," Roman said abruptly. Sweat had plastered his shirt to his back, and dust caked his boots. "We've got a few hours of daylight left so here's what we're going to do. Alma and David, start cataloging and crating the artifacts for transport. Bembe and Felix can organize the other men to start closing up the trenches while Jake, Enrique, and I secure the rest of the dig site." His voice hardened. "Until further notice, no one goes near the trench where we saw the snake. Any questions?"

"Yeah," Jake said, stepping forward, his chin thrust forward belligerently. "Who put you in charge?"

"We need to protect and close down the excavation in an orderly manner. I'm the logical choice." Roman's words were measured, reasonable, but there was steel beneath them.

"I don't agree." Jake crossed his arms, planting his feet wider. The stance of a man spoiling for a fight. "We've got weeks of funding left. I say we get back to work. Do what we can as long as we can. We don't need Kelling here. We know what to do."

"We don't have weeks!" David snapped. "The university is going to pull the plug as soon as they find out about Kelling!"

"Guys, maybe we should wait until we hear from—" Alma's attempt at mediation withered under the collective glare.

"Shut up," they growled in unison. She took a step back, color rising in her cheeks.

Enrique's head swiveled between Roman and Jake like he was watching a tennis match. Sweat trickled down his temple. "He's got a point, Jake. Maybe we should start thinking about securing the dig for next season."

"Let's vote on it," Roman said, trying to impose order on the chaos.

"I agree with Alma. We should wait to find out what happens to Kelling," Zen interjected, his casual tone a sharp contrast to the hostility crackling through the group.

Jake's eyes flared with barely contained rage. "You've been here, what? A few weeks? You're not even affiliated with the university." The words dripped with contempt. "You don't get a vote. I've got the most experience working with Kip. I'm putting myself in charge."

Zen's smile was easy, lazy even, but something dangerous glinted in his eyes. "Okay, if we're deciding based on experience then I vote for Bembe and Felix. They've been farming and living in this area for thirty-plus years." He spread his hands in a gesture of mock reasonableness. "All in favor raise their hands."

All eyes shifted to Bembe and Felix. The local men exchanged confused looks, shifting uncomfortably under the sudden attention. The tension in the air ratcheted up another notch.

Jake's face flushed dark red, the color spreading down his neck. Each word came out like a separate explosion: "Shut. The. Fuck. Up!"

"Make me." Zen's smile never wavered, but his eyes had gone cold and flat.

Enrique quickly stepped between them; hands raised. "Look, we're all upset. I think we shouldn't make any decisions today."

"I agree," Alma said, finding her voice again. Her gaze shifted uncomfortably between the men, like she was trying to gauge how close they were to exploding. "Why doesn't everyone finish up with what they were working on today and we can come up with a plan tonight?"

"Fine," Roman huffed, though his shoulders tightened with suppressed resentment. "But we close off the trench where we saw the snake, and no one goes near it."

Jake gave a terse nod, the motion jerky with suppressed anger. "Agreed."

The group began to fragment, the unease dissipating like smoke in the wind. But something else was building inside me, a pressure that had been there since I first arrived, since Nayla first disappeared. I couldn't stay silent anymore.

"Aren't you forgetting something?" My voice cut through their retreating backs. They turned as one to stare at me, and I felt the weight of their collective gaze like a physical thing. But I pressed on, the question no one seemed to want to answer. "What about my sister?"

The silence that followed was absolute. Even the jungle seemed to hold its breath. Above us, thunder growled a warning as if something very old and very hungry was coming our way.

LISA DIETRICH

CHAPTER SEVEN

Sacred water cascaded over Li Xul's shoulders, each droplet charged with ancient power. The cenote's surface rippled with forgotten memories as he traced protection glyphs in the air. The cave breathed around him—inhaling, exhaling—sending ribbons of mist dancing that pierced the cavern's throat.

Tonight, the veil thins, he thought, feeling the pulse of the otherworld against his skin. As he ventured deeper into the cavern, the sounds shifted from gentle whispers to the deep, resonant tones of the earth itself speaking.

In the Chamber of the Black Pool, Li Xul crouched before the ceremonial fire. His hands, steady despite the power building in his veins, scattered copal resin across the flames. The sacred smoke rose in thick coils, taking shapes that seemed almost deliberate—serpents and jaguars and faces with hollow eyes. The air grew heavy, pressing against his skin with the weight of centuries. Li Xul settled his mind into the ancient rhythms, letting his consciousness sink into the space between worlds. One by one, he began calling the ah puccob—the lords of death whose favor he sought. Each name was a key turning in an invisible lock, opening doorways between realms.

"Hun-Came," he whispered, his voice carrying the weight of generations of shamans before him. The fire dimmed to an otherworldly blue, acknowledging the presence of the god who feasted on decay and disease, whose very breath carried ill omens on the wind. The smoke thickened, carrying the sweet-rot scent of the underworld.

His fingers traced the obsidian blade at his side as he called forth Aj Sak T'el Ek'—Blood Gatherer. The air grew thick with the copper-tang smell of fresh wounds, and Li Xul's own scars began to throb in recognition. Then came Kisin, the Pus Master, whose laughter was the sound of flesh rotting from bone. The shadows in the corners of the chamber seemed to writhe with dark purpose.

Li Xul's hands trembled, but his voice remained strong. "K'ak' Upak'al," he intoned, invoking Bone Scepter and Skull Scepter together. The twin gods whose gaze could drain a warrior's strength appeared as shimmering distortions in the smoke, their presence making the very air feel thin and insubstantial. Finally, he called upon Ah Kak Xib Chaac—the Lords of Wing and Packstrap—who squeezed life from men's throats until their final breaths escaped in clouds of crimson mist.

Power surged through Li Xul's body like lightning through a copper rod. The air crackled with potential, heavy with the presence of so many death lords. Each breath drew their essence deeper into his being, their power radiating through his veins like liquid obsidian. He understood, as his ancestors had, the eternal cycle—death feeding life feeding death again. The moon above was proof that even the dead could rise, waxing full with each turning of the wheel.

With practiced precision, Li Xul drew his ceremonial lancet—carved from the tooth of an ancient jaguar—across the girl's forearm. In her drugged state she felt no pain. Blood welled up black in the firelight, spilling into a clay bowl marked with glyphs of containment and protection. The scent of his offering mixed with the copal smoke, creating an intoxicating perfume that made reality shimmer at its edges.

The jade amulet pulsed against his chest like a second heart as he pressed it to his lips. The carved surface grew warm, then hot, Hun-Came's power flowing into him like honey-thick venom.

Vision Serpent appeared first in his mind, slithering between worlds, its sinuous body shimmering through the tendrils of smoke. He felt its coiled body press upon him, thick and heavy, filling the sacred space with a living presence that bent the air itself. It led him down into shadows, where the boundaries between the realms melted away, and he could cross into the Underworld. Li Xul closed his eyes, feeling the delicate membrane separating this world from the next becoming almost translucent.

His blood sang with forbidden knowledge passed down through generations of Dream-walkers. As the last vestiges of his human form melted away, replaced by sleek muscles and fur, Li Xul embraced his true nature. The jaguar's roar that echoed through the chamber carried both warning and prophecy—the old gods were stirring, and the world of men would soon remember why they had once been feared.

LISA DIETRICH

CHAPTER EIGHT

I lay on my sister's cot unable to sleep. A toxic mixture of rage, resentment, fear, and helplessness burned my gut like acid.

Everyone was worried about Dr. Kelling, but that wasn't what was keeping me awake.

The memory of Roman's uncaring shrug, the flatness in his voice when he said, "Nayla's either dead or partying in some village," made my hands curl into fists even now.

The scene played again in my mind: my fingers grasping for the satellite phone as Roman held it just out of reach, my voice rising to a desperate shriek that scared even me.

Furious, I had tried to snatch the phone from him. He refused to give it to me. I ended up yelling and screaming at him like a child having a tantrum while he held the phone. It was Jake who intervened, eventually handing the phone to me.

Shaking and crying, I held the satellite phone in my hand only to come to the brutal realization that I had no idea who to call. Defeated, I returned the phone to Jake and retreated to my sister's tent, tears blurring my vision.

Alma followed, offering hollow comfort: "I'm sure she'll

turn up soon." Even she couldn't disguise her disbelief in her own words.

Nayla, where are you? The thought echoed in my mind like a mantra. *Please let me know you're all right.* Tears squeezed from my eyes, each one carrying a fervent plea to the universe and whatever gods might be listening—old or new, I didn't care anymore. Eventually, I tumbled into sleep.

The moonlight filtering through the tree canopy creates strange shadows that dance and twist with each movement of their branches, but my eyes are so attuned to the dark that I can see everything. I move with liquid grace among the trees, as the sounds and the sights of the night wash over me. My ears prick at the soft rustling of leaves and sounds of small rodents as they scurry along the jungle floor. I ignore them. It is my sense of smell that is leading me on this hunt.

I leap, landing softly atop a fallen log. I raise my head and bare my teeth. The pungent, musky scent of another jaguar permeates the air—I can taste him on my tongue, feel him in my bones. A low growl rises unbidden from my throat, primordial and fierce. He is close.

The dark water ripples as I slip into the river and swim toward my prey. Fur heavy with water, I silently pull myself onto the riverbank belly low to the ground. I become pure intention—pure action without thought. My body quivers with equal parts fear and anticipation as I inch through the undergrowth.

The night air presses against me, dense and thick. Then it hits me—the rich, metallic scent of fresh blood, the sound of soft flesh tearing. My muscles coil like springs, dagger-like canines ready to pierce skull and sever spine. The growl that escapes me is both a warning and a war cry as I charge.

Another jaguar, dark fur, eyes flaming red, blood dripping from his muzzle, stands over my sister's body. He recoils at the sight of me.

Rage and bloodlust surge through me like fire, burning away the last vestiges of my human self. I hurl myself into the clearing—

Only to land with a thud on soft earth. The jaguar has vanished like morning mist, leaving nothing but confusion in its wake. I shake my head from side to side, snapping and snarling at empty air.

I look down at my sister's broken body. "Nayla!" My roar, filled with rage and anguish, shatters the night.

I jolted awake on my sister's cot, sweat-soaked and trembling. A scream lodged in my throat like a trapped bird, the scent of death lingering in the air—or perhaps in my memory.

I looked over at Alma, sleeping peacefully in the cot across from me. *It was just a bad dream,* I recited to myself as I worked to slow my breathing and my racing heart.

What I needed was a cheery well-lit kitchen and cup of my mother's herbal tea to chase the lingering effects of my nightmare away, but I was in a tent, in the middle of the jungle somewhat limiting my options. Slipping quietly out of the tent with one of the lanterns, I let my feet carry me to the closest thing we had to a cheery well-lit kitchen.

The lantern cast a small circle of light on the plywood tabletop. I took a sip of water and listened to the wind rustling the dried leaves of the thatch roof overhead. The sound was soothing and reminded me of the soft lapping of waves on sand. If I closed my eyes, I could almost pretend I was home in California. But my thoughts, like a compass needle finding north, returned inevitably to Nayla.

From the beginning, Nayla embraced our Mayan heritage in a way that I never did. After our father's death, her fascination had become an obsession—particularly with the supernatural beliefs about wahyis and shapeshifters. By fifteen, she'd convinced herself our father's wahy had survived his death and was waiting for us in Guatemala. Maybe it was easier than accepting the truth: that our father had been a lawyer killed by the very people he'd chosen to defend. Becoming an archaeologist, studying the ancient Maya, was her way of keeping his memory alive.

Perhaps I wasn't so different from her after all. Despite the dreams, despite days of silence, I clung to the belief that Nayla was alive somewhere, waiting to be found. The image from my nightmare—the jaguar standing over her broken body—flashed through my mind. I tried to dismiss it as nothing more than a dream, but Zen's words echoed in my head like a warning: "You are a dream-walker."

"Are you okay?"

I jumped at his sudden appearance, though some part of me had known he would come. Zen's form materialized from the shadows as if I had conjured him with my thoughts. I glared at him. "Stay out of my head," I warned. "You can talk to me like a normal human being, or not at all!"

"Okay." He settled across from me, his strange eyes studying me with an intensity that made my skin prickle.

"What?" I snapped, crossing my arms.

"You had another dream." It wasn't a question.

"Don't start with that Dream-walker crap. I'm not in the mood."

"Niki," he said, my name soft on his lips. "I know you had another dream. I heard you scream—in my head. I heard you call for Nayla. That's what woke me."

I pressed my lips together in a thin line. *"No, you didn't."*

"So, you're allowed in my head, but I'm not allowed in yours?" His eyebrow lifted, and something in his expression made my heart skip.

"It was a dream, okay?" I said aloud. Then the words burst from me like water through a broken dam. "An awful, terrible dream! But it was only a dream! It doesn't mean anything!" To my horror, tears began spilling down my cheeks.

Somehow, I ended up in his arms, his warmth seeping into my cold skin as he held me, rocking me gently while my tears soaked his shirt. "Tell me about your dream," he murmured when my breathing had steadied.

"I... I saw Nayla." My voice quavered. "She was dead. You killed her."

Zen's body tensed against mine. "Niki, I wasn't in your dream."

I pushed him away. "Yes, you were!" I insisted. "I saw you! In my dream, I was a jaguar. I was hunting you. When I found you..." My voice failed. "You were...you were...eating her."

"That wasn't me." His eyes held mine, filled with concern and something darker. "I don't have the ability to walk in other people's dreams. I'm not like you."

"But it was you! You are the jaguar in my dreams!" I heard the childish note in my voice but couldn't stop. "I know you are the jaguar in my dreams!"

"I was the jaguar in your other dreams, because you wove me into those dreams," he agreed carefully. "But not this one. If I had been the jaguar, I would have shared the same dream. But I didn't. I didn't see Nayla. I didn't see you. The jaguar in your dream was not me."

I shook my head, but doubt crept in. He was right—this jaguar had red eyes not gold. "Nayla told me that dream-walkers can control dreams—their own and other people's. If I create a dream then we have to have the same dream?"

"Yes."

"You didn't have the same dream." Relief flooded through me as understanding dawned. A slow smile crept across my face. "I wasn't dream-walking. It really was just a nightmare."

Zen's eyes caught the lantern light, turning them into liquid gold. "Unless," he said softly, "you're not the only dream-walker at Choja q'eq."

"No," I whispered. "It was just a dream." The words came out hollow, each one a lie I desperately wanted to believe. My fingers traced the indent of my nails in my palms—when had I made fists? "Just because my father filled Nayla's head with stories about wayhis and dream walking doesn't mean—" My voice cracked. I couldn't finish the sentence, couldn't deny what I'd felt in that dream—the raw power, the certainty, the connection to something ancient and terrible.

The night seemed to deepen around us, as if responding to my unspoken fears. The hairs on the back of my neck and arms stood on end, a primal warning.

From somewhere in the depths of the jungle, a jaguar's roar shattered the silence, sending icy tendrils of fear skating along my spine. I shivered, the tremor running through my entire body.

"You're cold," Zen murmured, his expression etched with concern. His eyes, fathomless in the dim light, searched mine. "Let's go back to my tent. We can talk there."

He wrapped his arm around me, pulling me close. I leaned into him instinctively, breathing in his scent. I sought not just warmth from his embrace, but an assurance I knew, deep down, he couldn't give. Still, I let myself be enveloped by his presence, a temporary shield against the night and its lurking secrets.

CHAPTER NINE

When Jake caught me leaving Zen's tent the next morning, his face flushed red, his eyes scorching Zen like twin lasers. I felt a rush of heat creep up my neck, suddenly aware of how this must look.

"Good morning," Zen greeted him with a lazy smile, his voice still husky with sleep.

The muscle in Jake's jaw jumped. "Where's the Sat phone?" he asked, his tone accusatory.

"I have no idea." Zen's casual demeanor only seemed to infuriate Jake more.

"Quit playing games, Cazares. Give me the phone!"

"I don't have it. Ask one of the others." Zen's eyes flickered to me, a hint of last night's intimacy in his gaze.

Jake's gaze whipsawed to me, his eyes narrowing as he took in my disheveled appearance. "None of us have the phone, which is why I'm asking you." He held out his hand. "Hand it over."

Zen's expression hardened, his body tensing. I stood next to him acutely aware of his proximity. "I'm telling you. I don't have it."

"Bullshit! I heard you prowling around the site last night.

You're the only one who could have taken it!"

"Jake," I interjected, my voice slightly breathless. "He's telling you the truth. He doesn't have it. He was with me." The admission hung in the air, loaded with implication.

Jake turned to look at me, his eyes filled with disappointment and something else—jealousy? "Why won't you listen to me, Niki? I've tried to protect you, but you won't listen." His gaze shifted back to Zen. "If I find out you've been lying about the phone, I'm going to rip you apart."

Zen rocked back on his heels, the threat beneath his friendly smile unmistakable. "I sincerely doubt that." In a move meant to infuriate Jake, he casually tossed his arm around my shoulders, his fingers grazing the sensitive skin of my neck. "You ready for breakfast?" he asked, turning to face me, his eyes dark with unspoken promise.

With a flick of my fingers, I removed his arm, though my skin tingled where he'd touched me. "Yes." I turned toward Jake, trying to ignore the tension crackling between the three of us. "I'm sure the phone will turn up."

Everyone was already seated in the Dining Hall by the time we arrived, the local men at one table, the grad students at the other. Alma, Roman, David and Enrique turned as one to look at Jake, expressions expectant, as we approached. I saw him shake his head.

Roman slammed a fist on the table. "Where the hell is the Sat phone? Someone has to have it. It didn't just walk off by itself!"

"Did you look around the lab? Maybe it fell or someone moved it accidently," Alma suggested.

Roman shot a fierce look her way. "Of course, I searched the lab. The charging station is there; the phone isn't."

Doña Juana set a platter of scrambled eggs and tortillas on the table. Her dark eyes narrowing as her gaze flicked over me. She made the sign of the cross and hurried away.

In the morning light, my nightmare and idea of dream-walkers seemed like nothing more than superstition and scary fairy tales but Doña Juana's reaction to me made me realize that for some people the threat of witchcraft was all too real.

Last night I'd lain awake, my mind spinning in a million different directions. What I couldn't understand was how I could inhabit Zen's dreams before I'd even met him. If I was dream-walking, wouldn't I have to know the person whose dream I was entering? How else could I inhabit their dreams? Zen said that our spirit companions were linked by my dreams. What did he mean by that?

I shot a quick glance Zen's way, the memory of last night still vivid in my mind. He had curled himself around me in his narrow cot, his body radiating a delicious heat that seeped into my bones. The feeling of his chest rising and falling against my back, his breath warm on my neck, had sent shivers through me that had nothing to do with fear or cold.

"You are in control. You choose the dream," he had whispered in my ear, his lips brushing my skin. The low timbre of his voice had ignited something deep within me, a spark of desire I was still struggling to extinguish.

I forced myself to look away, my cheeks burning. I had no idea what his relationship was with my sister. Alma had insinuated that Nayla had thrown over Jake for Zen. Had they been lovers as well as colleagues? The thought sent an unexpected pang of jealousy through me. Nayla wasn't here to tell me so that made him kryptonite as far as I was concerned. Something to be avoided at any cost, at least until I could talk to my missing twin.

"Feeling better this morning?"

I looked up abruptly only to lock eyes with Zen. The corners of his mouth turned up into the faintest hint of a smile. Shit! Was he in my head again? I needed to figure out a way to stop that and sooner rather than later. *"Get out of my head!"*

He gave me a half shrug and turned to say something to

Alma.

I imagined a steel wall slamming down inside my head, shielding my thoughts from him, making sure that he could only enter if I gave him permission, and I was definitely not giving him permission.

I spooned eggs into my tortilla, allowing the conversation to flow around me. The others' fixation on the missing satellite phone seemed a bit extreme until I realized that without it, we had no way to communicate with the outside world.

"Wait. Are you telling me that we are stranded here?" I asked, giving voice to my anxiety.

David rolled his eyes. "I'm not sure if stranded is the appropriate term. It's not as if we're castaways on a deserted island. We can always hike out to one of the villages if we need to."

I pushed my half-eaten breakfast away, my appetite gone. "How far is the nearest village?"

"About fifteen kilometers," Enrique said, reaching for another tortilla. "But the nearest road—"

There was a sudden loud thump as something plummeted to the ground nearby. Doña Juana screamed.

Doña Juana stood rigid, her face ashen, pointing at something on the ground. One of the workers—Miguel, I thought his name was—crouched down to examine whatever had caught her attention.

"¡Una señal!" Doña Juana's voice trembled. "¡Malo! ¡Muy malo!" She frantically made the sign of the cross over and over again as if she were protecting herself from evil.

I leaned forward, trying to see what had caused her alarm. A dead quetzal bird lay on the packed earth, its iridescent green plumage dulled by death, its long tail feathers arranged in an unnaturally perfect spiral. The sight sent a chill down my spine—quetzals were rare, considered sacred by the Maya, and this one's positioning seemed deliberately ritualistic.

The local workers gathered around, speaking rapidly in

hushed tones that mixed Spanish with their native language. I caught fragments: "brujería," "mal agüero," and a name that made several of them cross themselves—"Li Xul."

Zen's body tensed beside me. When I glanced his way, his eyes had that strange, feral quality I'd seen in my dreams.

"It's just a dead bird," Roman announced loudly in Spanish, standing up. "Probably flew into a branch or was attacked by something and fell. Nothing to get excited about."

But Bembe shook his head, speaking urgently to Doña Juana in Spanish. I didn't catch all of it, but the words "Li Xul, Dr. Kelling" and "Señorita Nayla" were clear enough. The workers believed there was a connection between my sister's disappearance, Dr. Kelling's accident, the dead bird, and Li Xul.

"Es un mensaje," Doña Juana insisted, her dark eyes finding mine. "El guardián está enojado. La tierra está enojada."— It's a message. The guardian is angry. The land is angry.

Thunder rumbled in the distance and the air grew thick with the promise of rain. The workers exchanged knowing looks.

"It sounds like rain," Alma commented with surprise in her voice.

We turned as one and stared at the dark clouds gathering on the horizon. David squinted at the darkening sky. "It is too early in the season for rain."

"Apparently, not," Roman said dryly.

Alma's forehead creased with worry. "Raúl won't be able to land on the airstrip if it's too muddy. I'm not sure he can even fly if…"

"Alma's right. We should hike out now," Enrique interrupted, backing away from the dead bird. "Get help. Get a phone. Before—" He glanced at the gathering clouds, then at the pyramid looming over our camp.

"Don't be ridiculous," Roman snapped. "We have work to do. We need to secure the site—"

"The site can wait," David cut in, his voice sharp. "We need supplies anyway, and clearly we need a new satellite phone. We should hike out with the men. They know the way. It'll be safer in a group."

"I'll hike out," Enrique offered.

"No one is hiking out. It's just a dead bird and some unexpected rain," Roman said, his face set in stone.

"I'm not sure you have much say in who hikes out and who stays," Zen commented wryly.

I glanced over at Jake who was uncharacteristically silent, his eyes fixed on Bembe and the other men. I turned to see what had captured his attention.

Their stoic expressions said it all. They had no intention of staying. Whatever they believed was happening here, it had crossed some line in their cosmology. The dead quetzal was both warning and proof—the old powers were stirring, and they wanted no part of it.

As if confirming their fears, a low, resonant sound echoed from the direction of the ruins—like stone grinding against stone, though the day's excavation hadn't begun.

"Vámonos," Doña Juana said firmly, already gathering her things. "Ahora."

The men moved as one, collecting their belongings from their tents with practiced efficiency. No amount of arguing from Jake or reassurance from Roman could change their minds. Within an hour, they were gone, leaving behind half-empty coffee cups and the dead quetzal as mute testimony to their hasty departure.

The seven of us stood in the suddenly too-quiet camp as the first fat drops of rain began to fall. Then as if someone had turned on a fire hose, the pyramid and trees vanished behind sheets of water, and I couldn't shake the feeling that we were now cut off from the world in more ways than one.

"Still think we're not stranded?" I shouted over the noise of the deluge to David, but my attention was drawn to Zen, who stared at the dead quetzal with an expression I couldn't read.

Thunder cracked overhead like breaking stone, and somewhere in the jungle, something answered with a roar that sounded like a warning of impending danger.

David eyed the streams of water pouring from the thatched roof overhead. "We should have gone with Bembe and the others," he said voicing our anxiety.

"I just hope the tents hold up to this downpour, or we'll need to build ourselves an ark," Enrique commented.

Roman rolled his eyes. "It's just rain. What we need to do is secure the site. You and David should make sure the equipment in the lab is stored properly. A couple of extra tarps would be a good idea. Enrique and I will make sure all the trenches are covered. Zen, you can..." he paused.

Zen was gone.

Jake caught my eye. "Looks like Zen's gone to visit his grandmother. Again."

Roman ignored Jake's snarky remark and glanced up at the thatch roof, now leaking like a sieve. "Alma, why don't you and Niki collect our food and drink supplies. We'll need to protect them from the rain."

The incessant noise of rain pounding stone and earth made it hard to hold conversations. Alma and I quickly grew tired of shouting to be heard, so we mostly worked without speaking. Luckily, it turned out that most of the food supplies were already stored in critter-proof containers. Protecting the food supplies consisted of stacking crates and building impromptu shelving as we tried to move as much as we could up off the ground which was quickly becoming saturated from the torrential rain.

By late afternoon, the rain stopped but the earlier downpour had turned the excavation site into a series of muck-filled ponds interspersed with patches of thick boot-sucking mud. We gathered under the thatch roof of the Dining Hall, the only place big enough to accommodate all of us and surveyed the damage, staring glumly at the mess.

Enrique looked around. "This place isn't in too bad of shape. Other than a few leaks the thatch roof seems to have held up okay."

"Ugh! Why didn't you two get rid of the bird," David said when he caught sight of the dead quetzal still lying where it had fallen.

Alma made a mew of disgust and shuddered. Neither one of us had been willing to touch it while we were working, so we had left it where it lay.

David shook his head in disbelief. "You have got to be joking. Alma, you dig up skeletons and bones, how can you be afraid to touch a dead bird."

I kept silent, my eyes drawn to the bird's broken neck, its iridescent green feathers splayed like a grotesque piece of art on the packed earth. My sister had once told me that the ancient Maya considered quetzals to be divine messengers of the gods. I couldn't shake the feeling that Doña Juana was right about the quetzal being a message. I only hoped that the message wasn't meant for me.

"Oh, for Christ's sake." David pulled a pair of gloves from his back pocket, snapping them on his hands before bending over and scooping up the carcass. He strode to the edge of the clearing behind us and chucked the dead bird into the trees. Turning to face us, he mimed a washing motion with his hands as he grinned. "There, that's done. No need to worry your pretty little heads about the dead tweety bird anymore."

Jake and Enrique laughed. I did not. My eyes drifted to the spot where David had thrown the bird. A terrible foreboding seeped into my bones.

Roman cleared his throat. "Any chance you two found the Sat phone while you were cleaning up in here?"

We shook our heads.

He grimaced. "We need to take this place apart and find that phone. If we don't, we are stuck here until someone decides to send a plane our way."

I stared at him. "Are you serious?"

He nodded. "Very."

Enrique shook his head. "I don't get it. We've looked

everywhere for it."

"No, we haven't." Jake's blue eyes hardened. "I say we search Cazares' tent."

"I say we don't. Unless we search your tent first."

We turned around to see Zen, his mud splattered shirt and pants clinging to him like a second skin as he approached.

Jake's eyes raked over Zen like a razor. "Look what the cat's dragged in."

Zen answered with a slow feral smile before shifting his gaze to Roman. "I take it the phone is still MIA."

Roman answered with a curt nod.

"Okay, let's do it. Let's search everyone's tent, but Jake stays the hell out of mine." He turned and started walking toward his tent. "*We need to talk.*"

I flinched and stared fixedly at his retreating back, his voice echoing inside my head.

As I watched Zen disappear, a chill ran down my spine. My sister, the missing phone, the dead quetzal, the sudden storm—it all felt connected, pieces of a puzzle I couldn't quite grasp. And at the center of it all was Zen, with his cryptic words and ability to speak directly into my mind. I glanced at the others; their faces etched with worry and suspicion. We were cut off, tensions rising, and I couldn't shake the feeling that something ancient and dangerous was stirring in the jungle around us. As thunder rumbled in the distance, I made a decision. Whatever Zen had to say, I needed to hear it. With a deep breath, I followed him into the gathering gloom.

CHAPTER TEN

The lantern cast a warm circle of light inside the tent, creating an illusion of safety that couldn't quite dispel the oppressive darkness pressing against the thin fabric walls. Outside, the jungle pulsed with an unsettling silence, broken only by distant rustles that felt too deliberate, too watchful.

"Zen? Are you in there?" I asked, my voice barely above a whisper.

The front of the tent opened. He'd taken the time to shower off the muck and mud from his earlier foray into the jungle, and the scent of his shampoo made me want to run my fingers through his damp curls. I resolutely pushed the image from my mind as he stepped aside allowing me to enter. His eyes flickered past me, scanning the shadows outside before he zipped it closed.

"Make yourself comfortable." Zen lowered himself to the ground and stretched his legs, resting his back against a wooden crate.

I remained standing, keeping my distance from him and temptation. "Where were you this afternoon?"

"Looking for Nayla."

My heart leaped. "Did you find out where she is?" Hope

trembled in my voice.

He shook his head, his expression grave.

The air squeezed from my lungs. "Oh."

"It was the quetzal. I thought..." he said softly, his gaze turning distant.

"You thought what?"

He let out a long slow breath. "Nayla's wahy is a quetzal. I thought maybe she was trying to tell us something."

My brow furrowed in confusion. "What are you talking about?"

"Nayla is connected to the sun and dawn; her shadow spirit takes the form of the quetzal. Doña Juana was right— the dead quetzal was a message." He frowned. "I just don't know what the message is or who sent it."

A sudden flare of anger flashed within me. "Bullshit! I'm tired of this mystical nonsense! It was just a dead bird!"

Zen's eyes held mine firmly, unyielding. "You know that's not true," he said calmly but intensely. "I know you can feel it."

I closed my eyes, fighting against what I didn't want to believe. The image of the dead quetzal flashed in my mind again; its feathers arranged unnaturally on the ground like some grotesque offering. A chill ran down my spine, but I pushed the feeling away. "How do you know Nayla's spirit animal is a quetzal?"

He smiled tiredly. "Will you accept it if I tell you I just do?"

"Do I have a choice?"

He shook his head slightly. "No."

I sighed heavily, feeling trapped between disbelief and an undeniable pull toward truth. "You wanted to talk—so talk."

He patted the ground beside him. "Why don't you sit? This could take a while."

As I settled next to him, a low rumble echoed from the direction of the ruins—a sound like stone grinding against stone that sent chills down my spine. "What was that?" I whispered. "More thunder?"

"Another warning," he replied grimly. "I know you don't believe, but there are other forces at work here," he said slowly, his voice low and urgent.

A gust of wind rattled our tent as if responding to his words; it felt like something was watching us from beyond its thin walls.

"How much did Nayla tell you about...her research."

"Not much," I admitted.

His smile was grim. "It's time for a quick primer on Maya cosmology." He inhaled deeply and closed his eyes as if marshalling his thoughts before he began speaking. "The ancient Maya believed in the existence of supernatural beings who interacted in both the physical realm and the spiritual realm. Their gods could unleash terrible calamities in the physical world if angered. The role of the shamans— the aj ilonel or aj men—is to act as intermediaries between the living and the supernatural worlds, keeping the balance," he continued, glancing toward the entrance as though expecting something to emerge from the shadows. "Unfortunately, not all of these shamans use their powers for good."

I felt my heart race at his implication; dread settled in my stomach like lead. A gust of wind shook the tent, and for a moment, I could have sworn I heard my name whispered on the breeze. I shook my head, trying to clear it of these fanciful thoughts.

Zen's hand found mine, squeezing gently. "There's a shaman," he continued, his voice low and urgent. "Li Xul. The one Enrique mentioned yesterday. The locals fear him, and for good reason. He's using his powers for his own gain, disrupting the balance. And I think... I think he might be involved in Nayla's disappearance."

As Zen spoke, the shadows in the tent seemed to deepen, and I couldn't shake the feeling that we were being watched. The rational part of my mind scrambled for explanations, but with each passing moment, those explanations felt increasingly inadequate.

"David said Nayla might have gone to see Li Xul about the pectoral she'd found. But why would this shaman be involved with her disappearance?" I asked, my voice trembling. "I don't understand?"

Zen's eyes met mine, filled with a mixture of concern and something else—a fierce determination that both reassured and frightened me. "Because," he said softly, "I think your sister discovered something. Something that threatened him. Something Li Xul would kill to keep hidden."

My pulse quickened with unease. "What?" I whispered. "What did Nayla discover?"

"I don't know." His eyes locked onto mine with fierce intensity.

A vision from my nightmare flashed through my mind: Nayla standing with my father in an ancient cave entrance adorned with strange symbols—a place where wahy spirits might dwell—her face illuminated by an otherworldly glow.

"I need to go," I said abruptly. I felt as if an iron band was coiled around my chest making it hard to breathe. I stood.

Zen moved as if to get to his feet. "I'll walk you back to your tent."

"No!" I said, adding a belated, "Thanks, but I need time to think."

Clouds, buffeted by the wind and obscured the moon leaving me to carefully pick my way across the muddy archaeological site in darkness, my frayed nerves causing me to see and hear things in the night that made my heart skitter and skip in fear. I chided myself for my childish reaction to Zen's ghost story. I was letting my imagination run away with me. This was why I had refused to listen to my father's stories when I was young.

I'd spent my entire life rejecting the idea of a supernatural world populated by gods, demons, and sorcerers despite my father's stories and my sister's insistence that the stories were true. I wasn't ready to accept that dead birds and rainstorms were a sign of supernatural disturbance, but I couldn't quite shake the feeling that something was wrong, very wrong. The logical part of my brain rejected the idea of a supernatural realm, but another part of my brain felt the truth of his words with a visceral intensity.

I slipped into my sister's tent. Alma looked up from her book. "I was getting worried about you."

"Sorry. I was chatting with Zen."

A sly smile flitted across her face. "Chatting? Is that what it's called?"

"Yes. Chatting," I said firmly, cutting off all further conversation as I removed my clothes. I slid into my sister's sleeping bag, rolled onto my side and closed my eyes. Alma turned off the lantern and I listened to the creaking of her cot as she settled in for the night.

My mind was going a million miles a minute. Doña Juana wasn't wrong when she called my sister a witch. Nayla truly believed that she could influence events and people through supernatural means. She used to try and convince me that we were linked to the wider universe through our spirit companions and if I opened my mind to the possibilities I would be able to navigate between realms and worlds also. I had rolled my eyes at what I called her "Mayan fantasies." Given my disdain and skepticism of the topic, she eventually stopped talking to me about her abilities. Now I wish I had asked more questions.

Zen's insistence that I also had those abilities was troubling because I couldn't deny that I was experiencing things I could not easily explain. I felt jittery and off-balance as if the world was tilting underneath me. Underlying my feeling of unease, like a festering splinter beneath my skin, was the fact that my sister was still missing. I closed my eyes, forcing myself to breathe deeply as I tried to quiet my mind before drifting off to sleep.

The quetzal bird flits in front of me, flying low as if teasing me, the iridescent green, red, and blue of its feathers glittering like jewels in the bright sunlight. I leap softly onto the ground and follow it. I am filled with joy to see this beautiful bird. The bird flits among the trees, circling back to me when I fall behind, urging me forward.

She stretches her wings and glides beneath a tree branch just as a huge jaguar, eyes aflame, leaps from his hiding place and snatches her in his jaws. Rage erupts from me. This is my quetzal! I will not allow this to happen!

I call forth a torrential rain which pours like a biblical deluge from the sky, drowning the land below it. The jaguar finds himself suddenly swimming and struggles to keep his head above the water as he clutches my bird in his jaws. He turns toward me, his dark eyes rimmed with red, shocked and angry at this turn of events.

I watch in satisfaction as water sweeps over the jaguar's head. He releases the quetzal, sputtering and splashing as he struggles against the current, his eyes burning with hate and rage as the water carries him from my dream.

The water slowly recedes leaving behind a trail of slick red mud, uprooted plants, fractured tree limbs, and the broken body of the quetzal.

Lifting her broken body carefully in my jaws I carry her into the jungle where I lay her gently on the ground. I crouch next to my sister and weep.

I awoke with a shattered heart, tears streaming down my cheeks. My sister's name is a silent scream inside my head.

I slipped out of the tent as quietly as possible to avoid disturbing Alma. The air smelled of wet earth and decaying leaves. Gusts of wind chilled my skin in the night air, raising goose bumps on my arms and legs as I walked toward Zen's tent.

He was waiting for me. He folded his arms around me, holding me tightly and gently rocking me as if he were comforting a small child while I sobbed against his chest.

"I saw him in my dream. Li Xul. He's the other jaguar." I looked up at him, my face wet with tears. "He killed my sister."

He looked down at me, his cat's eyes glowing in the

moonlight. "Stay with me tonight," he said softly before leading me back to his tent.

We spooned together like an old married couple, Zen's arm draped protectively across my body. I pressed myself against him, feeling the strong slow beat of his heart as if it were my own, his breath warm against my skin.

The warmth of his hard lithe body next to mine was like a drug seeping into my bloodstream. It would be so easy to—I stopped myself, extinguishing the thought before Zen could reach into my head and hear it.

"Close your eyes. I will keep you safe tonight," he whispered, his voice vibrating under my skin like a plucked guitar string, his arm tightening around me. "Call me into your dreams and I will stand guard."

Exhaling deeply, I forced my eyes closed, reminding myself that Zen belonged to Nayla and allowed myself to surrender to the darkness as two amber eyes, glowing like flashlights, watched over me.

He was gone when I awoke the next morning. I was relieved. I was in no mood for company, not even Zen. My nightmare had left me feeling bruised and battered, the memory of the quetzal's death lay like a heavy stone on my heart.

I cautiously peeked out of the tent. There was no one about. Exiting quickly, I scurried along the muddy trail to the latrine before backtracking to my sister's tent.

Jake was waiting for me in front of the tent. When he caught sight of me, he quickly hid something behind his back, grinning like a Cheshire cat, the early morning sun turning his blonde ponytail into spun gold. "Good morning," he chirped.

"What do you have in your hand?" I asked suspiciously.

"I'll give you three guesses."

I was in no mood to play games. "I don't know." I eyed him for a moment while he waited expectantly. "You found the satellite phone," I begrudgingly guessed.

"No, but I do come bearing gifts." His smile widened.

I sighed heavily. "Jake, I'm tired and I don't want to play games." I moved as if to pass him, but he stopped me.

With a showman's flair, he whipped his hands from behind his back and offered me a toothbrush. "This is for you, my lady."

I greedily snatched it from his hand. "Oh my, god! How did you know?"

Jake looked pleased with himself. "Alma mentioned something. I remembered coming across this when I was searching the field lab yesterday."

"The field lab?"

"Yep. We archaeologists use a surprising number of dental tools in our work. They are very useful for scraping off stubborn bits of dirt and rock from artifacts."

I studied the toothbrush dubiously. "This hasn't been…"

His eyes flashed with merriment. "No. It's still in the package. I can also get you a dental pick if you need one of those."

I clutched the toothbrush as if it were a cherished prize. "Thank you, thank you, thankyou." I'd been rinsing my teeth with bottled water, now I could actually brush my teeth. "You have no idea how happy this makes me!" I told him.

Jake looked pleased. "You're welcome."

"I hate to be greedy, but is there any chance you found some extra toothpaste to go with this?"

He shook his head. "Sadly, no. But…I'm willing to share mine." He gave me a sly look and winked. "See you at breakfast." He sauntered off whistling a happy tune.

It was a little thing, but my encounter with Jake and brushing my teeth, even without toothpaste, felt like a victory over my terrible dream from the night before. Yes, I was still in the middle of the friggin jungle with no way of communicating to the outside world. Yes, there was still no sign of my sister. But somehow, in the light of day with semi-clean teeth, it was easy to pretend that my dream was the result of my overactive imagination, my sister was happily ensconced in a town somewhere, and Li Xul was nothing more than a bogeyman in a child's fairy tale.

Everyone had gathered at the dining hall. Alma and Enrique were scrambling eggs and making tortillas on the kerosene stove. David, Roman, Zen and Jake sat at the table studying a paper map.

"How'd you sleep last night?" Alma asked with a quick flick of her eyes toward Zen.

"Fine. Thanks," I replied, not taking the bait.

She grinned. "Enrique and I volunteered for breakfast duty. If you want caffeine your choices are warm coke or coffee."

"Coffee."

Alma nodded to the battered metal percolator perched on top of the stove. "Help yourself."

Enrique looked up from where he was cracking eggs into a bowl. "By the way, Jake volunteered the two of you for clean up."

I located a ceramic mug in one of the crates and poured myself a cup of coffee. "I'm down with that."

"Good to hear." He paused and looked over at the table. "Did you hear that, Jake? You and Niki are on clean up."

Jake gave him a thumbs up.

Skirting the crates, I made my way to the table. The guys were involved in what sounded like an intense discussion. Zen slid over to create a space for me on the bench.

"I agree with David. It's stupid to wait around here until someone decides to come look for us. We should hike out to the nearest town," Jake continued heatedly.

"You have no idea what you're asking us to do," Zen said. "This isn't some nature park with groomed trails."

Roman shook his head. "Zen's right. It's too dangerous. Besides, this is where they will come to look for us."

"That's the whole point. When are they going to come looking for us?" Jake argued. "We could be here for weeks."

"We should have left with Bembe and the others,"

David said.

Roman gave David the side eye. "Not helpful, David."

"Breakfast is served." Enrique and Alma dropped a platter of scrambled eggs and tortillas on the table.

Roman rolled up the map and slid it to the end of the table.

Jake grabbed a tortilla and filled it with eggs. "So, what? You think we should just sit around here and wait until we don't have any supplies left?"

"It won't come to that, Jake," Alma said. "Dr. Kelling will send a plane for us."

"Assuming he didn't die," David mumbled.

Roman glared at him. "Once again, not helpful."

Alma passed me the plate of tortillas. "People know that we're here. They'll figure it out eventually. The university knows we are at Choja q'eq. They'll send someone out here. Though, Pastor Miguel's village isn't that far. We could hike out to it."

Roman shot an angry look her way. "I say we wait for a plane."

Jake shook his head angrily. "You don't get it. No one is going to rescue us. We're on our own. Our only option is to hike out. Alma's right. Pastor Miguel will have resources we can access."

"How far away is Doña Juana's village?" I asked.

Jake nodded approvingly at me. "Santilq'ol is only a day's hike from here."

"It doesn't matter how far it is since we don't know if we can find it," Roman replied.

"It's not on the map?"

"In a word, no. We don't have GPS out here. We'd be hiking blind. And even if we could find the village, there's no guarantee that we'll be able to contact anyone outside of the village. It's not like there's going to be a cell phone tower nearby." Roman's voice dripped with sarcasm.

"The best we could hope for would be to get someone from the village to guide us to the Cobán or one of the other towns, but even with a guide I wouldn't want to hike fifty miles through the jungle. We're not equipped to do that," David added.

"We don't need to get a guide. We've got one right here." Jake stared pointedly at Zen. "Don't we, Zen?"

We all turned and looked at Zen. He returned our gazes, his eyes calm, his expression unreadable, and said nothing.

Jake's eyes flashed angrily. "What? You've got nothing to say? You've been prowling around the jungle since you arrived here. Why don't you take us to meet your grandmother? The one you were supposedly visiting when Nayla disappeared."

I inhaled sharply at the mention of my sister's name.

Jake's eyes darted my way, before sliding back to Zen. "What about it, Zen? Are you willing to be our guide?"

"No."

"No?" Jake said with a frown, bristling with barely contained anger. "Why not?"

As we stared at him, waiting for his reply, Zen took a sip of his coffee. "Like David said, we're not equipped to hike through the jungle."

"Okay. How about this? We don't hike through the jungle. You do," Jake said with a malicious smile. "You hike out to find help while the rest of us wait here."

"No."

Alma placed her hand on Jake's arm. "Jake, that's a lot to ask of someone. It's dangerous out there."

Jake shrugged off her hand. "So what? He's been out there before. He knows the way."

Zen's eyes narrowed. "You have no idea what you're asking."

"Then enlighten us," Jake challenged, leaning forward. The tension at the table was palpable. I glanced between Jake and Zen, sensing there was more to this confrontation than just finding a way out of the jungle.

Roman cleared his throat. "Look, we're all stressed. But we need to stick together. Sending someone into the jungle alone is too risky."

"I agree," Enrique chimed in, his usual easygoing humor replaced by genuine concern. "We don't know what's out there."

I couldn't help but think of my dream and the jaguar with the red-rimmed eyes. I shuddered involuntarily. Zen noticed.

"There are things in this jungle that you can't begin to understand," he said, addressing the group but looking directly at me.

Jake scoffed. "Fine. If Zen is too chicken to hike to the village. I'll do it." He turned to me. "Niki, what do you say? Should we go find Nayla?"

My eyes widened in surprise. "What?" My heart rate bumping up a notch. "Me?" I squeaked.

He reached across the table and grasped my hand. "This is something we should have done as soon as Nayla went missing. Doña Juana's village is not far from here. Let's go. We can hike out today. Nayla knew how to get there. She'd been there before. I'm sure that's where she is."

Before I could even answer, Zen spoke up. "Niki is not going with you."

I scowled at Zen. "You don't get to tell me what I'm going to do."

The others kept silent, their eyes darting between Zen, Jake, and myself.

Jake ignored the others. His blue eyes fastened on me with an intense sincerity. "Niki, I know you're worried about Nayla. Let's do something about it. Something that should have been done the day she disappeared. Let's find her. Let's find your sister." Jake squeezed my hand encouragingly.

"I don't know." I glanced nervously at the wall of vegetation circling the archaeological site. "What if we get lost or what if they send a plane and we miss our chance to get out of here."

Zen glared at me. "Don't be stupid, Niki. You're not

going with him."

Nayla's face floated before my eyes. If Zen was right, and my dreams were some sort of message, well, the message was clear. My sister was in danger. I had no choice. I had to do whatever it took to save her. I held Zen's stare for a moment, lifting my chin defiantly, before turning to face Jake. "When do you want to leave?"

LISA DIETRICH

CHAPTER ELEVEN

Li Xul paced the damp cave floor, his rage palpable in the flickering torchlight. The night's events replayed in his mind, each detail fueling his anger and confusion. He had sent his wahy, the powerful jaguar spirit, to eliminate the quetzal—the girl's wahy. It should have been a simple task, a mere flexing of his considerable power in the dream realm. But something had gone terribly wrong. The sister —the twin, the one he had been told was powerless—had somehow intervened.

In the spirit world, he had watched her move through the trees with the grace and stealth of a jaguar. It was impossible. Her birth sign should not have granted her the ability to manifest as the sacred feline. The day of one's birth determined their wahy, immutable as the stars themselves. Yet there she was, defying all he knew to be true. And then, incomprehensibly, she had transformed into water itself.

The memory of his wahy struggling against the flood she created made his fists clench in fury. How had she commanded the elements with such ease? Such power should have been beyond her reach.

"Impossible," he muttered, his voice echoing off the

cave walls. "It cannot be her."

Yet the evidence was undeniable. She had not only seen his wahy but had fought it off, protecting her sister's spirit. Such a feat should have been beyond her capabilities.

Li Xul's mind raced with the implications. If this girl truly possessed the power to challenge him, to defy the very laws of the spirit world he had spent decades mastering, then everything was at risk. His carefully laid plans, his accumulated power, his control over the region—all of it could crumble if she realized her full potential. He needed answers. He needed to know how she had acquired such abilities, and more importantly, how to strip them from her.

The balance of power had shifted, and he felt control slipping through his fingers like sand. As he contemplated his next move, a shrill sound cut through the cave's heavy silence. Li Xul froze, his eyes darting to the source of the noise. There, on a makeshift altar of stone, lay the satellite phone. It was ringing. For a moment, Li Xul stood motionless, staring at the device as if it were a venomous serpent. Then, slowly, a cruel smile spread across his face.

Perhaps this unexpected call would provide the very answers he sought. With deliberate steps, he approached the altar, his hand reaching for the phone. Whatever came next, he would be ready. The girl may have won this skirmish in the dream realm, but Li Xul was far from defeated. The real battle was only beginning.

CHAPTER TWELVE

I zipped the top of my sister's daypack closed, my fingers trembling slightly. Inhaling deeply, I rolled my neck to try and loosen the knot that had formed between my shoulder blades. Going into the jungle with Jake was reckless and dangerous, but I had no choice. I had to find my sister. Exhaling forcefully, I stood, resolutely slipping Nayla's day pack over my shoulders. It was time. I stepped out of the tent.

Zen leaned against a tree, arms crossed, watching me. His stillness was unnerving, almost inhuman. His green-gold eyes watched me with an intensity that made my skin prickle.

"Don't try to talk me out of this," I warned him, more sharply than intended.

One corner of his mouth tilted upward, but the smile never reached his eyes. "I wouldn't dream of it." He held out his hand. "Give me your pack."

I grasped the shoulder straps tightly. "No!"

"I'm not going to take it from you. I just want to check your supplies."

I hesitated. Something in his tone made the hair on my

neck rise. Not danger, precisely. But something close to it.

I eyed him suspiciously. "Why?"

He sighed heavily. "Because you are going hiking in the jungle. Because you need to be prepared. Because I want to make sure you are safe. Because you have no experience with this sort of thing. Because…"

"Fine," I interrupted.

I begrudgingly handed the daypack over to Zen. He unzipped it and began rooting around inside. He shook his head.

"You've no first aid supplies, no rain gear, no food, and one measly bottle of water."

"Jake said the hike to the village is only a few hours."

Zen's mouth tightened. "Jake is an idiot."

He bent over and unzipped the backpack lying at his feet. He began pulling out items and transferring them to my pack. "These are water purifying tablets." He held up a foil packet. "The directions are on the back. This is a waterproof poncho." He lifted my pack with one hand, testing its heft. "If you think you can manage the weight, you should add at least one more bottle of water."

He held it out to me, eyeing my shorts and T-shirt. "You also need to change your clothes. See if you can find a light-weight long sleeve shirt and you'll want to cover your legs."

"In case you didn't notice, it's 80 degrees and humid. Why would I want to wear long sleeves?"

"Bugs." He eyed me up and down. "Trust me, you don't want to have all that sweet succulent flesh exposed to the ticks, bot flies, and mosquitos that are going to find us in the jungle."

I rolled my eyes at him, but did as he said, ducking back into the tent to rummage through my sister's clothes until I found something I thought would work. A pair of dark green hiking pants and a dry-fit long-sleeved shirt.

When I returned, Zen gave me a nod of approval and handed me the daypack.

I meekly shouldered the pack. "I'll go get another bottle

of water from the Dining Hall."

Zen slung his backpack over his shoulders, following me as I walked.

I glanced back at him. "What are you doing?"

"Keeping you safe," he said, with a lift of his eyebrow, his eyes challenging me. "You didn't think I was going to let you do this without me, did you?"

My first reaction was to angrily deny that I needed his help, but I stopped myself. He was right. I would feel safer if Zen came with Jake and me.

The atmosphere at the Dining Hall crackled with unspoken tensions. Alma, David, and Roman sat on one side of the table, Enrique and Jake sat across from them. I noticed that Enrique had added a backpack to his customary ensemble of board shorts, t-shirt and backward baseball cap. He eyed Zen as we approached.

"Looks like we've got a quorum," Enrique said, grinning and breaking the electric silence. "Zen, I take it you'll be joining us."

Zen's nod was minimal. Controlled.

Jake's body went rigid, his eyes boring into me. "I wasn't expecting you to bring an entourage."

I shrugged. "Not my choice." I went over to the cooler and grabbed a bottle of Gatorade, stuffing it in the side pocket of my sister's daypack.

Jake abruptly got to his feet. "We need to get going."

Alma walked over to me and gave me a hug. "If Nayla shows up here, we'll let her know where you are."

"Thanks."

Enrique stood and leaned over the table to fist bump David and Roman. "See ya on the flip side, bros. If the troops get here first, send them our way, otherwise we'll send them to you once we get back to civilization."

"Let's go." Jake shot a resentful look Zen's way before grabbing his pack and leading us to the tree line. He paused to unsheathe a machete.

"Once more into the breach," I murmured under my

breath as I stared into the darkness between the trees, a darkness pulsing with unknown threats.

"What?"

Apparently, Enrique was not a lover of Shakespeare. I returned Enrique's quizzical look with a tight smile before squaring my shoulders and following Jake into the dense foliage.

The "trail" to the village was nothing more than a faint depression among the bed of decaying leaves covering the ground. We walked in a single file line, the thick air wrapping around us like a heavy wet blanket. The ground felt spongy under my feet as if the rain from yesterday had not yet been absorbed by the earth.

Jake, resentful of Zen's presence, sullenly slashed at the woody vines and tangle of branches, as Enrique tried to lighten the mood with jokes and banter. Eventually, even he fell silent. The thick tree canopy blocked the sun, making it feel as if we were hiking in a hot green cave; a cave echoing with various hoots, screeches, squawks, and the sound of a million buzzing insect wings.

We'd been following Jake for about three hours, when Zen finally spoke. "Jake, I've got a compass with me. We should check to make sure we're headed in the right direction."

Jake stopped and turned around to face us, wiping sweat from his brow with the back of his hand. "If you want to take the lead, it's all yours." He held out the machete.

Zen shrugged. "No thanks. You're the one who knows where we're going. I'm just making a suggestion."

The straps of Nayla's daypack dug into my shoulder muscles, now painfully uncomfortable. I took advantage of our stop to shrug off the daypack and drink some water, letting my gaze wander. Vegetation pressed in on us from all sides. I had no idea what "trail" Jake was following, but I had long ago lost any sign of it.

With a shudder, I used the back of my hand to brush off a cluster of small red ticks clinging to my sister's pants, grateful that I'd listened to Zen about protecting my legs. Some kind of bug buzzed and whined near my ear. I searched in the pack for the bottle of bug repellent and rubbed some on the back of my neck, pants, and ankles.

Enrique had also dropped his pack on the ground and drank greedily from his water bottle. "Wouldn't be a bad idea to make sure we're headed in the right direction, Jake," he commented, replacing the cap on his water bottle.

"Shut up," Jake growled. He opened his pack and began rummaging through it. He froze in shocked surprise and looked up, his gaze shifting guiltily among us, before hastily zipping his pack closed again. "I don't have the compass."

Zen eyed him with disdain. "Good thing I brought one also." He opened his pack and pulled out a compass.

Jake moved closer, peering over Zen's shoulder. "We've been heading east," Zen said, his voice unnervingly calm. "I thought you said the village was northeast."

Jake's face flushed. Not with simple embarrassment. With something darker. "I know where we're going. We stay on the trail."

"What trail?" I asked, unable to keep the frustration out of my voice. "I haven't seen anything resembling a trail for hours."

As thunder rumbled overhead, I felt it—a strange resonance deep in my bones. Not fear. Something closer to recognition.

"We need to find shelter," Zen said, his voice calm but urgent. "It's going to be dark soon, and we can't risk getting even more lost."

Jake opened his mouth as if to argue, then closed it, nodding reluctantly. Zen took charge, leading us to a small clearing where the trees provided some cover.

"We'll camp here for the night," he announced. "Enrique, help me gather some dry wood if you can find any. Jake, see if you can clear a space for a fire. Niki, set up whatever shelter we have."

As the others moved to their tasks, I realized with a

sinking feeling that we hadn't brought any tents or sleeping bags. The best I could do was to string up the ponchos between trees to create a makeshift shelter.

When Zen saw what I'd done, he gave me a nod of approval. "Good thinking."

My face flushed with pleasure at the compliment. "Thanks. I used my Girl Scout training."

"Girl Scout training? I thought they mostly sold cookies," Zen said with a lift of his eyebrow.

"We did sell cookies. But we also went camping. Once. Then I quit. I don't like camping."

Zen threw back his head and laughed. I couldn't help but join in. None of my friends back home would ever believe that I was spending the night sleeping in the jungle of my own volition.

By the time darkness fell, we had a small fire going, thanks to Zen's waterproof matches. We huddled around it, the ponchos providing us with the illusion of protection. I only hoped we didn't have another rainstorm.

"So much for a few hours' hike," Enrique muttered, warming his hands by the fire. Jake sat silently, staring into the flames.

"We'll head back to Choja q'eq at first light," Zen said, passing around some energy bars he'd packed. "We should be able to follow our own trail back."

As I chewed the tasteless bar, my thoughts turned to Nayla. Was she out here somewhere, lost and alone? Or had something worse happened to her?

I shivered, moving closer to our meager fire. It was going to be a very long night.

I must have dozed off because when I awoke, the fire had burned down leaving only a small collection of embers. My neck and muscles were stiff from the exertion of hiking and sleeping on the cold hard ground. I sat up and rubbed my arms for warmth, glancing around our makeshift campsite as my eyes became accustomed to the dark.

I quietly got to my feet, stepping over Zen's sleeping

form, and placed the last of the wood we'd collected on the embers.

Enrique stretched and raised himself to a sitting position. I sat next to him. We both held our hands toward the meager flame.

"We need more wood," Enrique said softly as he pushed himself to his feet. "I'll go get some. You stay here and make sure the fire doesn't go out."

I poked the embers with a stick, sending a shower of sparks drifting upward into the night air. I couldn't see Enrique, but I could hear him as he gathered twigs and branches in the tangle of vegetation surrounding us.

Zen stirred and sat up, brushing the hair out of his eyes. "Where are Jake and Enrique?" he asked.

"Enrique is getting more wood. I don't know where Jake is."

From somewhere in the dark, I heard a deep throaty cough. It sounded vaguely human, except it was very low and very deep. Zen froze.

"Enrique?" I called nervously. "Is that you?"

"Quiet. Don't move," Zen whispered. "Stay by the fire."

The low booming cough sounded again. This time, however, it was followed by a deep rumbling snarl.

I felt my blood run cold. Zen held up his hand, motioning for me to stay still.

The jungle had become eerily silent, even the insects had stopped their incessant buzzing. It was as if every living thing in the jungle was holding its breath, waiting.

From the other side of the fire pit there was another booming cough, throaty, deep, and powerful. It cut through the silence like a knife. I flinched, startled by the proximity of the sound.

"I've got enough wood to make our fire really roar," Enrique announced as he lumbered toward us, a collection of branches and twigs filling his arms.

In a sudden blur of fur and muscle, a snarling jaguar launched itself onto Enrique's back, sinking its teeth into his neck. Enrique screamed and fell to the ground as Zen jumped to his feet and hurled himself at the big cat.

I stood and watched helplessly as the snarling, writhing mass of fur and limbs rolled across the ground away from the fire.

Jake materialized from the surrounding darkness, machete in hand, staring in shocked horror at Enrique's bloody body.

"Do something!" I screamed at him.

The world suddenly tilted sideways as I was abruptly torn from my body.

I smell the biting metallic odor of blood mingling with the musky stench of the jaguar and the smell of my own sweat and fear. Claws and teeth flash. I am screaming with rage and frustration as my prey rolls and twists beneath me. I desperately try to kill my prey, roaring with pain as sharp claws rake my flesh. The weight of the animal knocks the breath from my lungs as we fall to the ground.

I look into fierce yellow eyes and it is as if time has stopped. The cat's quivering muscles bunch as if to attack, but I lunge upward sinking my teeth in the soft flesh of his throat, tasting the warm salty blood as it trickles down my throat. My stomach churns with nausea and something else, an intense craving for more.

No!

I ripped myself from my dream, my legs folding beneath me as I fell to the ground weeping. With a certainty that defied logic, I knew that nothing about this moment was accidental. Something powerful and ancient had awakened and I was somehow connected to it.

CHAPTER THIRTEEN

The fire crackled weakly, casting flickering shadows across our makeshift camp. Enrique's labored breathing punctuated the eerie silence of the jungle night. I huddled close to the flames, my body trembling not from cold, but from the lingering shock of my... vision? Possession? I couldn't find words to describe what had happened. The taste of blood still lingered in my mouth, a coppery reminder of the jaguar's savage attack. But it hadn't been the jaguar, had it? It had been me. Somehow, impossibly, I had become the predator. I glanced at Zen, his shirt torn and stained with blood.

His eyes met mine, filled with a mixture of concern and something else— recognition, perhaps? As if he understood what had happened to me.

Jake paced at the edge of our camp, machete still in hand. He seemed unscathed, but his face was pale, his jaw clenched tight. "We need to get out of here," he said, breaking the tense silence. "We need to head back to the dig."

Zen shook his head slowly. "We can't move Enrique. Not that far. He's too badly injured."

"So, what, we just sit here and wait for the jaguar to come back?" Jake's voice rose, edged with panic.

"It won't come back," I said softly, surprising myself.

Both men turned to look at me. "How do you know?" Jake demanded.

I swallowed hard, avoiding their gazes. "I just... know."

I closed my eyes, memories of the attack flooding back.

"She's right. It won't be back," Zen said quietly. He leaned back, resting against a fallen log with a groan of pain.

Jake's face contorted with a mixture of fear and disgust. "What the hell is going on here? You know something, don't you?" He pointed accusingly at Zen.

Zen met Jake's glare steadily. "I know that the jungle can be dangerous. I know that we can't move Enrique. I know that we're not doing anything tonight."

"Screw that," Jake spat. "I'm getting us out of here, with or without you."

As they argued, I found myself drifting, their voices fading into the background. Something had awakened inside me, something ancient and powerful. And somehow, I knew it was connected to Nayla's disappearance. We were part of something bigger, a cosmic game I was only beginning to understand. I looked up, interrupting their heated exchange.

"We stay," I said firmly. "At least until morning. Enrique needs us, Zen is in bad shape and...it would be stupid to try and travel while it's dark."

Jake and Zen fell silent, their rivalry momentarily forgotten as they stared at me.

"I didn't mean that we should leave now," Jake commented sullenly. "I'm not stupid."

I ignored him.

Zen held my gaze and nodded. "There's a first aid kit in my pack. Enrique's lost a lot of blood. See if you can find something to stop the bleeding," he said before closing his eyes.

I eyed his blood-soaked shirt. "What about you?"

"I'll be fine," he replied without opening his eyes.

***

When the sun finally rose, it brought with it a heavy morning mist that curled around the trees and vegetation, wrapping the jungle in a thick white blanket. I rubbed my arms for warmth and scooted closer to the fire as the forest awoke. I could hear the various hoots, calls, and whistles of birds and monkeys, but they remained nothing more than faint shadows flitting above us in the mist-shrouded branches.

Jake stirred the glowing embers of our fire with a broken tree branch before tossing it into the flames. The wood was damp from the mist. The fire spluttered and smoked.

Zen roused himself, and painfully got to his feet, wincing. I looked him over. The jaguar's teeth and claws had left deep gashes on his shoulders, back, and chest. Last night, he had let me treat the worst of them with the antibiotic ointment I'd found in his first aid kit which I hoped would prevent them from becoming infected.

There wasn't much we could do for Enrique. He lay next to the fire where we'd half carried, half-dragged him last night, eyes closed, skin deathly pale, his breath shallow and erratic. The jaguar had managed to sink his teeth into the back of his neck and shoulder. The puncture wounds had been deep and bled a lot. I had covered him with one of the waterproof ponchos, in the hope that it might keep him warm, but I wasn't sure it was doing him much good.

"Where are you going?" Jake challenged Zen as he walked away from our camp.

"To take a piss. You good with that?" Zen replied evenly.

Jake watched Zen leave, his face hard and angry. When Zen was out of sight, he turned toward me. "We need to get out of here. You and me."

"Jake," I said tiredly. "Give it a rest." I was cold, hungry, thirsty and in no mood to put up with his petty jealousy.

He grabbed my arm, his eyes staring at me with a ferocious intensity. "Listen to me, Nikki. I'm serious. Zen can stay with Enrique. The two of us will hike to the village and get help. It's the only reasonable plan."

I brushed his hand from my arm. "You couldn't find the village yesterday, what makes you think you can find it today? When Zen comes back, we'll talk about it and decide on a plan."

Jake's expression darkened. "You're making a mistake to trust that guy. He's the one that is dangerous. Not the jungle."

I returned his gaze. "You had the machete, but it was Zen who tried to save Enrique last night. I'll stick with dangerous."

Jake's eyes blazed angrily. "You've made the wrong choice."

I opened my mouth to retort, but the words died on my lips as movement caught my eye. Zen was emerging from the mist, but he wasn't alone. Six men, dressed in t-shirts, loose cotton pants, and rubber rain boots, followed behind him. Two of the men carried a long sapling on their shoulders, the carcass of a dead jaguar swinging below it. The other four men wore machetes and had rifles slung over their shoulders.

My heart raced as I instinctively shrank back. Jake tensed beside me, his hand moving toward his own machete.

"It's okay," Zen called out, his voice calm but authoritative. "They're here to help."

As the group approached, I couldn't help but wonder if this was what Jake had meant by the "wrong choice." Had Zen known these men were out here? And more importantly, could we trust them?

The men's eyes darted between us, lingering on Enrique's prone form. One of them, older than the rest, stepped forward and spoke rapidly to Zen in language I didn't recognize. Zen nodded, replying in the same language.

I glanced at Jake, whose face was a mask of suspicion and barely contained anger. It was clear that whatever was happening, it was far beyond what any of us had anticipated when we set out to find Doña Juana's village yesterday.

According to Zen, the men were willing to take us to their village. There was a brief argument, the older man shaking his head when I pointed to Enrique.

"We can't leave him, Zen," I said, locking eyes with him. "Tell them. We will not leave Enrique."

Zen nodded.

I'm not sure what Zen said, but an agreement was reached. The men quickly and silently went to work using their machetes to hack at vines and saplings to make a stretcher for Enrique. Zen and one of the men gently rolled Enrique onto the stretcher and lashed him in place with another vine.

"Looks like you and I have first shift," he said with a curt nod at Jake. Jake shot a venomous look my way, before reluctantly scrambling to his feet.

"I can help," I offered.

Zen gave me a tight little smile. "Don't you worry, you will be."

Our progress was slow and painful. The mist had quickly burned off leaving a humid heat in its wake while we hiked. As the heat built, my clothing stuck to me, chafing my skin while sweat dripped from my forehead, blurring my vision and burning my eyes with a toxic mix of insect repellent and human salt.

Zen, Jake and I rotated positions carrying the stretcher every half hour or so. I dreaded each time it was my turn. The muscles in my shoulders and arms ached, the rough bark of the handholds scratched and inflamed the skin on the palms of my hands. I couldn't help but think how painful it must be for Zen, each time he lifted the stretcher, it reopened the wounds causing them to weep, staining his shirt red.

To make matters worse, neither Jake, Zen, nor I had had anything to eat or much to drink for hours. I was feeling so weak that I began to worry that I wasn't going to make it to the village. My heart pounded and I wheezed for breath as I struggled to keep up with our Maya guides. I panted and staggered forward, willing myself to keep moving my feet one step at a time. At one point, exhausted and close to muscle failure, I stumbled. The stretcher tilted dangerously and only Jake's quick reflexes kept the stretcher, and Enrique, from spilling onto the ground.

Realizing that I needed a break, the older man signaled for us to stop. With a grunt of relief, Jake and I set Enrique down. I straightened up, rolling my shoulders and neck. I flexed my stiff, swollen fingers, my hands aching as blood rushed into them and shook off my pack with a hiss from the pain.

Two of our guides scrambled up a couple of nearby trees, cutting sections from the thick brown vine curling around the trunks. They slid down the trees. One of them made two quick slices with his machete and offered the woody vine to me.

"Agua," he said timidly.

I licked my dry, cracked lips and accepted his gift, unsure what to do.

He mimed holding the vine above his mouth. I imitated his movements and clear liquid dripped from the vine. I drank greedily letting the cool liquid soothe my parched throat. When I finished, I wiped my mouth with the back of my hand, nodding my thanks to him. "Gracias."

He smiled shyly as I handed the vine back to him. Zen broke our last energy bar into small pieces and passed them around to everyone.

When we had finished, one of the men wordlessly lifted Enrique's stretcher, taking my place, and we resumed our single file march through the forest.

As we pushed deeper into the jungle, the canopy became denser, casting us in an eerie twilight. The sounds of unseen creatures echoed around us. We ducked under low hanging vines and clambered over rocks and rotting logs, my limbs heavy with fatigue as I numbly put one foot in front of the other and hoped and prayed, we would stop soon.

Then, as if by magic, a narrow path marked by two stakes with jaguar skulls stuck on top of them suddenly appeared in the middle of the forest.

"We're close to the village," Zen said.

Jake grunted a reply. I was too tired, hot, and thirsty to answer.

The path wound its way through the trees and vines until it ended in a small clearing ringed with five thatched huts. Two young peccaries, tethered to stakes, lay sunning themselves in the center of the clearing. Several women in colorful skirts looked up expectantly from where they were grinding corn on stone metates. One of the men shouted a greeting to the women. At the sound of their arrival, the village came to life.

Dogs began to bark, naked children tumbled out of the huts only to stop and gaze in open-mouthed surprise when they caught sight of Zen, Jake, and me. The women jumped up and hurried over to the men and quickly took charge of the dead jaguar.

The men carrying Enrique paused and slowly lowered his make-shift stretcher to the ground. An old woman hobbled toward us. Her skin was brown and wrinkled like worn-out leather, her hands gnarled and bony. She paused in front of us, her eyes, cloudy with cataracts, focused on Zen.

He bowed his head. "*Grandmother.*"

His words echoed in my head though he had not spoken. Grandmother? Was this the grandmother Zen had visited when Nayla disappeared?

She acknowledged his words with a nod before bending over to examine Enrique. "*I can do nothing for this one.*"

I heard her words clearly.

She reached toward me, cupping my face in her

calloused hands. A wave of dizziness overcame me, and I stumbled, my vision blurring. The world around me seemed to shift, colors becoming more vivid, sounds more intense.

I could hear the old woman's voice, though her lips weren't moving. "*The jaguar's mark is upon her*," she said, her cloudy eyes fixed on me. "*She is a child of two worlds. She is a child of jaguar. She is a child of moon. Connected to light and shadow, to the seen and unseen, to life and death.*"

I felt a chill run down my spine despite the oppressive heat. The jungle around us seemed to pulse with an otherworldly energy, the air thick with unseen presences. The villagers' eyes, all focused on us now, held a mixture of fear and reverence.

Zen stepped closer to me, his hand on my elbow steadying me.

The old woman's gaze shifted between Zen and me, a knowing look in her eyes. "*The balance is shifting*," she said, her voice echoing in my mind. "*Something ancient and powerful awakens and grows restless.*"

I wanted to protest, to deny any connection to these strange events, but the words caught in my throat. The memory of my transformation into the jaguar flashed through my mind, vivid and undeniable.

"*Hija de la Luna, you will come with me*," she commanded, releasing me. She turned and began to hobble slowly toward one of the huts.

As if I had no will of my own, I obediently followed behind her.

CHAPTER FOURTEEN

I entered the old woman's hut, Zen and Jake following silently behind me. The interior was dim, lit only by the flickering flames of a small fire pit in the center. Shadows danced on the walls, adorned with strange symbols and dried plants. Gourds, clay pots, and plastic five-gallon buckets lined crude wooden shelves, their contents a mystery.

The old woman crouched next to the fire and pointed a gnarled finger at me, gesturing for me to sit on the hard packed dirt floor. She then motioned Zen over to a woven mat of dried leaves near the fire, ignoring Jake who hovered uncertainly nearby in the doorway.

Zen's movements were careful, deliberate as he lowered himself to the ground. He removed his tattered shirt, exposing the deep claw marks that marred his smooth skin. The dagger-like pendant around his neck gleaming white against his skin in the firelight.

With practiced hands the healer began to examine Zen's injuries. He winced as she probed the edges of the wounds. She pointed at a clay pot on one of the shelves. I retrieved it for her, watching silently as she scooped out a pungent salve and applied it to the deep gashes that mapped his chest like angry rivers. He hissed in pain, his muscles tensing.

She spoke to Zen in her native language, her dark eyes darting toward Jake.

"Jake, she wants you to bring Enrique in here," Zen translated through gritted teeth as the healer worked the medicine into his arm.

"We'll get him," I volunteered, turning toward the exit.

"*Daughter of the Moon, you will stay.*" Her fierce gaze pinned me in place.

"How are you able to talk—" I began, but she cut me off with a sharp look.

"*Quiet! Others must not know that you have this gift.*"

Jake looked between us in confusion.

"She's right." Zen exhaled forcefully through his nose as the healer prodded the gash on his chest. "Holy shit that hurts! Jake, get Enrique. Niki needs to stay and help with the medicines."

Jake's eyes narrowed, shooting a suspicious look at Zen.

"It's okay, Jake. I'll stay and help. You get Enrique."

With a curt nod in my direction, Jake disappeared through the doorway.

"*How is it that I can understand you?*" I asked.

Her focus remained on her work applying the salve to Zen's wounds, but I heard her words clearly. "*Those of the forest do not need words to communicate.*"

I had no idea what she meant. Those of the forest? I locked eyes with Zen, my expression questioning.

Zen winced and closed his eyes.

I watched in silence as the old woman worked, wanting desperately to ask her what she meant, but lacking the courage to do so.

Jake returned with two men carrying the stretcher with Enrique. I gasped aloud when I saw him. He lay motionless, his skin unnaturally pale. He didn't so much as flutter an eyelid when they laid him on the dirt floor.

"*Can you help him?*" I asked desperately.

The old woman's expression softened slightly as she squatted next to Enrique, touching his forehead and heart. "*Your friend hovers between worlds*," she answered me without speaking. "*Death circles him like a hungry vulture.*" She shook her head slowly. "*His spirit has already begun its journey. We can only ease his passing.*"

Tears welled in my eyes as her words sank in. Enrique was dying, and there was nothing we could do for him.

The old woman stood slowly and shuffled over to her collection of herbs and dried plants while I stared bleakly at Enrique's prone form.

Jake dropped onto the ground next to me, his eyes roving restlessly around the room, taking in everything but Enrique's unnaturally still body and unsteady breathing. "Do you think…" he began, his voice faltering.

"There's nothing she can do for him," I whispered, my voice catching as I blinked back the tears.

Hearing us, Zen roused himself. With a slight grimace of pain, he stood and gently cut away the vines securing Enrique to the stretcher. When he finished, he sat beside Enrique, resting his fingers lightly on the top of Enrique's hand, the salve causing his bare skin to glisten in the firelight.

A hot flush spread through me at the sight of his lean muscles beneath his gleaming skin. I forced myself to look away only to meet the knowing gaze of the healer. Embarrassed, I stood and walked over to where Enrique lay, settling myself on the ground next to Zen.

"I don't want him to feel alone," he said simply.

I nodded, my throat too thick with emotion to speak.

The three of us sat in mournful silence as we stared into the flames of the fire, listening to Enrique's shallow irregular breathing and the rhythmic, meditative sound of the old woman's stone mortar and pestle.

"Mamá?" A woman stood in the doorway carrying a large metal pot. She held out the pot like an offering, the aroma of something hot and savory wafting from it, causing my stomach to grumble with hunger.

With a nod from the old woman, the young woman placed the pot near the fire and retrieved several serving bowls from the shelves. She filled the bowls carefully, handing one to each of us. I was so hungry I could have eaten seconds or even thirds but I realized that was not an option. So, I savored my stew, slurping every drop, barely managing to refrain from licking the bowl clean when I had finished.

While we ate our meal, the old woman squatted next to Enrique, chanting softly to him. She lit a small bundle of dried leaves, wafting the aromatic smoke over his body. When we had finished eating, the old woman spoke to Zen and the other woman in her native language.

"She wants Niki to stay with her. Jake and I have to leave," Zen translated. "She's asked her daughter to take us to their family's hut. Jake and I will sleep there."

At the thought of being separated from Zen and Jake, a sudden flare of anxiety fizzed through me. "I don't understand, why do I need to stay here? Why can't I go with you?"

The old woman's cloudy eyes fixed on me with an intensity that made my skin prickle. "*The jaguar's spirit stirs within you, my daughter, but you must learn to control it, or it will consume you. You seek your true path. Tonight, you will stay with me. I will guide you on your journey.*"

Zen's eyes met mine, softening as he noted my trembling hands. "*You'll be okay,*" he reassured me. "*She's a gifted healer. You can trust her, Niki.*"

After Zen, Jake, and the girl left, the old woman sent me outside to empty my bladder while she prepared a special medicine for me. When I returned, I noticed that she had covered Enrique with a woven blanket. She motioned for me to sit near the fire.

"*Now,*" she said, in a rhythmic voice that echoed through my mind, "*we begin.*"

She handed me a chipped ceramic mug. I could see dried

chopped plant bits floating in the discolored liquid. I eyed it suspiciously.

"*Drink.*"

I sipped cautiously at the tepid liquid. It left a bitter earthy taste in my mouth.

"*You must drink all of it.*"

Grimacing, I closed my eyes and poured it down my throat.

When I was finished the old woman nodded approvingly. She pointed to a second hammock hanging from the rafters overhead. "*Go to sleep. I will be here to guide you on your journey.*"

I laid back in the hammock and breathed through the waves of nausea rocking my body. My eyes traced the tendrils of smoke drifting toward the dried leaves of the thatch roof as my legs and arms began to tingle.

My spirit detaches from my body and floats skyward with the smoke. I drift backward through time and space, my soul flickering like a star twinkling in the dark. The moon waxes and wanes. The tides rise. The tides fall. I am the daughter of the moon, she who controls the rhythms of life.

Voices wash over me, coming from nowhere and everywhere at once. I see men, women, children, glide past. Thousands of years of sorrows. They march and sing as one, a haunting melody of ancient secrets. Dressed in white they dance among standing stones. Dressed in woven cloth and adorned with feathers they lay offerings at the foot of stone altars. Soldiers with swords, staffs, and guns block their path and I watch, with tears streaming down my cheeks while their bodies fall, their blood feeding the red earth as the sky turns to night.

My father and sister appear before me; they link arms and begin to sing a defiant chorus calling for me to bring forth my light and wash the earth clean.

An owl hoots from somewhere in the darkness. A wave of dizziness overtakes me, and I am suddenly upside down, looking backward at myself. I feel the shadow of Hun-Came pass over me and cold burns my body like an icy flame.

A jaguar appears, emerging from the shadows like a specter. His neck arches as he sniffs the air searching for prey, and his dark, red-rimmed eyes lock onto me. The jaguar curls back his lips into a malevolent smile, revealing long dagger-like canines. The air around me thickens, charged with a supernatural energy that makes my skin crawl. Li Xul, Li Xul, Li Xul—the name hammers inside my skull.

I whimper and call out in fear.

The old woman takes hold of my face in her gnarled hands and presses her forehead to mine. I hear her voice inside my head. "Daughter of the moon, Daughter of the Jaguar, you must not show fear. You must be stealthy and courageous. You will wrap yourself in moonlight. You will hide in the trees and slip unseen into the rivers of time. You are the hunter! You are the jaguar!"

My skin is tingling, icy fire courses through my veins. I hear my sister's voice. "There can be no rebirth without death." I exhale and let go. My bones shift and break apart beneath my skin, changing shape and rearranging themselves like strange puzzle pieces.

I am dying. I am reborn. I am the jaguar! I am the hunter!

The drone of insects and chatter of cicadas, the high frequency squeaks of small mammals, the rustling of the wind in the leaves, assault my ears. I raise my head and catch a scent—sharp and intoxicating. It shoots into my bloodstream like a drug, unleashing something primal within me. I growl low in my throat not as a warning but as an urgent call for him to come closer.

He approaches slowly, cautiously. His green-gold eyes are filled with fierce heat as he crouches low to the ground, hard muscles bunching beneath his gleaming dark coat, the pattern of rosettes rippling across his fur like shadows dancing on black water.

I stand still, vibrating with need as he twines his body around mine, growling low in his throat. His musky scent fills the air around us— a heady mixture that ignites a need within me. My fur bristles in anticipation as I let out a raspy grunt—an invitation.

He rubs his head against my flank, nipping me, caressing me with his rough tongue as I stand perfectly still, the hairs on the back of my neck erect, my muscles quivering with the need to have him inside of me.

With one fluid motion, he grabs my neck—powerful jaws holding me gently in place—and mounts me. A blast of molten heat blazes *through me and I throw back my head as a primal roar rips from my throat.*

I awoke riding the crest of the orgasm, the bones in my body liquifying, my mound and inner thighs slick and wet. I leaned over the hammock and vomited onto the dirt floor as electric shivers coursed through my veins, too weak to even lift my head.

LISA DIETRICH

CHAPTER FIFTEEN

Li Xul paced the dimly lit cave, his anger palpable in the flickering torchlight. The jaguar pelt across his shoulders weighed heavily tonight, its energy restless against his skin as the vision replayed in his mind, each detail fueling his rage.

The girl was more powerful than he had anticipated. Her strong connection to the spirit world was undeniable. But it was the revelation of the power of her dual heritage that truly unsettled him. A daughter of the moon and the jaguar. Celtic druid blood of her mother mingling with the ancient power of her father's people. Such delicious irony that the very thing he sought to destroy had merged to create something far more dangerous.

Li Xul clenched his fists angrily. He had been close, so close, but the old woman must have sensed his presence, must have recognized the shadow he had cast across the girl's mind. She knew too much, understood too well the ancient ways. He could not allow the old healer to help the girl discover her true powers.

He drew a deep breath, inhaling the copal incense that clouded the air, his fingers tracing the obsidian blade at his belt—the same blade that has spilled the blood of countless sacrifices. He lifted the blade, watching firelight dance along its edge.

He would not rest until the old woman's life force fed his power, and this accursed bloodline was extinguished. He touched the jade amulet he wore, his fingers tracing the engraved image of Hun-Came. Sometimes, to honor the old ways, one must eliminate those who remembered them too well.

CHAPTER SIXTEEN

My mouth tasted like death, and my skull throbbed with the echoes of last night's visions as we stood at the edge of the village. Jake and Zen worked in tense silence, shoveling dirt onto Enrique's grave while acrid smoke stung my eyes. The villagers gave me a wide berth as they passed, their eyes downcast, shoulders hunched while placing stones atop the fresh earth. I couldn't blame them. After my drug-fueled X-rated trip last night, I smelled worse than the village peccaries and I probably didn't look much better than one either.

Sighing, I approached the grave with my own stone, its weight solid and real in my hands. I placed it carefully on the mound of dirt, whispering a prayer—to whoever might be listening, including the ancient powers I could no longer deny existed. The ones that had somehow turned me into a jaguar and given me a front-row seat to my own erotic spirit walk.

I returned to my place by the fire and stood behind the old woman. I could feel Zen's eyes on me like physical touch, searching for—what? Some sign of the jaguar spirit that had possessed me? I kept my eyes fixed on the burial, refusing to meet his questioning looks.

The old woman—how was it possible that I still didn't know her name—sang and chanted. My head throbbed, the pain rising and falling in time with the healer's voice. She tossed a handful of something onto the fire and a spicy pine scent infused the spiraling smoke. Hot tears pricked the back of my eyes, though I was not sure if they were for Enrique or myself.

"She's adding sacred copal, pine resin, to the fire," Jake whispered into my ear. "The ancient Maya believed smoke carried messages to the gods."

I nodded without really hearing him, too aware of Zen's presence on my other side. He hadn't spoken a word to me all morning, but the electricity crackling between us said more than enough. Heat crept up the back of my neck as fragments of last night's vision flashed through my mind— sleek black fur, powerful muscles, golden eyes burning with an all-too-human intensity. I forced my attention back to the ceremony. The old woman's voice had taken on a rhythmic quality that reminded me of...other things.

Get it together, Niki.

But how could I, when everything I thought I knew about reality was unraveling? The vision of Nayla and my father surfaced unbidden, and my stomach lurched. Nayla was with my dead father? Did that mean she was dead? Or was it a trick of the tea—like the way I transformed into a jaguar and...

No. Not thinking about that part.

I felt Zen shift restlessly beside me, half-expecting him to interject a snide comment inside my head, but he was uncharacteristically quiet.

My eyes slid sideways. *"What? You've got nothing to say?"*

"I've got plenty to say, but I'm not willing to say it here." His eyes fixed on the fire.

"I want you to stay out of my dreams!" I kept my eyes forward.
"Niki, do you really want to have this conversation here? Now?"
"Yes," I hissed under my breath.

Jake looked over at me. I gave him a weak smile before

turning my gaze back toward the fire.

"Niki, you are the dream-walker. You control dreams. I'm just along for the ride. And I do mean ride."

"*Shut up!*" I cut him off, even as my body remembered the feeling of fur against fur, of the urgent need and heart-stopping primal release that left me weak and trembling. To my utter humiliation, my body reacted to the memory with an intense craving that left me weak-kneed and breathless.

I could feel Zen beside me, shaking with silent laughter.

The words burst out in a hiss before I could stop them: "I don't want this! I don't want any of this!"

The old woman's chanting stopped. She turned, her cloudy eyes fixing on me with unnerving precision. *"You cannot run from your destiny,"* her voice whispered in my mind. *"The jaguar spirit has chosen you. You have a sacred responsibility."*

My hands began to tingle, phantom claws trying to emerge from my fingertips. I curled them into fists, pressing them against my thighs as waves of nausea rolled through me. The copal smoke thickened, or maybe that was just my swimming vision. Everything felt unreal, as if I were caught between dreaming and waking. I swayed, gulping the hot, heavy smoke-filled air and closed my eyes, fighting to keep the bile from rising in the back of my throat.

A high-pitched scream pierced the air. A young girl stood rigid, pointing at the fire where the copal smoke had taken on an impossible shape—a jaguar, crouched and ready to pounce. As I watched in horror, its smoky head turned to face me directly.

"K'in and Ix B'alam," the old woman intoned. *"Fire Jaguar awakes."*

A burning heat slicked my skin, and I fell to my knees, retching, every cell in my body crying out in agony as Nayla's *wahy* flew into me and buried itself in my heart.

There can be no rebirth without death.

Jake and Zen caught me before I hit the ground. My head was jackhammered in two as another wave of nausea hit, and my legs gave out completely. I heard the din of frightened voices echoing through a haze of pain.

Jake's arm wrapped around my shoulders, but his familiar presence felt wrong, like my body was rejecting anything that wasn't part of this new reality I was being forced into.

"We need to take her to Grandmother's hut," Zen said.

"Back off! I've got her," Jake barked, as he pushed Zen aside and scooped me into his arms.

He carried me to the hut and gently deposited me on the ground, the smoky interior swimming before my eyes. I collapsed beside the fire, my head threatening to split apart, my heart already had.

The old woman followed us inside; her weathered face creased with concern. She spoke sharply to Jake in her native tongue.

"She wants you to go," I managed to whisper, each word sending daggers through my skull.

Jake's hand tightened on my shoulder. "I'm not leaving you." The protectiveness in his voice would have touched me a day ago. Now it felt like sandpaper against my raw nerves.

"Jake." I forced myself to meet his eyes. "You're not helping. Please."

Something shifted in his expression—hurt, understanding, resignation. "Fine. But I'm finding a way to get us out of here." He shot a final distrustful look at the old woman before striding out.

The moment he left, some of the tension eased. I dropped my head into my hands, feeling the healer's cool fingers press against my temples. The pain began to recede like the tide going out, leaving exhaustion in its wake.

"*You must tell her.*" Her words slipped into my mind like smoke. I hadn't even noticed Zen enter the hut.

"*I will, Grandmother. Now you must rest.*"

The old woman rose stiffly, Zen offering her a steadying arm as she hobbled over to her hammock. She rolled herself into it and closed her eyes, exhaustion etched into her deeply lined face.

Zen lowered himself to sit across from me. The firelight caught his eyes, causing them to shine like flashlights—too similar to the jaguar's gaze from my dream. My skin prickled with awareness.

"I am so tired of this." The words came out raw, honest. "I want my old life back."

"I know." Simple words, but the compassion in them nearly broke me.

I drew in a shaky breath. "Is Nayla dead?"

"I don't know."

I placed a hand across my heart. "I felt her. At the fire. When the jaguar looked at me, I felt her...spirit...her wahy," I said, pronouncing the last word reluctantly.

Zen's expression was gentle. "Maybe she's reaching out to you the only way she can."

With a feeling of resigned acceptance, I tilted my head in the direction of the healer. "What does she want you to tell me?"

He was quiet for a moment, as if gathering his thoughts. When he spoke, his voice was low. "Her name is Rosa." His eyes flicked to the old woman. "When she was young, she lived in a community at the edge of the jungle. They were subsistence farmers—had been for generations. At least they were until a foreign mining company found minerals under their land."

I knew how this story went. I'd heard it over and over again from my father. "Let me guess— they refused to sell."

"Yes. Rosa's father and the other farmers resisted. The government sent soldiers." His eyes grew distant. "Twenty people died, including her father and two of her brothers. She was young then, but she led the survivors here, into the heart of the jungle. They've been here more than thirty years now, calling themselves the People of the Forest. Their purpose is to protect this place—not just the trees and rivers, but also the spirits that give this place life."

I glanced at the old woman's sleeping form. "Is she really

your grandmother?"

One corner of his mouth lifted in that crooked smile that made my heart stutter. "Rosa is everyone's grandmother."

"That's not an answer."

His eyes met mine, serious now. "Am I related to her by blood? No. Your father was the one who brought me here and introduced us."

I stared at him in shock. "My father? You knew my father?"

"Yes. I was eighteen," he said quietly. "I was having... issues. The kind that made people think I was crazy. Your father performed a ritual—"

"Stop!" The word came out sharp enough to cut. "My father was a lawyer. He protected indigenous communities through legal channels. He didn't perform rituals."

"He was both, Niki." Zen's voice remained gentle, but firm. "A lawyer and an aj ilonel—a Day Keeper. He maintained harmony between worlds, using both legal knowledge and sacred tradition."

"You sound just like Nayla." I was tired of my world shifting, tired of discovering my life had been built on half-truths. "Did you tell Nayla that you knew our father?"

"Yes."

The echo of my sister's message burned in my chest: *There can be no rebirth without death.* And suddenly I knew with bone-deep certainty that finding Nayla wasn't just about saving my sister anymore. It was about understanding what I was becoming. My old life—the one based on reason and logic—was dead and buried and a new life—a life where I no longer knew the rules—had replaced it.

The fight drained out of me.

"I know." Zen's eyes, glittering like sunlight on water, held my gaze.

A piercing wail jolted me. Across the hut, Rosa thrashed in her hammock, her thin frame rigid with terror. Her eyes snapped open, cloudy white and unseeing, fixed on something beyond the physical world.

"Abuela!" I rushed to her side, but Zen was already there, his hands gentle on her shoulders.

"Li Xul," she gasped, clutching his arm. The rest came out in rapid language that I couldn't follow, but the name Li Xul sent ice down my spine.

Zen spoke to her softly in her language while I hovered uncertainly nearby. Gradually, her breathing steadied, though her fingers remained locked around Zen's wrist. When she finally turned to look at me, her eyes were clear and sharp with urgency.

"*Sit*," she commanded, her voice hoarse. When I hesitated, she patted the ground beside her hammock. "*There is no time. We begin now.*"

I lowered myself to the packed earth, acutely aware of the way the shadows seemed to writhe in the dying firelight. Rosa reached out with a trembling hand and pressed her palm against my chest, right over my heart.

"*Your wahy is strong*," she said, her words careful and deliberate. "*But strength without protection is like a door without a lock. It invites thieves.*"

"Li Xul,*"* I whispered, remembering those burning eyes in my dreams.

She nodded grimly. "*He is a dream-walker, like you. But his heart is twisted with greed. He believes that by taking your wahy, he can claim its power for himself. You must not allow that to happen. You must destroy his source of power before he destroys you.*"

My hand crept up to cover hers, still pressed against my heart. "*What can I do?*"

"*Close your eyes*," she instructed. "*See your heart. Not the flesh and blood, but the sacred space within where your wahy dwells.*"

I did as she asked, trying to visualize my heart as more than just an organ. In my mind's eye, it became a chamber of living stone, warm with an inner light.

"*Now build walls*," Rosa's voice guided me. "*Strong walls. Walls that nothing can break.*"

I imagined steel rising up, thick and impenetrable. But it felt wrong—too modern, too manufactured for something so primal.

"*No*," the word slipped into my mind as she read my thoughts. "*Not metal. Older. Stronger. The walls of the ancient temples were built with limestone sealed with sacred jade. See them rise. Feel their power.*"

The steel in my mind melted away, replaced by massive blocks of limestone. Jade glowed in the seams between them, pulsing with the same rhythm as my heartbeat. I could almost smell the copal smoke, feel the weight of centuries.

"*A door,*" she continued. "*Make it of ceiba wood, blessed by seven generations of Day Keepers. See the glyphs of protection carved deep. Feel their meaning.*"

The door took shape, solid and ancient, marked with symbols that seemed to move when I wasn't looking directly at them.

"*Now the lock.*" Her fingers pressed harder against my chest. "*Think of what matters most. What you would die to protect. This is your key, and no one—not even another dream-walker—can forge a copy.*"

Nayla's face appeared in my mind, but not as I'd last seen her. Instead, I saw her as a child, gap-toothed and grinning, holding out her hand to lead me on another adventure. The love I felt in that moment crystallized into something solid and real—a lock that sealed itself into the ceiba wood with a sound like a final heartbeat. I placed my sister's wahy inside the temple I created and locked it tight. Nayla had sent her wahy to me for safekeeping. She was in trouble and I was going to do everything in my power to protect my sister.

"*Good.*" Rosa's hand fell away, leaving my skin tingling. "*Every night before you sleep, check your walls. Strengthen them. Remember the lock. Li Xul is powerful, but even he cannot break bonds forged of love and sealed with jade.*"

I opened my eyes to find both Rosa and Zen watching me intently. The old woman's face was lined with exhaustion, but her cloudy eyes were fierce with determination. Whatever she had seen in her vision, she wasn't sharing it—but the urgency in her voice told me all I needed to know.

"*What did you see?*" I asked anyway. "*In your vision?*"

She shook her head once, firmly. "*Some knowledge is a burden that must be carried alone.*" Her gnarled fingers found mine, squeezing with surprising strength. "*Remember what I have taught you. The wahy of the Fire Jaguar is sacred—a gift from powers older than memory. Guard it well.*"

Zen reached for my hand. The moment his fingers touched mine, electricity sparked between us. That primal need from my dream roared to life, and I could almost feel fur rippling beneath my skin.

Jake burst into the hut before I could snatch my hand away. "I've found a guide. He'll take us as far as Santilq'ol, Pastor Miguel's village." His eyes fixed on our joined hands, his face hardening. "We leave tomorrow."

The certainty in his voice grated against everything inside me that had changed. Tomorrow felt like another lifetime—one where I was still just a lawyer's daughter who didn't know about jaguar spirits or Day Keepers or the price of rebirth. One where I couldn't feel the jungle's ancient power thrumming in my blood, calling me to a destiny I wasn't sure I wanted but could no longer deny.

LISA DIETRICH

CHAPTER SEVENTEEN

I lay in the hammock, eyes opened, the pre-dawn chill raising goosebumps on my skin. The first rays of dawn were creeping through the doorway, but they brought no warmth. I shivered, remembering the feeling of Li Xul's presence in my dreams, like smoke and shadows given form. He had been there, poking and prodding my defenses, but I had built a dream of my choosing and locked him out.

I built my dream, the way I had learned as a child fighting to keep the nightmares away, by creating a world of beauty in my mind. I had the strength of Nayla's wahy to fortify me. In my dream, Nayla and I were in our backyard playing on our swing set. Soft sunlight illuminated my mother's garden with its blooming flowers and vegetables. I added the tinkle of wind chimes and filled the air with the scent of warm earth and green plants. My father stood at the grill, laughing at something my mother said. He was wearing the apron that Nayla and I had given him for Christmas. The one that said, "Papá Numero Uno." My father turned to look at me, his dark eyes filled with love and tinged with sadness. "It is not your fault. Do not blame yourself."

My father's words left me feeling unsettled as I remembered my dream. *What wasn't my fault? Nayla's disappearance? Enrique's death?*

"Niki!" Jake whispered through the open doorway.

I scrambled upright in the hammock, nearly tipping myself onto the dirt floor. "What?"

"We leave in one hour."

"Okay." I rolled out of the hammock and began gathering my things.

Zen, Jake, and I stood in the center of the village, waiting for our guide, Gorgonio. The young peccaries had been tied to their stakes again. As I watched them snorting and rolling in the dirt, I wondered where they spent their nights. Left out at night they would have been easy prey for a wandering jaguar.

"Rosa's family takes them into their hut." Zen's words slid into my head, answering my unasked question. *"Along with a pet monkey and two small parrots."*

"Must have made for an interesting couple of nights."

A faint smile played on his lips. *"Not as interesting as my dreams. Speaking of which…I missed you last night."*

I whipped my head around and glared at him. "Stop it!" I hissed.

Jake's eyes shifted between the two of us. "Am I missing something here?"

"No!" Zen and I answered at the same time.

"Okay. If you say so." Jake looked down at his watch. "I'm going to see what's keeping Gorgonio."

We watched Jake's retreating back and Zen turned to face me. "We need to find time to talk about you and me. That dream you had…"

"That dream was a hallucination," I cut him off even as my body remembered every intoxicating sensation of that encounter. "Brought on by whatever was in the tea. Nothing more."

His hand brushed mine, sending electric sparks shooting down my spine. "You know that's not true."

I snatched my hand away and turned my eyes forward, resolutely avoiding his gaze. "Here comes Jake."

Jake and a short, stocky man, I could only assume was Gorgonio, headed toward us. Even from this distance, I could tell that Jake was pissed off. A young girl trailed behind the two men, oversized rubber rain boots on her feet and a string bag over her shoulder.

"Looks like Rosa's granddaughter Imul is planning on joining us."

Jake halted in front of us. "Zen, tell the girl that she isn't coming." He jerked a thumb in the direction of the healer's granddaughter.

Zen glanced over at her. She had stopped about ten feet behind Jake and Gorgonio. She met Zen's gaze with a defiant lift of her chin. "Not sure that's going to do much good."

Jake's jaw jumped. "Then tell Gorgonio to tell her!"

Gorgonio shifted uncomfortably from one foot to the other, his eyes shifting between Zen and Jake.

"I expect he already has," Zen commented easily. He lifted his daypack and slipped it onto his shoulders. "Should we get going?"

Jake speared him with a glare. "We are not hiking through the jungle with a little girl. It's miles to Santilq'ol and I 'm not carrying a child."

Zen nodded briefly in the direction of Imul who stood staring stubbornly at the men. "I suspect that little girl could walk circles around you, Jake."

Jake bent over and picked up a rock, brandishing it threateningly at Imul. She stood her ground; chin tipped defiantly up at him. He threw it at her. She jumped back and the rock landed with a heavy thud in the dirt at her feet.

"Jesus, Jake!" I grabbed his arm and yanked it back, fury blazing through me. "You could have hit her!"

"I wasn't going to hit her. I just wanted to scare her off." His eyes searched mine, pleading for understanding. "It's too dangerous for her to come. You know that. Look what happened to Enrique. You know she can't come." His eyes flicked to Zen. "Since he won't be the responsible adult, I needed to do something."

"You didn't need to throw a rock at her," I seethed. I turned toward Zen. "Can you please talk to her. Make her understand that she can't come with us."

"I'll try."

Zen and Gorgonio walked over to the little girl. She watched them approach warily. The two men spoke, the girl said nothing, simply dropped her gaze to the ground.

"Okay," Zen said, when they returned. "Vamanos!"

I looked over my shoulder before we slipped into the thick vegetation. Imul stood where we'd left her, her dark eyes watched us without wavering.

As we ventured deeper into the thick vegetation, the sounds of the village faded away, replaced by the cacophony of jungle noises.

Gorgonio led the way, his machete occasionally slicing through stubborn vines. Jake followed close behind, with me in the middle and Zen bringing up the rear. After twenty minutes, my clothes were already sticking to my skin from the humidity. The canopy above was so thick that it felt like twilight, even though it was mid-morning.

About an hour into our trek, the hairs on the back of my neck stood up. I couldn't shake the feeling that we were being watched. I glanced over my shoulder, but Zen's reassuring presence was all I saw. As we continued, the feeling persisted. Every rustle of leaves, every snapping twig made me jump. I tried to rationalize it—we were in the jungle, after all. There were bound to be sounds. But the prickling sensation at the nape of my neck wouldn't subside.

"Everything okay?" Zen asked, noticing my unease.

I hesitated. "I just... I feel like someone's following us."

Overhearing my words, I noticed Jake's hand move instinctively to the machete at his belt.

Suddenly, Gorgonio stopped, holding up a hand. We froze, straining our ears. Zen's eyes narrowed as he scanned the dense foliage around us. There it was—a faint rustling, too deliberate to be the wind or an animal.

In a flash, Zen darted into the underbrush. There was a yelp, followed by the sound of a brief struggle. When Zen emerged, he was holding a squirming figure by the arm.

It was Rosa's granddaughter, Imul.

"Well, well," Zen said, a mix of amusement and exasperation in his voice. "Looks like we have a stowaway."

Jake cursed under his breath. "I told you she couldn't come!"

Imul stood defiantly, chin raised, despite the leaves and twigs tangled in her hair. Her oversized boots were caked with mud, and her string bag was bulging with what I assumed were supplies.

I knelt down to her level. "Imul, why did you follow us? It's dangerous out here." Zen translated my words. Imul's response was rapid and passionate.

"She says Abuela told her to go with us," Zen explained. "She says she can help us."

Jake ran a hand through his hair in frustration. "We can't take her with us. We have to go back."

I looked at the determination in Imul's eyes, then at the dense jungle around us. We'd been walking for over an hour. Going back would cost us precious time—time Nayla might not have. "Maybe..." I began hesitantly. "Maybe she should come with us."

Jake stared at me incredulously. "You can't be serious."

"Think about it," I argued. "She's already here. Going back will waste hours. And she clearly knows how to move through the jungle—she followed us without us noticing for this long."

Zen nodded slowly. "She's right, Jake."

Jake looked from me to Zen, then to Gorgonio, who shrugged noncommittally. Finally, he threw up his hands. "Fine. But she's your responsibility."

I turned back to Imul and smiled. "Looks like you're coming with us, after all."

As Zen translated, a smile broke across Imul's face. She reached into her bag and pulled out a small, carved obsidian figure of a jaguar, pressing it into my hand.

"For protection," Zen translated as Imul spoke. I closed my fingers around the figure, feeling its rough edges.

"Thank you," I said softly. We resumed our journey, now with Imul walking beside me.

"Tell me about Fire Jaguar," I said aloud.

Imul glanced up at me, a questioning look on her face. I shook my head and pointed to Jake to let her know that I was speaking to him. She made a face, expressing her low opinion of Jake. I hid my smile as Jake looked over his shoulder at me.

"Are you thinking about the trick the old lady did with the smoke?" He continued without waiting for me to respond. "Ak' b'al is known as the Jaguar God of Terrestrial Fire, also known as the Jaguar God of the Underworld, associated with the Night Sun."

"The Night Sun?" I asked. "You mean the moon?"

"No. According to the ancient Maya, the Night Sun is the form that the sun takes when it travels under the earth at night, before it rises the next morning." Jake tapped Gorgonio on the shoulder and asked him in Spanish to stop, saying we needed a quick water break.

Gorgonio nodded and disappeared into the vegetation.

Imul looked up at me and I mimed drinking water. I unbuckled my daypack and slid it from my shoulders, rolling them to release the tight muscles. Zen and Jake did the same. I offered my water bottle to Imul, but she pressed her lips together and shook her head.

"Zen, please tell her she needs to drink something."

"I can try, but I can't guarantee I'll be successful." He crouched down so that he was eye-level with Imul and the two of them began what sounded like an intense negotiation.

I uncapped my water and drank, eyeing the two of them, noticing how good Zen was with the little girl. He spoke to her calmly and listened carefully to what she said. He was going to be a great father one day. With a pang of wistful longing, I realized how much he reminded me of my father.

"So," Jake said loudly, drawing my attention back to him. "What exactly do you want to know about Fire Jaguar?"

I turned to face him. "I don't know. Anything you can tell me. You said Fire Jaguar's associated with the underworld. Does that mean she's like Hun-Came, a god of death?"

"She?" Jake's eyebrows rose in surprise. "Hmm. That's interesting. Most archaeologists assumed Fire Jaguar was a male god. The image has been found on warrior shields indicating a god of war or a protector of warriors. But the image has also been found in murals and vases that make that unclear. There's at least one image of Fire Jaguar being attacked by people who are trying to set the god on fire."

"That doesn't sound very god-like," I said with a lift of my eyebrow. "I mean, I thought the Mayan gods were supposed to have special powers. Why would people want to burn their own god?"

"I don't know." Jake took another swig of his water. "Maybe Fire Jaguar was the god of their enemies? Maybe they weren't attacking and it was a ritual of some sort? It's hard to tell when you're working with images from faded murals and broken shards of pottery."

Jake's information wasn't much help. According to Rosa, I had been chosen by Fire Jaguar. What the hell was I supposed to do with that? What did that even mean? I had so many questions and not a lot of answers. Frustrated, I turned to see how the negotiation between Zen and Imul was progressing.

It didn't appear that Zen had had much success convincing our young stowaway to drink from his water bottle. Fortunately, Gorgonio returned carefully carrying several sections of the same type of woody brown vine we had drunk from on our earlier trek. He handed one to Imul who drank from it.

Satisfied that our little charge wasn't going to faint from dehydration, I nodded my thanks to Gorgonio. "Gracias por cuidar a la niña."

When we resumed our journey, Imul fell into step beside me, her presence both comforting and unsettling. The hot humid air pressed against my skin as Gorgonio slashed vines and branches cutting a path through the thick vegetation. I looked down at Imul wondering why her family hadn't prevented her from following us.

"Abuela told me to go with you because Fire Jaguar chose you," Imul said suddenly, her voice barely above a whisper. Zen translated, his eyes meeting mine with a mixture of curiosity and concern.

I clutched the obsidian jaguar figure in my pocket. "What does that mean, Imul? What did Abuela want me to do?"

As Zen relayed my questions, Imul's face grew serious. She spoke rapidly, her hands moving in intricate gestures. Zen listened intently, his brow furrowing.

"She says the Fire Jaguar is your guardian," Zen translated. "And that you and Fire Jaguar will keep her safe."

Jake scoffed ahead of us. "The old woman is playing you for a sucker. I bet she's hoping that you'll lay some cash on the kid because of your guilty conscience."

Imul didn't understand, but Jake's tone made the ugly meaning of his words obvious. Her small hand reached up and anxiously clutched mine.

I gave her hand a reassuring squeeze. "Shut up, Jake."

I caught Zen's eye, unspoken tension crackling between us like electricity.

We continued our hike under towering trees dripping with lush moss and vines, the canopy providing welcome shade from the hot Guatemalan sun. On several occasions, we passed the remains of decaying Mayan ruins. Their pitted limestone walls knotted with creepers and vines, nearly swallowed by the surrounding vegetation. Whenever we came to a river or stream, Gorgonio ferried Imul across on his back.

On one occasion, Gorgonio abruptly threw out an arm

to stop me before I waded into the river. "Peligro." He pointed to a long snake covered in black triangle markings. "Barba Amarilla," he whispered, his eyes tracking the poisonous snake as it slithered across our path and disappeared into the wet leaves making me wish I too had worn a pair of rubber rain boots.

Eventually, we found ourselves walking on a narrow trail cut into the jungle. The trail steepened as we climbed over a small pass, dropping back down into a valley where we encountered a tiny settlement squatting on the shore of a wide river. We had arrived at Santilq'ol.

LISA DIETRICH

CHAPTER EIGHTEEN

I don't think I'd ever been so happy to arrive anywhere in my life. I wanted nothing more than to find a lovely hotel, soak my tired aching muscles in a hot bath and fall into a soft bed.

The sun was setting as we emerged from the dense jungle into the settlement of Santilq'ol. The town sprawled before us—a patchwork of several dozen homes built from an assortment of cement blocks, adobe bricks, and wood, topped with a mishmash of stained clay tiles and rusty tin roofs.

As we entered the main plaza, the white plaster façade of a church loomed over us, dominating the landscape. My heart quickened. This was Doña Juana's town, and somewhere within these walls lived the pastor Nayla had come to see.

Women in vibrant red skirts and intricately embroidered huipil tops moved through the streets, some carrying baskets of produce, others leading children by the hand. Near the riverbank, a group of women scrubbed clothes against smooth stones, their laughter carrying on the evening breeze.

"We'll head over to the church. The rectory doubles as

a hotel for visitors," Jake explained, adjusting his pack.

As we approached the church steps, I noticed Jake lagging behind, fiddling with something in his pocket. Curiosity piqued, I fell back to walk beside him. "Everything okay?" I asked.

Jake startled, quickly shoving whatever he was holding deeper into his pocket. "Yep," Jake replied breezily as the church doors swung open.

A lean man, dark hair graying at the temples, wearing simple black clothing and a white clerical collar stepped out, his eyes alighting on Jake. He greeted him heartily, clapping him on the shoulder. "Hello, Jake. What a pleasant surprise. What brings you to our humble parish?"

"We've had a few problems at Choja q'eq, and we could use your help." Jake tilted his head in our direction. "Would you be able to put us up for the night and help us arrange transportation?"

The pastor's piercing eyes scanned our group. "Of course. All of God's children are welcome at Santilq'ol," he said, his voice smooth. His eyes rested on me with a dark penetrating gaze as he introduced himself. "I'm Pastor Miguel."

As I looked into the pastor's face, an inexplicable chill ran down my spine. There was something about him— something hidden beneath the surface—that set my nerves on edge. Imul must have felt my tension because her small hand found mine once again.

His mouth quickly curved into an apologetic smile. "Please accept my apologies. I can see that I've made you uncomfortable. I don't mean to pry, but I can't help but feel that we've met somewhere before."

Jake chuckled. "This is Niki Balam, Nayla's sister. They're twins."

"Ah. Yes. I see the resemblance." Pastor Miguel extended his hand. "I'm pleased to welcome you to our humble parish."

Pastor Miguel turned out to be a charming host and I

decided that my initial reaction to him was just a figment of my very tired imagination. He had us all laughing as he regaled us with a brief history of the town, founded by Catholic priests in the 1800's. "The village's name translates to 'Holy crap,'" he explained with a good-natured laugh as he showed us to our rooms. "Which goes to show you that not even men of God cannot avoid the call of nature."

The pastor led us to a room filled with used clothing, toys, and packaged food. "U.S. charities send us things for the church. We distribute them to the community." He eyed our dirty, ragged clothes. "Please, help yourselves. I'll show you to your rooms after you find what you need. You can leave your clothes in the bathroom. I'll have Josefina and Maria launder them. They will be returned to you in the morning."

The rooms were basic—a bed and a clothes rack—but clean. The indoor plumbing consisted of a shared bathroom with a real shower. I almost wept with joy at the sight.

"We even have hot water—well tepid—," Pastor Miguel amended with a rueful smile. "But there is plenty of soap. Towels are in the cupboard. Just toss them in the basket when you're finished."

I quickly elbowed my way past Jake and Zen, towing Imul behind me. "Ladies first," I announced breezily, as I locked the door behind us.

I turned on the shower and joyfully scrubbed the grime and sweat from my scalp and skin while Imul watched with wide eyes. She initially resisted showering and using the strange soaps and shampoos, but I eventually convinced her to bathe.

When I helped her put on the "new" dress we'd found for her in the charity bin, she couldn't stop staring at herself in the mirror. It was the first time she'd ever seen her own reflection and she was fascinated by it. In the end, I practically had to drag her out of the bathroom.

On our way to our room, Imul and I met Zen in the hallway. Imul smiled shyly up at him, as he admired her new clothes. Liquid heat flooded my body when his gold-flecked eyes slowly looked me up and down. "You look good, too," he whispered. He leaned toward me, his eyes boring into mine. "*We need to talk.*"

"Later," I hissed between clenched teeth. With a tug on Imul's hand I hurried back to our room.

Pastor Miguel had prepared a simple but hearty meal for us in the church's small dining room. The table was set with mismatched plates and cutlery, giving it a homey feel. Imul's eyes were wide with wonder as she took in the unfamiliar setting.

"Please, sit," Pastor Miguel gestured warmly. "I'm thrilled to have visitors. It's not often we get newcomers in Santilq'ol. Though I do have some sad news to share with you."

He gestured toward the open bottle of wine on the table. "Please, help yourselves," he said as we settled into our seats.

Jake offered to fill Pastor Miguel's glass who responded with a nod. He took a sip of wine before speaking. "I thought I would let you know that I contacted the hospital. Unfortunately, Dr. Kelling is in a medically induced coma. Apparently, there were some complications. They are still hopeful that he will recover, but they won't know for some days yet." He paused. "I let the authorities know about the situation at Choja q'eq and asked the authorities to check on your friends.

I do apologize. I had no idea that your situation was so dire. Juana and the men failed to mention anything to me when they returned. I'm afraid I just assumed that the excavation site had closed for the season."

His expression turned somber. "I think that someone should contact the university about your friend Enrique's death so that his family can be notified. I'd be happy to help with that if you like."

Jake looked down at his plate. "Damn," he said under his breath. "I can do that."

Zen exchanged looks with me. I let a moment pass. I felt bad about Dr. Kelling and Enrique, but I had more pressing concerns. "Pastor Miguel?" I asked, my chest tight with anxiety.

The pastor turned to look at me, his eyebrows raised expectantly.

"My sister, Nayla?" I asked in a rush of words. "I don't know where she is and I'm hoping you might be able to help me find her."

The pastor's eyes flicked to Jake then back to me, his expression faltering for a moment. "Your sister's not at Choja q'eq?"

"No. She left the archaeological site about a week ago and we don't know where she is. Doña Juana said she came to see you before she left. I was hoping she might have said something to you about her plans."

Pastor Miguel's expression changed to one of sympathy. "I'm sorry to hear that she's missing. I wish there was something I could tell you, but I'm afraid there isn't. Your sister did come to me several weeks ago, seeking guidance, but..."

"But what?" I pressed.

He sighed, frowning slightly as he set his glass on the table. "Your sister was very troubled. I offered to counsel her, but she wasn't interested. She left rather abruptly, I'm afraid." His words were carefully chosen.

"Did she say anything? Anything at all about where she might go or what her plans were?"

He shook his head. "No. I'm sorry."

"It's just that..." I inhaled deeply trying to keep my emotions in check. "It's just that I'm really worried about her."

Pastor Miguel offered me a gentle smile. "I imagine you are. I wish I could be of more help, but your sister was... quite determined to continue her journey alone."

I nodded, disappointment settling in my stomach.

Pastor Miguel's eyes fixed on Imul. "So, who have we

141

here?" he asked, his eyes bright with false cheer as he changed the topic of conversation. "Imul seems a little young to be affiliated with the university."

I felt an insistent fluttering under my rib cage and the world shifted and blurred for a moment then the image of a jaguar shimmered before my eyes. I gasped. When I blinked, the vision had faded.

I glanced around the table only to find everyone was staring curiously at me. I caught Zen watching me, his expression a mix of concern and something else—something that made my pulse quicken.

I took a sip of water. "Sorry. I...I think I'm more dehydrated and tired than I realized." Imul's small hand found mine under the table. Her eyes darting nervously between Pastor Miguel and me.

I smiled weakly at Pastor Miguel, not quite able to erase the image of the jaguar from my mind. "Her name is Imul. She..."

"She was a stowaway. One of the children in the village where we stayed," Zen interrupted me mid-sentence. "By the time we discovered she'd followed us, it was too late to return her to her family. She's kind of attached herself to Niki, but Gorgonio will take her home to her family tomorrow."

I stared at Zen in surprise.

"*We need to talk.*" Zen's smile never faltered, but the voice in my head was unyielding.

Pastor Miguel's eyes drifted around the table, his expression sympathetic. "It sounds like it's been quite a trying adventure for all of you. Hopefully, our humble church can offer you some respite and comfort."

Two local women shyly entered the dining room bearing plates of hot food. "Ahh, perfect timing." The pastor's smile widened. "May I introduce all of you to Maria and Josefina. They prepared this delicious meal for us. Shall we bow our heads and say grace?"

Pastor Miguel tried to engage us in conversation during

our meal, but I was bone-weary, both physically and emotionally drained from the events of the last few days. I excused myself as soon as I'd finished eating and dragged myself to my room, an anxious Imul sticking to my side like a small barnacle desperately clinging to the hull of a sinking ship.

Mustering a weak smile of reassurance, I demonstrated how to brush our teeth with the bottled water and fresh tube of toothpaste Pastor Miguel had thoughtfully supplied. Without Zen to translate, our ability to converse was limited but we managed. Afterward, I tucked the very tired little girl into the bed we were to share, laying down next to her. She fell asleep almost immediately, still holding tightly to my hand.

I was exhausted, but sleep eluded me, and I stared at the ceiling, my mind spinning in a dozen different directions as the soft pulse of Nayla's wahy beat beneath my breastbone.

There was a soft knock on my door. I slipped out of bed, careful not to wake Imul.

Zen stood in the hallway, looking better than he had a right to. Clean shaven he looked decidedly less feral and dangerous.

His mouth quirked into a lopsided grin. "May I come in?"

I glanced over my shoulder at Imul. "I don't want to wake her."

Zen reached out and grabbed my hand. His touch sent a cascade of sparks rocketing up my arm that settled like liquid heat in my belly. "Please. It's important."

I hesitated for a moment before stepping into my room. Zen entered, closing the door softly behind him.

He stood close, his presence overwhelming in the small space. The faint scent of soap and something distinctly *him* made my pulse quicken.

"What?" I crossed my arms over my chest, trying to create some semblance of distance between us. But it was futile. The memory of the dream—the heat of his touch, the primal connection—flared in my mind, unbidden and unwelcome.

"You know what," he said, his voice low and rough. His gold-flecked eyes locked onto mine, holding me captive. His gaze dropped to my lips for a fraction of a second before returning to my eyes. "We need to talk about the dream."

"That dream was a drug-induced hallucination," I snapped, even as my body betrayed me by leaning slightly closer to him. "It wasn't real."

"It felt real enough." His voice was quiet but insistent.

I swallowed hard, my throat suddenly dry. "It doesn't matter what I felt. It doesn't change the fact that it wasn't real."

Zen stepped closer, his hand brushing against mine. The contact sent a jolt through me. "You're wrong," he murmured. "It *was* real—and so is the connection between us."

"Stop," I whispered, shaking my head. "I can't do this with you."

"Why not?" His voice was soft but relentless. "Because you think I was with Nayla?" The mention of her name hit me like a slap.

"Weren't you?" My voice cracked despite my best efforts to keep it steady.

"No." The word was firm, absolute. "Nayla and I were friends—nothing more."

I wanted to believe him but doubt still gnawed at me. "Then why do I feel like you're hiding something?"

Zen hesitated, his jaw tightening as if he were wrestling with some inner conflict. Finally, he exhaled sharply and ran a hand through his hair. "Because there *is* something I haven't told you."

My heart thudded painfully in my chest. "What is it?"

He looked at me then, his eyes burning with an intensity that made it hard to breathe. "I was born under the sign of the jaguar, too," he said quietly. The words hung in the air between us, heavy with meaning I didn't fully understand.

"What does that even mean?" I asked, my voice barely above a whisper.

"It means we're connected," Zen said, his voice low and urgent. "The jaguar is more than just a symbol—it's a force that binds us together. I am in your head because we are connected. Your dreams are a gateway to a different realm, a world in which we are bound to one another. Your dreams aren't hallucinations. They are visions. What you see in your dreams is real. What you felt in your dream—it's real."

I shook my head, taking a step back even as his words ignited something deep inside me—a flicker of recognition, of truth. "This is crazy," I said, though my voice lacked conviction.

"It's not crazy," Zen insisted, stepping closer again until there was barely any space between us. His hand came up to cup my cheek, and despite myself, I leaned into his touch. "You know it's not. You are a Jaguar. We are both hunters."

I stared at him. My last name translated from the Mayan language means Jaguar, but I had just realized that Zen's family name was Cazares—you must hunt.

Before I could respond—before I could decide whether to push him away or pull him closer—a sharp knock echoed down the hallway.

"Niki?" Jake's voice called out from behind the door to my room. "Are you awake? We need to talk."

I jerked back from Zen as if burned, guilt flooding through me even though we hadn't done anything wrong.

Zen dropped his hand reluctantly but didn't move away. His eyes searched mine. "I'll tell you everything," he promised in a low voice meant only for me. "But not here— not now."

I stood for a moment, my heart racing and my mind spinning. "Stay here," I whispered. "I'll deal with Jake."

I plastered a smile on my face, opened the door and stepped out into the hallway, quickly closing it behind me. "Imul is asleep. I don't want to wake her."

"Sure. Whatever." Jake's face was alight with suppressed

excitement. "I spoke with Pastor Miguel. He said he'll help us arrange transportation to Cobán."

As much as I wanted to get out of the jungle, I couldn't leave. Not yet. "Jake, I'm not going anywhere until I find my sister."

"I know you're worried about Nayla. Believe me, I am too and this is how we find her," Jake said, fervently. He spread his arms wide. "We can't possibly search the entire jungle on foot. The authorities have access to planes, helicopters, and search teams. We need to go to Cobán. It's the only way that we're going to find your sister."

CHAPTER NINETEEN

Pastor Miguel greeted Imul and I with a warm smile as we entered the small dining area the next morning. "Good morning, ladies," he said, as he stood and chivalrously pulled out two chairs for us. "Did you sleep well? I know the rooms are basic, but I do hope you were comfortable."

I nodded, stifling a yawn as I sat. "Yes, we were. Thank you. It felt great to sleep in a real bed last night."

The pastor's smile widened. "I am glad to hear that. We are a bit isolated here, so it is always such a pleasure to have visitors. We do try to spoil them. Coffee?"

"Yes, please."

Pastor Miguel poured a cup of coffee into my mug and returned to his seat at the head of the table. "And for the little señorita, perhaps some chocolate al mixto?"

He placed a small mug in front of Imul, who sniffed it suspiciously. He proceeded to mime sipping it, licking his lips, and rubbing his stomach. Imul laughed.

"*You look exhausted.*" Zen watched me from across the table.

"*I didn't sleep well last night.*"

The truth was, I hadn't slept at all. After sending Zen away, using Imul as an excuse—though we both knew it was more than that—I had collapsed into bed, bone-weary. But each time I closed my eyes, my carefully constructed dreamscapes shattered into nightmares. Giant bats with razor-sharp wings sliced through the air. Knives flew like deadly rain. Enormous serpents struck from shadows that shouldn't exist. Behind it all, orchestrating my terror like a maestro before his symphony, loomed Li Xul, his flame-filled eyes boring into my soul. No matter how I fought, I couldn't expel him from my dreams. My only escape was to wrench myself awake, again and again, as the night stretched endlessly before me.

I'd spent the night staring at the ceiling, my heart racing each time I drifted toward sleep, desperately trying to understand what had changed. My carefully constructed defenses were no longer keeping him out and I didn't know why. Li Xul hadn't just infiltrated my dreams—he'd stripped away my ability to control them, a power I'd wielded since childhood. I'd never encountered another dream-walker, so I had no framework for fighting one. But if I was going to protect myself and my sister, I would have to learn.

"*Neither did I.*" Zen's amber eyes searched mine, making something flutter in my chest—something I didn't want to examine too closely. "*Let me in, Niki. Walk in my dreams tonight or let me into yours. We'll both sleep better if you do.*"

His eyes seemed to see straight through me. For a moment, I wavered, desire and fear warring for dominance. No. Zen Cazares was a distraction I couldn't afford. At least not until I could figure out what was happening to me.

I turned away from him, grateful for the arrival of Josefina and Maria who began setting plates of food before us: pan dulce, fresh tortillas, scrambled eggs, sausage, fresh fruit, and spiced beans—a veritable feast. I thanked the two women and complimented them on the food. They smiled and ducked their heads shyly before retreating to the kitchen without a word.

Imul, who was thoroughly enjoying her hot chocolate, allowed me to fill her plate while Pastor Miguel regaled us with stories of the town's history. His charm was undeniable, and once again I found myself relaxing despite the nagging feeling of unease I'd felt from my sleepless night.

Suddenly, the pastor's eyes lit up. "Oh! I almost forgot." He reached behind his back and produced a small, cloth doll. The small doll wore the red skirt and embroidered huipil of the local women. Her black braids were made from yarn and wrapped with colorful ribbons in a style similar to Josefina and Maria.

Imul froze, her eyes wide, shining with hope as she stared at the doll.

Pastor Miguel grinned. "I thought this poor little dolly might need a friend." He offered the doll to Imul who glanced at me for permission. I smiled and nodded. She snatched the doll and clutched it to her chest as if she was afraid he might change his mind.

"That's very kind of you," I said, touched by the gesture.

Pastor Miguel waved off my thanks. "Of course. Now, I have some good news for the rest of you. The authorities will be flying to the archaeological site today to check on your friends."

Jake leaned forward, his expression eager. "That's great. Any chance you were able to arrange transportation for us?"

"Jake, I know you are eager to be on your way, though selfishly I do wish I could persuade you to stay longer," Pastor Miguel said, his eyebrows raised inquiringly as he glanced around the table at the three of us. "Ah. I can see from your faces that this is an argument that I won't win. Well, what I can offer you is the use of our parish boat. Abram and José can take you as far as the road. It's how we connect with larger towns. Unfortunately, our truck is in for repairs, so they won't be able to drive you to Cobán, but I can make some calls to arrange a ride for you." He dabbed his mouth with his napkin. "Please enjoy your coffee, there is no need to rush. I am afraid I need to excuse myself to attend to some pressing parish business, but I'll make a few inquiries as soon as I am free. I should think that you will be able to leave sometime early this afternoon."

We thanked him. He stood and with an avuncular pat on Imul's head took his leave.

I caught Zen's gaze as he watched our host depart. His expression was unreadable, but I could sense his restlessness.

***

The river was wide and sluggish, its waters swirling around wide flat stones worn smooth by generations of local women washing their clothes. The parish boat was little more than an old motorized canoe with peeling paint and mismatched wooden planks for seats.

José and Abram, the counterparts to Maria and Josefina, were to accompany us down river. Abram settled himself at the back of the boat, taking command of the motor. José took his place at the prow, a rifle slung casually across his shoulder. Their eyes met briefly, exchanging a look I couldn't decipher.

I eyed the rifle with some trepidation as I carefully climbed into the canoe, the wooden planks shifting treacherously beneath my feet.

Pastor Miguel offered me a steadying hand. Noting my fearful glance at the rifle, he gave my hand a reassuring squeeze. "There's really nothing to worry about. Abram and José have made this trip dozens of times. The rifle is just a precaution."

I smiled wanly at him, not quite able to shake the feeling that something in his tone rang hollow.

The small boat groaned under our combined weight as Pastor Miguel waved us off from the bank. Jake, still angry that Gorgonio had disappeared before we were able to leave Imul with him, positioned himself at the stern near Abram, his eyes fixed intently on the horizon. Zen and I occupied the middle section, with Imul perched between us, her small legs swinging over the edge of the seat. The air was thick with humidity, promising another sweltering day.

Imul's eyes were wide with wonder, her small hand still clasped tightly to mine, her doll tucked safely under her other arm. Despite our inability to communicate, she met each strange new experience—from sleeping in a proper bed to this boat ride—with complete trust that I would keep her safe. The weight of that trust pressed heavily against my chest. I glanced down at her small fingers intertwined with mine, hoping that her confidence was not misplaced.

Somehow, I was going to have to find a way to return her safely to her family. I glanced over at Zen. I'd have to talk to him about it later because right now I needed to prioritize finding my sister.

The merciless sun beat down, draining what little energy I had left. I sat quietly, letting Imul's excited chatter wash over me as Zen pointed out various wildlife. A family of turtles basked on a half-submerged log, their shells gleaming like wet stones. A massive catfish rippled in the murky water as it passed beneath our boat. A grumpy river otter, startled by our approach, dove with a splash that made Imul squeal with delight. Her joy was infectious, and I found myself smiling despite my exhaustion.

We'd been traveling for more than an hour when the distinctive whump-whump-whump of helicopter blades shattered the humid stillness. I looked up to see it, a small spec in a cloudless sky. José and Abram exchanged another of those inscrutable looks, but this time I caught something darker in their eyes. Without warning, Abram angled the boat toward the riverbank.

"What are you doing?" Jake demanded.

Abram ignored him and continued pointing the boat toward the shore.

"What the hell?" Jake surged forward, rocking the boat dangerously as he tried to place his hand on the tiller. "You're supposed to take us to the road!"

The two men ignored him completely. Abram guided the

canoe to shore with practiced efficiency, cutting the motor as José hopped onto the bank. The rifle, no longer casual, swept up to cover us with clear intent. The message was unmistakable: get out.

None of us moved. The only sound was the distant throb of the helicopter as it circled above the jungle canopy.

Zen's thoughts slipped into my mind, calm but urgent. *"You carry Imul. I'll get the packs. Be ready."*

I gave him an imperceptible nod, drawing Imul closer to me. My heart hammered against my ribs.

Jake's face flushed dark with rage. He lunged for the tiller, trying to wrestle control from Abram as the canoe tilted dangerously. "This is complete bullshit!" The words exploded from him, spittle flying. But there was something else in his voice—something that sounded almost like fear.

José's face hardened as he leveled the rifle at Jake's chest. "¡Salgan! Now!"

"Jake." Zen's voice cut through the tension like a blade, measured and controlled. "The man has a gun. If he wants us off the boat, we're getting off the boat." His eyes never left José as he addressed me. "Let's go."

I stood carefully, cradling Imul against me as I stepped into the shallow water. My hiking boots sank into the soft riverbed as Imul's arms tightened around my neck like a vice. She suddenly let out a cry and struggled in my arms, reaching out toward the boat.

We'd left the doll in the boat. "Zen, the doll."

Zen nodded. "I'll get it."

"I'm reaching for our packs," Zen announced in Spanish, his movements slow and deliberate as José watched through the rifle's sights. He tossed our bags onto the bank, scooping up Imul's doll before following us into the water.

Zen handed the doll to Imul, who wordlessly squeezed her tightly as she trembled against me.

Jake remained rooted in place, his entire body vibrating with barely contained fury. But beneath the anger, I caught a glimpse of calculation in his eyes as they darted between the rifle and Abram.

"Jake, please," I pleaded, fear making my voice crack. "Just get out of the boat."

The muscle in his jaw jumped erratically. His hands clenched and unclenched at his sides.

"Don't do anything stupid." Zen's voice carried a warning edge. "Not with a gun pointed at us."

For a moment, I thought Jake might actually try to fight. Then, with a snarl of rage, he snatched up his pack and lurched onto the bank, water spraying in his wake. He immediately began tearing through his bag, muttering under his breath as Zen, Imul, and I watched Abram reverse the engine. José maintained his position at the prow, rifle trained steadily on our group until they disappeared around a bend in the river.

Zen hefted his pack onto his back. "Jake, we need to get moving."

"Motherfuckers!" Jake's voice cracked with fury, ignoring Zen. "I'll show them. God damn it, where is it?" He upended his pack, dumping the contents onto the muddy ground. "When I get through with them—"

"Being angry isn't going to help us get out of here." Zen's words carried an undercurrent of tension I'd never heard before.

"Maybe not. But this will!" Jake triumphantly held aloft a satellite phone—the same one that had mysteriously disappeared from the archaeological site. His lips curved in a savage smile. "After I make this call, those bastards are going to wish they'd never—"

What happened next seemed to unfold in slow motion. Zen's face transformed into a mask of cold fury, his amber eyes blazing with an intensity that stole my breath. He launched himself at Jake with devastating speed. They crashed to the ground in a tangle of limbs. Zen's fist connected with Jake's face with a sickening crunch. In one fluid motion, he wrenched the satellite phone free and hurled it far into the river's murky depths.

Jake rolled to his hands and knees, blood streaming from his clearly broken nose and dripping onto his shirt. His face contorted with rage. "You bastard!" he spat, blood staining his teeth. "You have no idea what you've just done!"

I stepped between them, anger and confusion warring in my chest. "What the hell is going on?" I demanded, my voice sharp enough to cut glass. I whirled on Jake. "Why do you have the missing satellite phone?" Then to Zen. "And why did you just throw it in the river?"

The thunderous approach of a low-flying helicopter drowned out any response, its shadow passing over us like a giant predator.

"Niki!" Zen's voice carried an urgency I'd never heard before. His golden eyes locked onto mine with frightening intensity. "We need to get out of here. Now!"

I hesitated, torn between the need for answers and the fear in Zen's voice.

"*Trust me.*" The words carried a weight that seemed to stop time itself. Without waiting for my response, he scooped up Imul, cradled her against his chest and sprinted into the trees.

With no real choice, I plunged after them into the jungle's embrace. Zen ran like a man possessed, and adrenaline surged through my veins as I struggled to keep pace. Terror and anxiety kept my legs pumping and my muscles firing. Branches whipped at my face and arms, leaving stinging welts in their wake. I had no idea what we were running from, but Zen's fear was infectious, spreading through me like wildfire.

The helicopter's roar grew deafening as it skimmed the canopy above us. I made the mistake of looking up, searching for it through the leaves. My foot caught on an exposed root, and I crashed to the ground with a cry that was equal parts surprise and pain.

The impact drove the air from my lungs in a rush. As I lay there gasping, the world around me began to change. The spectral outline of a massive jaguar materialized, its coat rippling with ethereal flames that cast no light. My heart stuttered in my chest.

The air thickened, becoming almost gelatinous as a heavy vapor rose from the earth itself. It swelled and surged, rolling across the jungle floor like a white tsunami. Everything it touched transformed—trees, shrubs, and rocks became ghostly versions of themselves, familiar shapes turned alien and wrong.

"Zen!" His name tore from my throat, equal parts plea and warning as I staggered to my feet.

"Niki?" His voice seemed to come from everywhere and nowhere, distorted by the supernatural mist that continued to rise around us. Each syllable echoed strangely, as if spoken underwater.

"Over here!" Panic edged my voice as the mist swirled higher.

"Don't move. I'll find you." The certainty in his words offered a lifeline.

The jungle fell unnaturally silent, even the helicopter's thunder seeming muffled and distant. I wrapped my arms around myself, trying to hold back the tide of fear as I waited in a world turned to fog and shadows, praying that Zen would find me before whoever was hunting us did.

The spectral jaguar paced at the edge of my vision, her fiery coat flickering like a warning. Or a promise.

LISA DIETRICH

CHAPTER TWENTY

Li Xul stood at the edge of the cenote, his reflection rippling in the dark water below. The sacred pool had once been a place of sacrifice, where the ancient ones fed their gods with blood and pain. Now it served as his sanctuary, a nexus of power where the boundaries between worlds grew thin.

He pulled the jade medallion from his jacket—Hun-Came, Lord of Death, rendered in gleaming stone. The archaeologists had labeled it a mere artifact, something to be catalogued and stored. They hadn't felt its pulse, its hunger. They hadn't heard its whispers.

But the girl had sensed it. Nayla. She'd come to him with the carved jade artifact, but when he'd held it in his hand, she saw him for what he was. Her eyes had widened in recognition. In fear. That's when he knew he had to silence her.

Li Xul's fingers tightened around the carved jade. He'd built his empire through careful calculation, using the old magics to enhance his modern operation. The drugs, the human trafficking, the illegal mining—they were merely tools, means to an end. Each death fed his power. Each soul claimed brought him closer to true immortality.

But now the sister threatened everything. She had slipped through his grasp, again.

The girl was a problem. A problem he needed to solve. He kicked a stone into the cenote, shattering his reflection. She was strong—stronger than any adversary he'd faced. When he'd invaded her dreams, expecting to crush her mind with ease, she'd fought back. Worse, she'd escaped him, wrenching herself awake again and again. No one had ever resisted him like that.

"You're troubling yourself over one girl?" A voice like dry leaves rustling through empty tombs whispered from the god. "You who commands death?"

"She is more than just a girl," Li Xul growled. "She walks in dreams. And like her sister, she carries the old blood."

"Then take it. Drain it. Add her power to your own."

Li Xul smiled, feeling the familiar surge of dark energy flowing from the Mayan god of death, Hun-Came. Yes. The dream-walker's power would be sweeter for having been taken by force. And once he had both sisters...

Li Xul tucked the jade medallion back into his jacket and pulled out a small leather pouch. The bones inside clicked together as he shook them—fragments of sacrificial victims recovered from the cenote's depths. He cast them onto the stone platform, reading the patterns they formed.

"Soon," he murmured. The bones showed him glimpses: the dream-walker running through mist, the protective circle of her companions fracturing, blood seeping into thirsty earth. "Your power will be mine, little dream-walker. The old gods will feast again."

He gathered the bones and stood, his shadow stretching long across the platform as the sun dipped toward the horizon. In the jungle below, his men were already mobilizing. They knew these paths, these hidden places. The dream-walker might have escaped his nightmare, but she couldn't outrun his reach forever.

He'd take care of the old woman tonight. His men would handle the cleanup, erasing any trace of their presence.

Let the girl run. Let her think she had a chance. In the end, it would make breaking her all the sweeter.

Li Xul rubbed his fingers along the smooth jade through his jacket, feeling its cold pulse against his chest. Power. True power. Not the petty authority of governments or cartels. Not the temporal influence bought with money and blood. But the power of the old gods themselves. The power to master death itself.

The dream-walker was the key. Her blood would open the final door.

In his mind, he could already taste her fear.

CHAPTER TWENTY-ONE

The sound of helicopter blades faded to a distant echo as the mist rose higher, then disappeared completely. The jungle remained unnaturally silent, save for the faint dripping of moisture from leaves and the hollow sound of my own breathing.

"Zen?" I called out again, peering nervously into the mist as it thickened around me, pulsing with otherworldly energy. My voice seemed to be swallowed by the supernatural fog.

The wisps of swirling vapor rose and curled around themselves, taking shape before my eyes. I watched, fascinated and horrified, as the ghostly specter of Fire Jaguar appeared, padding silently toward me. She turned her massive head, golden eyes fixed on the curtain of white blanketing the trees to my left. When I turned to look, Zen emerged from the swirling mist, Imul clinging tightly to him.

"Niki, are you okay?" he asked, his voice laced with concern.

I nodded, unable to speak. I turned back to look at Fire Jaguar, but the image had dissipated into wisps of shadow and light, leaving me wondering if I'd imagined it entirely.

"Good. We need to move," Zen said urgently. "The mist

will give us cover, but we can't stay here."

I turned to face him. "What is going on? Who are those people in the helicopter? Why are we running?"

Zen's eyes glowed intensely in the half-light. "There are only two organizations who own helicopters out here: the military and the narcotraficantes. That wasn't a military helicopter."

My mouth fell open. I stared at him completely stunned. "Drug traffickers?" My heart leaped to my throat. "We left Jake! We need to go back. We left Jake with those people! He could be in danger."

Zen's expression hardened. "Jake can take care of himself."

I glared at him, shocked by his lack of compassion. "I know you don't like Jake, but how can you be so cold? He could be killed!"

Zen sighed heavily. "Niki, why do you think Jake had the phone?"

"I don't know."

"He has the phone because he's involved."

My brain made the leap. "You think Jake is trafficking drugs." I shook my head. "That can't be true."

Zen sighed heavily. "Look I know it's a lot to take in. I'll explain everything. I promise. But right now, we need to put as much distance as we can between ourselves and the people in the helicopter. Trust me."

There was that word again. Trust. Did I trust him? I wasn't sure. I hesitated.

Imul struggled in Zen's arms and reached for me, her precious doll in one hand, her eyes wide with fright.

I made my decision. "Okay. I'll carry Imul."

Imul buried her face in my neck with a whimper as I wrapped my arms snugly around her and settled her on my hip. "Let's go."

My mind reeled as we hiked through the mist-shrouded forest. We walked in silence. I had no idea where we were going, trusting Zen and Fire Jaguar to lead us to safety. I only hoped my trust was not misplaced since I had lost all capacity to discern truth from fiction. Was it true about Jake? Had I really seen the image of Fire Jaguar? Or were Zen and my mind playing tricks on me?

As we walked, the mist swirled around us, seeming to guide us, parting to reveal safe passages and thickening behind us to obscure our trail. At first, I'd welcomed the cool mist as a respite from the heat but the damp seeped into my bones, chilling me. I felt unsettled, as if we had crossed a threshold into a world where myth and reality intertwined.

Finally, after a long while we emerged into a small clearing, the late afternoon sun's rays thinning the mist, returning color once again to our world. Much to the relief of my aching arms and back, Imul decided that she was ready to walk.

I set her down and stretched. "How about a rest break?" I asked Zen.

He nodded, slipping his backpack from his shoulders with a wince, the heavy pack grazing his healing wounds.

"You, okay?"

"I'm fine." His tone made it clear that this discussion was over.

I held up my hands in mock surrender. "Okay."

With a curt nod, Zen unzipped his pack. He removed a water bottle and held it out to me.

I accepted it, unscrewed the top and took a gulp before returning it to him. Part of me wanted to sink down onto the ground and rest my tired, aching legs, but I was afraid if I did, I wouldn't want to stand up again. So, I remained on my feet. "I can't help it. I am worried about Jake. What if you're wrong?"

Zen's face was impassive. "I'm not." He drank greedily from the bottle before replacing it in his pack. "We can't stay in the open like this. We need to keep moving while we still have the light. I want to find us some shelter before it gets dark."

"How can you be sure about Jake?" I challenged him.

"Look. I'll explain everything tonight. But right now, we need to get going."

I had no choice but to accept his terms. I looked over to call for Imul, but she was nowhere to be seen.

My heart leaped into my throat. I whipped around frantically searching for her. "Imul!"

The clearing suddenly seemed vast and empty. Panic clawed at my chest as I spun in circles, searching for any sign of the little girl. "Imul!"

Then the world blurred around me, colors bleeding together like wet paint. Fire Jaguar materialized before me, more solid than I'd ever seen her. Her coat rippled with flames that cast no heat, her golden eyes boring into mine. She turned and padded toward a rocky outcropping I hadn't noticed before.

"This way," I called to Zen, already moving to follow the spectral cat.

Zen didn't question me, falling into step behind me as the great cat led us to a thin fissure in the rock face. It looked barely wide enough for an adult to squeeze through.

"Imul?" I called softly, peering into the darkness.

A giggle echoed from within, followed by the sound of her speaking softly to her doll. Relief flooded through me.

"The opening widens inside," Zen said, examining the fissure. "It looks like it might lead to a cave system."

I squeezed through the narrow opening, letting my eyes adjust to the dimness. The passage opened into a much larger space, and I gasped. We weren't in a natural cave— we were standing in what appeared to be an ancient temple chamber. Faded glyphs covered the walls, barely visible in the dim light filtering through the fissure. At the far end, a crude stone altar bore the unmistakable carved image of a jaguar wreathed in flames.

Imul sat cross-legged near the altar, completely absorbed in playing with her doll, seemingly unaware of the panic she'd caused.

"It's a temple. It belongs to Fire Jaguar." I breathed, running my fingers over the ancient carvings. "How did Imul know how to find this place?"

"Maybe she was led here, just like you were," Zen said quietly. "This could be a safe place to rest for the night. The entrance is defensible, and no one would think to look for us in here."

I nodded, but my stomach growled loudly, reminding me that none of us had eaten since morning. Zen must have heard it because he shrugged off his pack.

"There's a left-over buñuelo in my pack. You and Imul can share it. I'm going to try to find us some more food," he said, pulling out his water bottle and a small knife.

Fear gripped me at the thought of him leaving. "What if the helicopter comes back?"

He stepped close, his hand warm on my shoulder. "I won't go far, and I won't be gone long. I promise." His amber eyes held mine. "You're safe in here."

I glanced at the jaguar carved into the altar. "What about you?"

"I'll be careful." He squeezed my shoulder once before releasing it.

I watched him squeeze back through the fissure. In the dim light of the cave, Imul continued to play with her doll, humming softly to herself.

The carvings on the walls seemed to shift in the shadows, and I could have sworn I heard the distant sound of a jaguar's roar echoing through the ancient chambers.

I scrounged through Zen's backpack and found the sweet roll he'd saved from breakfast. I gave it to Imul who gobbled it hungrily. My lack of sleep and the tension of the day caught up with me. Exhausted, I lowered myself to the ground next to Imul and leaned back against the cool rock wall, closed my eyes and listened to Imul happily chattering to her doll as I tried not to count the minutes to Zen's return

Hunger claws at my belly, a primal ache that demands satisfaction. The jungle whispers around me as I move like liquid shadow through

the undergrowth. A familiar scent catches my attention —musky, alive. My muscles respond instinctively, my body dropping low to the earth. The pizote emerges, whiskers twitching, unaware of its fate. Time slows. I feel every heartbeat, every twitch of muscle as I launch forward. My claws sink deep, meeting the resistance of flesh and bone. The kill is swift, efficient. Hot blood floods my mouth, and with it comes a surge of pleasure so intense it borders on ecstasy. Power courses through my limbs as I tear into the meat, and for a moment, I am pure instinct, pure predator.

I snapped awake with a violent shudder, the copper taste of blood still sharp on my tongue. My heart hammers against my ribs as I pressed my hands to my mouth, half-expecting them to come away bloody. The cave's shadows seemed to pulse around me, and the carved jaguars on the walls appeared to watch with knowing eyes.

"Just a dream," I whispered, but the words felt hollow. It hadn't felt like a dream at all. I had been the jaguar—had known its hunger, its power, its savage joy in the kill. The sensations had been too vivid, too real. Even now, I could feel phantom echoes of muscles I didn't possess, of senses beyond human perception.

Zen's words and the healer's words echoed in my mind: *You are a jaguar. You have been chosen. You cannot escape your destiny.* The carved eyes of Fire Jaguar stared at me from the stone altar, and for a moment, I swear they gleamed with golden light. I pressed my palms against my eyes, trying to block out the sight. I'd made my peace with dream-walking and spirit companions—those things felt distant, mystical, safe. But this... this was visceral, primal. The taste of blood lingering on my tongue, the ghost-memory of muscles bunching and stretching, the electric thrill of the hunt still singing in my veins—these weren't visions. They were transformations. My father's blood, my family's legacy, was reshaping me from the inside out, and no amount of rational explanation could make that feel safe or sane.

Balam. Jaguar. Not just a name, but a birthright. Part of me wanted to run from this cave and never look back. But the other part, the part that still thrummed with the power of the hunt, knew it was far too late for that. The jaguar was in my blood, in my bones, in my very name. Fighting it felt like fighting gravity—exhausting and ultimately futile.

A low rumble echoed through the chamber—whether from deep in the earth or from my own throat, I was no longer sure.

Imul looked up from her doll, her dark eyes wide with concern. I tried to smile, but it felt more like a grimace. She scooted closer, pressing her small warm hand into mine. The simple human contact helped ground me but didn't entirely dispel the wildness thrumming beneath my skin.

With a quick smile of reassurance for Imul, I pushed myself to my feet and paced the small chamber, trying to shake off the lingering sensations. The carved images of Fire Jaguar seemed to follow my movement, taking on new meaning. I pressed my fingers against the ancient stone, tracing the outline of a leaping jaguar. The rock felt warm beneath my touch, though that must have been my imagination.

What was happening to me? I was exhausted, hungry, and trapped in a cave dedicated to a jaguar deity—of course my mind would conjure images of hunting. But that didn't explain the lingering taste of blood, or why my body felt both foreign and more alive than ever before. The boundary between my reality and my dreams had become frail and insubstantial, and I was no longer certain which side I was standing on.

CHAPTER TWENTY-TWO

I gazed down at Imul's sleeping form and covered her with the rain poncho from Zen's pack.

A sound from the entrance made me whirl, my body instinctively dropping into a crouch. For a split second, my senses sharpened impossibly—I could smell earth and green growing things, hear the whisper of cloth against stone, taste the approaching presence in the air. Then reality snapped back into place, leaving me dizzy and disturbed by my reaction.

"It's just Zen returning. Just Zen," I whispered to myself like a mantra.

Zen squeezed through the narrow entrance, our eyes met, and something electric passed between us. I wondered—not for the first time—who exactly I had chosen to trust. My eyes lingered on his bare chest, tracing the ragged claw marks on his smooth tawny skin as he crouched next to me carefully removing the assortment of fruits he'd wrapped in his shirt.

"It's not much but I found some jocote and some nance berries." He looked up at me, his eyes luminous in the strange light. His mouth and chin were stained with the remnants of something, the color almost black.

I reached over and touched his face. As soon as my fingers brushed his mouth, an electric charge rocketed along my arm like a liquid flame burning my body with heat and desire. I couldn't have removed my hand if I'd wanted to.

Zen's eyes locked onto mine and he leaned toward me, his expression questioning.

"Yes," I whispered, desire sparking inside of me, hot and raw.

With a quick glance at the sleeping Imul, Zen stood and helped me to my feet.

He led me to the crude stone altar, lifting me to sit on the smooth stone. He gently cupped my face. "Are you sure?" he asked, his voice low and rough.

Instead of answering, I closed my eyes, wrapped my legs around him and lunged toward him, licking the stain on his mouth with my tongue, the biting metallic taste of blood causing me to half-groan, half-growl with desire.

I could feel the hard heat of him through my clothes as he pressed himself between my legs, his mouth devouring mine. I was shaking with an almost feral need to have him inside of me.

His hand slid under my shirt, unclasped my bra and found my breasts. He rubbed his thumbs over my nipples in slow circles. *Too slow.* I needed him now! I wanted him now! In one frantic motion, I ripped my shirt over my head craving the feeling of his skin on mine.

"Please," I begged breathlessly.

He froze, his breath ragged, his eyes boring into mine. His eyes raking my naked torso with a hungry heat that made my bones melt.

He stepped out from between my legs and cradled one foot. His hands slid down my inner thigh to my hiking boot, making quick work of unlacing it and dropping it on the ground. My legs trembled under his touch, as he removed my other boot. He slid his fingers under the waistband of my pants and slowly, fingers trailing along my thighs rolled them down my legs. I moaned in ecstasy at his touch.

I sat naked, legs splayed, my eyes fixed on him with a savage intensity, shuddering with need. His hands snaked up my legs, his fingers fluttered against my mound, now wet and slick with longing as he leaned in to nuzzle my neck. Wrapping his hands around my hips, he pulled me closer, his mouth trailing kisses from my neck to my breast. When his mouth found my nipple, I arched my back shivering as ripples of pleasure coursed through me.

"I want you now," I growled low in my throat.

His eyes blazed gold as they locked onto mine. With one hand he unbuckled his belt, dropped his pants and thrust himself inside of me.

I wrapped my legs around his hips and rode him like he was a bucking bronco as a spasm of intense release roared through my body. He followed, shuddering with a low groan of pleasure as he wrapped his arms around me. Utterly spent, we clung limply to each other like two shipwreck survivors.

I rested my head against his shoulder, feeling the slowing of his heartbeat for several minutes before placing a hand on his chest and gently pushing him away. "Holy fuck."

I could see the glimmer of his animal-white teeth in the dim light as he smiled. "My sentiments exactly."

A throaty grumble of contentment reverberated through the cavern. Fire Jaguar.

"Did you hear that?" I asked.

Zen cocked his head to one side listening. "Hear what?"

"Never mind." I groped around the altar for my shirt and bra, my body and face flushing hotly, this time from embarrassment. "I don't usually do things like this. In fact, I never do things like this."

Zen handed me my pants and my boots. "Well, then I'll count myself lucky."

I turned my back on him as I dressed, fighting feelings of remorse and shame that suddenly seemed to be flooding through me. "Oh my, god. We didn't even use a condom." I looked over my shoulder at him. "Please tell me you don't have an STI."

Zen let out a low rumbling chuckle. "You're tough on a man's ego. This is where you're supposed to say it was the best sex I've ever had. But just so you know, I'm clean as a whistle."

I exhaled in relief. "That's something at least."

What had just happened to me? Having crazy sex without protection was so unlike me. It was like I'd been possessed by—did supernatural beings have sex? Fire Jaguar? I closed my eyes, breathing deeply as I tried to ground myself before I lost it completely.

"Are you alright?" Zen asked.

I glanced over at Imul who had slept through our entire episode of carnal sex. That was a relief. I already felt guilty about any emotional scarring she may have acquired during our adventure this afternoon, I didn't want to add to it by having her watch Zen and me going at it.

I turned back to face Zen. "Actually, I don't think I am. I don't know what's wrong with me. I don't know who I am anymore. I'm hallucinating during the day. I'm seeing jaguars everywhere; I just had unprotected sex in a cave and... you...you have blood on your face." My voice cracked.

Zen rubbed a self-conscious hand across his chin. "I know that it can be overwhelming, but…"

A bark of incredulous laughter escaped me. "Overwhelming? That's one word for it. Though *insane* might be a better choice."

"You're not insane, though I know there are times when it can feel like it." His expression was filled with empathy.

I walked over to Imul and sat next to her. Zen followed, lowering himself to the ground beside me. He offered me one of the plum-like fruits.

"Thanks." I bit into the tart tangy fruit. I had no idea how to interact with Zen after what had just happened. "Did you hurt yourself?" I asked awkwardly, eyeing the dried blood still clinging to his chin.

"What?" He rubbed his hand across his chin.

I nodded. The night air was cooling quickly. "Look. I just want to say that what happened...it's not who I am. Okay? I don't know what came over me."

Zen reached for my hand. "Hey. You don't need to apologize or explain."

I tugged my hand from his. "Let's talk about something else." I reached for another jocote fruit. "Why don't you tell me what is going on. Who are the people in the helicopter and why do you think Jake is trafficking drugs?"

Zen took a long drink from his water bottle. "Li Xul."

"Li Xul?" I asked with a lift of my eyebrow. "The shaman? What does he have to do with the people in the helicopter?"

"Li Xul is a shaman and a major drug trafficker. Though he doesn't limit himself to drugs. He also traffics people, stolen artifacts, and gold from illegal mining operations."

My mouth fell open. I stared at him completely stunned. "How do you know this? And why do you think Jake is involved? I know he had the phone," I said quickly before he could answer. "But there could be a dozen other reasons why he had the satellite phone."

"There could be, but there aren't. Why hide the fact that he had the phone unless he needed it to make phone calls that he didn't want anyone else to know about?"

I shook my head. "I just don't believe it."

"Look, I know it's a lot to take in. But someone's been using the shipment of artifacts from Choja q'eq to smuggle drugs and gold."

I stared at him. "How could you possibly know this?"

His green-gold eyes locked onto mine. We stared at each other in silence. After a moment, he came to a decision. "I'm with the D.E.A."

If he had told me he was a unicorn or a mermaid, I wouldn't have been more stunned. I didn't even know how to react. "The D.E.A. as in The Drug Enforcement Agency of the United States?"

"Yep. I was sent here to investigate and identify the source of the contraband coming through the university."

It seemed so improbable that it could only be a joke, but then as I thought about it, I realized it actually made sense—Alma talking about how Zen kept himself aloof from the others. David and Roman complaining about his lack of archaeology skills. The antagonism between him and Jake. And Nayla. Was my sister working with Zen?

"Did Nayla know?" I asked, my pulse quickening.

He gave me an almost imperceptible nod. "Not at first. But she caught me in the field lab, going through one of the shipments. She threatened to report me to Dr. Kelling. I had to tell her."

"You told my sister!" Anger boiled up inside of me seeking a target. "Jake was right! You're the reason my sister is missing! You made her part of your investigation and now she's..." I choked on my words.

Zen held my gaze. "I know you're worried about Nayla. I am too. But I did not involve her in my investigation."

"Bullshit." I spat the word out, rage building in my chest. "I know my sister. She would have jumped at the chance to help you."

"She was involved," Zen said quietly. "But not the way you think. She came to me." He paused, choosing his words carefully. "She said something else was going on, something bigger than drugs."

I let out a harsh laugh. "Let me guess—she told you some story about the jade pectoral and Hun-Came."

"Not exactly. She did believe that Choja q'eq was ground zero for an ancient spiritual war, but she thought that Li Xul was channeling old power—power that let him infect people's minds." Zen's eyes reflected the firelight as he spoke. "She believed that Li Xul wasn't content just to kill people with drugs or poison them with cyanide from his mining operations. I think she was right. I think he's a dream-walker, like you. He can enter people's thoughts, twist them, make them believe things that aren't true." Zen leaned forward, his voice dropping. "Nayla was convinced he killed your father."

I shot to my feet, trembling with fury. "You are unbelievable. My father wasn't killed by some drug-trafficking shaman channeling ancient Mayan gods. He was murdered by a mob of superstitious, angry people!"

My voice had grown louder, waking Imul who half-alseep whimpered and sat up. I sank down next to her and placed a comforting hand on her back, murmuring to her to go back to sleep. She clasped her doll to her chest and rolled over, closing her eyes again.

Zen waited until Imul's breathing had deepened before speaking. I could tell he was working hard to keep his voice level and low. "A mob of people who had been convinced your father was practicing witchcraft and killing their children—when in fact it was chemicals leaching into their water from nearby mining operations that was making them sick." His amber eyes locked onto mine. "Why would they think that, Niki? Who planted that idea in their heads? Someone had to have the power to influence their perceptions."

The implications of his words raised goosebumps on the back of my neck. I remembered my recent dreams, the way Li Xul had slipped into my mind. My anger drained away as quickly as it had come.

"No," I whispered, but even as I denied it, pieces were falling into place. "My father..." My voice cracked. "He was trying to protect the village from the mining operation. He was gathering evidence about the water contamination."

Zen nodded slowly. "And Li Xul couldn't let that happen. It was easier to let the village destroy itself—and your father—than risk exposure."

I felt sick. All these years, I'd blamed ignorance and superstition for my father's death. But if Zen was right, if Li Xul really had that kind of power... "Is that why Nayla disappeared? Because she figured this out?"

The silence that followed my question was answer

enough.

"I've been having visions. Not just dreams but visions when I'm awake. Visions of a jaguar, where I become the jaguar. I feel what the jaguar feels. I see things through the jaguar's eyes. Tonight, when you were out, I had another one. I could taste the blood, I...I was literally blood-thirsty. I wanted more." My hands trembled with the implication of what I was admitting aloud. I glanced over at Zen, afraid of what I might see in his face, of what his reaction might be. "What if Li Xul is putting these thoughts and images in my head and I can't stop them?" I whispered.

Zen watched me carefully, his expression unreadable, then leaned back against the rock, exhaling slowly. "Li Xul isn't responsible for your visions. There are things about me you don't know, Niki. Things that might change the way you understand all of this."

I stared uncomprehendingly at him. "Like what?"

He hesitated, rolling a jocote between his fingers as if searching for the right words. "I had a choice when I was younger. I could have been something else, something... dangerous. But I sought out your father instead. He understood things most people don't. Things about what I am."

Something about the way he said it sent a shiver through me. "What do you mean, what you are?"

Zen glanced at me, then past me, into the darkness beyond the firelight. "You're not the only one who walks between realms. You are seeing what I see. Feeling what I feel." His voice was barely above a whisper. "Your father knew the old ways. He helped me when I was younger, when I didn't understand what I was becoming. He taught me control."

A chill crept up my spine. "What are you talking about?"

His golden-green eyes flickered in the firelight, unreadable. "Did you ever wonder why I show up in your dreams as a jaguar?"

I stared at him, my heart pounding, too afraid to ask the

question I needed to ask.

The air between us thickened, my breath caught in my throat. This was ridiculous. Impossible. And yet—hadn't I felt it myself? I had sensed something lurking beneath the surface when I first saw Zen. My rational mind rejected what he was telling me. The idea that wahyob and naguales existed, that there were humans who could transform into animals, was something I could not allow myself to believe.

"Those are just stories," I whispered.

Zen gave a small, enigmatic smile. "The stories exist for a reason. You know they do. You've known what I am, you just haven't been willing to accept it."

"No." I shook my head.

"When Enrique was attacked, you were with me." He tapped his temple. "I felt you inside my head. You know I'm telling the truth." His gaze, intense, feral, pinned me in place, willing me to accept the impossible.

The revelation crashed over me like a wave, leaving me breathless and disoriented. The memory of my teeth sinking into the soft flesh, the hot blood trickling down my throat and the greed for more was—Zen? Holy fuck! Zen was a wahy ba'alam, a nagual—a shapeshifter. I had no idea how to react. Or even if I should react. Threatening a wild animal could be dangerous. I glanced at Imul. Did I have to worry about her safety? About mine?

"Why are you telling me this now?" I asked, my voice barely steady.

"Because you need to know," he said simply. "And because, sooner or later, you're going to have to decide what you believe—about me, about yourself, about us, and about the battle we're in."

I stared into those glowing amber eyes and made my decision. Jaguars, shamans, and the gods, be damned! As soon as I knew that Imul was safe, I was finding my way to Cobán and getting the fuck out of Guatemala.

LISA DIETRICH

CHAPTER TWENTY-THREE

At sounds of the jungle awakening, I sat paralyzed oblivious to the chirring, hooting, trilling of various monkeys and birds, hearing only the words of Zen's confession echoing in my mind. Shapeshifter. The word itself seemed to pulse with ancient power, with danger. I watched him now through new eyes, searching for signs I'd missed—the fluid grace of his movements, the predatory stillness when he listened, the golden-green eyes that sometimes caught the light at impossible angles. My rational, academic mind warred violently with what my instincts had recognized from the beginning: the jaguar had always been there, watching from behind Zen's human facade.

The boundary between human and animal, between myth and reality, had shattered, leaving me adrift in a world where nothing was as I'd believed. Zen said we were linked, that we were both hunters. I didn't want to dwell on what that might mean or the fact that my father's stories might be real or what it might mean for me. It was easier to pretend that last night—none of it—had happened and focus on the practicalities of our situation. Which as it turned out, wasn't hard.

I woke in the morning with stomach cramps. I thought it was from the fruit I'd eaten last night, but when I went out to relieve myself and saw the blood, I realized it wasn't. On the plus side of things, I wasn't pregnant, on the negative side—well, I was going to have to figure out a way to deal with this new complication. Unfortunately, my daypack with my emergency supplies was still by the river where I'd left it when we fled from the helicopter.

When I returned to our cave, Zen, Imul, and her doll sat cross-legged on the ground engaged in what looked like a deep philosophical discussion.

"I need the first aid kit," I announced.

Zen looked up at me, his expression concerned. "Are you hurt?"

I shook my head, an embarrassed heat creeping up my neck. "I..um...It's a female thing. I need some gauze bandages."

To his credit, Zen seemed unfazed by my *situation*.

I wondered briefly if his ease around bodily functions and blood was related to his animal nature—the jaguar part of him that existed beyond human social taboos. Was anything about our interaction normal now that I knew what he was?

Zen dug through his pack and handed the kit to me. "Pastor Miguel let me restock from his supplies. Take what you need."

"Thanks." I ducked around the stone altar and found a private place to take care of things. By the time I'd put myself together, all I could think of was how much I hated camping. I would have given almost anything for a tampon, hot shower, clean clothes, a bottle of ibuprofen, a bed, and a decent meal.

"Nayla, I could kill you for dragging me into this."

An annoyed grumble echoed from deep within the cave.

I started laughing. *Why not?* I thought. After experiencing hallucinations, flaming jaguars, drug traffickers, DEA agents, and shapeshifters, why not add my sister's voice in my head just to make things that much better. *"Now? Now you decide to show up? As if I don't have enough problems already."*

I waited for my sister to reply, but there was nothing but silence. My head dropped into my hands. A puff of something sad and lonely vibrated in the hollow space of my ribcage.

Sighing heavily, I slowly straightened and dragged myself back to where Zen and Imul were waiting for me.

I blindly followed Zen through the jungle, trusting that he would lead us back to Rosa's village as Imul skipped and scampered beside me. Keeping to my vow to focus only on the practicalities of our situation, I forced myself not to think about Zen's revelation from last night. Imul and I needed this man, this human man, to survive.

Zen and I agreed that we needed to return Imul to her family before we did anything else, and the little girl was thrilled to be going home. A few times, she yelped happily and scampered into the underbrush only to return with some roots she'd dug up or edible fruit she found, generously sharing her bounty with us as we hiked.

Each time we came across a stream or river, Zen refilled his water bottles, dropping purifying tablets into them. At first, Imul eyed the murky brown water in the bottles suspiciously, refusing to drink it and pointing to the vines overhead. Only after Zen patiently explained that without machetes we could not easily cut them, did she deign to drink it. I didn't blame her. It was like swallowing warm mud, but it was all we had.

We eventually stopped at a wide river. Zen consulted his compass. "We need to cross."

I made a face as I stared unhappily at the wide expanse of sluggish brown water. "How?" I asked.

Zen grinned. "One step at a time."

Imul and I waited anxiously on the banks as Zen waded into the water, holding his pack above his head. At mid-river the water was up to his shoulders. I caught myself studying his movements in the water, searching for something inhuman in the way he navigated the current. Was this how he'd always moved, or was I just seeing him differently now that I knew? The jaguar was a powerful swimmer—was that helping him now, even in human form? I had so many questions about how his dual nature worked, I pushed the thought aside. Now was not the time.

When he reached the opposite side of the river, he dropped his pack on the opposite side before making the return trip to where Imul and I waited anxiously for him.

"How much of you is human?" The question slipped out before I could stop it.

Zen's eyes met mine. "All of me is human, Niki. And all of me is jaguar, too. It's not one or the other."

I smiled nervously. "So, I guess that means that I don't have to worry about you eating me for dinner?"

"Not unless you're asking about oral sex."

It was supposed to be a joke, but neither of us laughed. Zen held my gaze, searching for something, I wasn't sure what. After a moment, he turned from me and crouched in front of Imul. "Princess, your chariot awaits."

She solemnly handed her doll to me for safe keeping, before climbing onto Zen's back and wrapping her hands around his neck.

"You ready?" he asked, his expression carefully blank.

I sighed heavily and nodded. With one last scan of the shore, I stepped into the water.

By early afternoon, Imul's little legs had given out, though to be honest, my legs weren't far behind. It was only by sheer determination I kept putting one foot in front of the other as Zen and I traded carrying Imul and his pack for what seemed like hours. I was so relieved when we finally found the trail marked with the jaguar skulls and smelled the smoke from the cooking fires that tears filled my eyes. Buoyed by success, we hurried along the path to the village, Zen in the lead.

Before we entered the village, he skidded to an abrupt

stop and turned quickly, holding up his hand. "Stop!" he hissed through his teeth.

Imul and I immediately froze, my heart beating against my rib cage like a drum. We stared at him, eyes wide with fear.

He held up a finger to his lips, then mouthed the words, "Don't move."

I nodded and he disappeared into the undergrowth. I drew Imul close to me.

Imul pointed after Zen, making it clear that she wanted to go with him.

I shook my head.

She slid from my back and gazed up at me, her face set in the stubborn expression I'd come to know so well over the last few days. She wanted to go home, and we were telling her she had to wait. Her small mouth frowned unhappily, her eyes shifting between me and the path that led to her village.

Then, faster than I would have thought possible, she took off, her small legs sprinting for home.

"Damn!" I chased after her, both of us skidding to a halt at the edge of the village—or what was left of the village.

I stared in horror at the smoldering ruins before me. The clearing looked like a war zone. A blue smoky haze hovered over the charred remains. The buildings had been burned and left to smolder in blackened heaps of ash and wood. The stones from the cooking hearths had been viciously kicked and scattered across the clearing. Only Rosa's hut had been left unmolested. One of the peccary stakes had been placed in front of the healer's hut, a cloud of flies buzzed around the dead flesh of the thing impaled on it.

It took me a moment to realize what I was looking at— Rosa's severed head on a pike. My stomach lurched as a salty bitter taste rose from the pit of my stomach, filling my mouth. I rolled my head to the side, retching and shaking uncontrollably.

Imul let out an earth-shattering wail. She ran toward the

horrible thing on the pike screaming and crying, just as Zen burst from behind a screen of leaves and branches.

He stopped abruptly when he saw us. His eyes shone fiercely. "I told you to stay put!"

With trembling arms, I lifted a sobbing Imul and cradled her against me, hoping to shield her from the sight of her grandmother as she sobbed inconsolably. "She took off. I tried to catch her but…"

"Get her away from here," he barked, his face taut with rage and grief.

I moved away mechanically, clutching the sobbing child to my chest. Part of me wanted to collapse next to her and surrender to my own tears, but I forced myself to keep moving. My eyes kept darting to Zen as he surveyed the destruction, his face tight with controlled rage. Yesterday, I would have seen only a man grieving for friends. Today, I saw something else—something wild and dangerous beneath his human exterior.

Part of me wondered if the jaguar in Zen was raging now, hungry for vengeance against whoever had done this. I stared at him, searching his face for signs of the predator I now knew lived within him, half-afraid I'd see that animal fury breaking through his human control before nodding numbly, and carrying Imul, walking back the way we'd come. Not quite able to shake the primal fear that whispered he was something I couldn't trust. And yet, what other choice did I have?

The little girl's sobs tore at my heart as I sank down onto a fallen log, cradling her against my chest. I stroked her hair and rocked her gently, murmuring soft nonsense words, though I knew nothing could ease this kind of pain.

The sound of voices made me stiffen. I clutched Imul tighter, ready to run, but then I heard Zen call out in Q'eqchi.' A moment later, people began emerging from the jungle—the villagers, carrying what few possessions they'd managed to save. Their faces were drawn with exhaustion and fear.

Gorgonio rushed forward when he saw us. An older woman began speaking rapidly, gesturing toward the village. Though I couldn't understand her words, the terror in her voice needed no translation. Zen listened intently, his face growing darker with each word.

"What happened?" I asked when she finished.

"They came in the night," Zen translated, his expression giving away nothing of the emotional turmoil roiling below the surface, but his voice tight with anger. "Men with strange green eyes that glowed in the dark. Night vision goggles," he explained. "They grabbed Rosa's daughter and son-in law and dragged them outside. When Rosa came out to help, they killed her. Made an example of the three of them. Said it was a message for anyone who would dare disrespect Li Xul."

My legs gave out and I sank back onto the log. "Because we were at the village. Because she helped us." The words felt like ashes in my mouth.

"No." Zen's voice was sharp. "Because Li Xul wants to destroy anyone who might stand against him. Rosa was a healer, a keeper of old ways. She was already his enemy."

But I couldn't shake the guilt that coiled in my stomach like a poisonous snake. If we hadn't come here, if we hadn't brought danger to their doorstep...none of this would have happened.

More villagers were arriving now, their shocked murmurs turning to wails of grief as they saw the state of their homes. Zen spoke with several of the men, then turned to me. "They want to bury their dead. We should help."

I nodded. It was the least we could do. The next few hours passed in a blur of grim activity. The men carefully removed Rosa's head from the stake, wrapping her remains in clean cloth. Others began clearing debris, salvaging what they could from the ruins. The women gathered children away from the worst of the destruction, trying to comfort them even as they wiped away their own tears.

I worked alongside the men, moving stones, gathering

scattered possessions, helping to dig graves. My muscles screamed in protest, but I welcomed the pain. It felt like penance.

By sunset we had interred the bodies. "They'll have a ceremony tomorrow morning," Zen explained.

While we buried the dead, the women resolutely focused on caring for their families. Gorgonio invited Zen and I to join him and his family at their fire pit where his wife baked yams dug from one of the gardens.

Exhausted, I gratefully dropped to the ground. Imul crawled into my lap, and I wrapped my arms around her and rested my chin on the top of her head, the fire providing much appreciated warmth and light as the air cooled and night closed in around us.

Gorgonio's wife, who caught me washing out the ace bandage I'd been using as a menstrual pad after dinner, quietly slipped me a bundle of soft cloth when we returned. I smiled at her gratefully.

We spent the night sleeping in the open clearing of what had once been a thriving village but was now a collection of family hearths feebly flickering in the middle of a dark forest.

I woke in the darkest part of night to find the fires had burned low, leaving only glowing embers that cast a dim red light over the sleeping villagers. The jungle was unnaturally quiet—no insects chirping, no night birds calling. Even the wind had stilled. Something had drawn me from sleep, though I couldn't say what.

Then I saw it—a flickering at the edge of the clearing, like heat waves rising from sun-baked stone. The air seemed to ripple and tear, revealing glimpses of another place, another time. I tried to look away, but my body wouldn't respond. The vision pulled me in, as inexorable as a tide.

I found myself standing in an ancient plaza, its stones weathered by centuries. Two figures faced each other across a ceremonial ball court—one wreathed in flames that took the shape of a great jaguar, the other surrounded by writhing shadows that formed themselves into skeletal wings and a grinning skull. Fire Jaguar and Hun-Came, locked in an eternal battle for balance.

Their power clashed in waves of searing heat and bone-deep cold. Where they met, reality itself seemed to crack. Through these fissures, I caught glimpses of other times, other battles—armies of ancient warriors clashing in battle, indigenous activists marching, soldiers executing kneeling men. The pattern repeated itself through centuries: protection versus corruption, preservation versus destruction, justice versus power.

I saw Li Xul, the red-eyed jaguar clearly then, Hun-Came's power flowing through him like black mercury. And behind him, a vision of environmental devastation—forests reduced to toxic waste, rivers running with poison, people twisted by corruption both spiritual and physical. This wasn't just about drugs or gold or artifacts. It was about the soul of the land itself.

The scene shifted again, and I saw myself as I could be—standing with Fire Jaguar's flames dancing around me, my lawyer's mind melded with jaguar instinct, wielding both human law and ancient power. The power to protect, to preserve, to bring justice—it was there for the taking, if I had the courage to accept it.

The vision released me with a jolt. I sat up and gasped for air, my heart hammering in my chest. The fires still burned low, the villagers still slept, but everything had changed. I looked down at my hands, remembering how they had glowed with Fire Jaguar's power in my vision. Then I thought about the ruined village around me, at the fresh graves we'd dug, at the sleeping children who deserved a future free from devastation and fear.

Running away to Cobán wasn't an option anymore. The battle between Fire Jaguar and Hun-Came had found new champions, whether we wanted it or not. Li Xul had already chosen his side. Now it was my turn.

I felt Zen's presence before I saw him, a warm solidity

in the darkness. "You're cold," he whispered. He wrapped his arms around me and held me, sharing the warmth of his body. He didn't speak, but I knew he understood. Tomorrow, we would need to make plans, gather allies, prepare for what was coming. But for now, I sat in the darkness, watching the embers glow like tiny mirrors of Fire Jaguar's flames, and felt the power stirring in my blood.

The jungle's night sounds slowly returned, but they seemed different now—not random noise, but a rhythm, a heartbeat, a reminder that everything was connected. The law of the jungle and the law of man weren't so different after all. Both were about maintaining balance, protecting the weak, and bringing justice. I had trained to do that in one world. Now I would have to learn to do it in both.

The next morning, we gathered around the three fresh graves—Rosa, her daughter, and her son-in-law. Imul held my hand firmly, but the rest of the villagers gave me a wide berth, their eyes sliding away from me fearfully.

"Do they blame me?" I asked Zen, my heart still aching with the thought that Rosa's death was somehow my fault.

Zen gave my other hand a squeeze. "No. They don't blame you. They know me, but you are powerful and scary. Someone best to be avoided."

"But I'm not," I protested.

"Fire Jaguar chose you. Abuela told them that you are the one who will free the forest from Li Xul."

I stared at him both stunned and shaken. Had Rosa really told her people that I was going to defeat a powerful shaman and his army of killers? Zen held my gaze.

"Right. No pressure," I mumbled under my breath.

Zen gave my hand another squeeze. "Whatever happens. I'll be right beside you."

The villagers began to sing, a low, mournful sound that seemed to rise from the earth itself. I didn't understand the words, but I felt their power. They were not just grieving songs, but prayers of protection, of defiance.

Gorgonio approached us after the ceremony, lifting

Imul in his arms. He spoke quietly to Zen, who translated: "They'll be moving the village deeper into the jungle, somewhere Li Xul's men can't find them. Imul will live with Gorgonio's family. I've explained that she can't stay with us. She understands."

Imul's sad dark eyes dented my heart. When I reached out to tenderly squeeze her hand, she buried her face in Gorgonio's shoulder, refusing to look at me. I couldn't blame her. She'd lost her family and now I was abandoning her, too. I turned to look at the smoking ruins of her home. "Will they be safe?"

"Safer than staying here." Zen's eyes met mine. "Safer than staying with us."

I nodded, a lump forming in my throat as I watched Gorgonio walk away carrying Imul in his arms.

"We should leave now, while there's still light. We need to keep moving. We're the ones Li Xul really wants," Zen said.

He was right, but leaving felt like running away. I touched one of the grave markers gently. "I'm sorry," I whispered, though I knew the dead couldn't hear me.

As we turned to watch the villagers leave, I saw something move at the edge of my vision—a flash of flame-touched fur, gone before I could be sure it was real. But somehow, I knew Fire Jaguar was watching, bearing witness to both the destruction and the survival of her people and the land.

A loud wail knifed through the air and I turned quickly. Imul had wriggled free of Gorgonio's arms and barreled toward me like a very small homing missile. She threw herself at me wrapping her arms around my knees sobbing uncontrollably. I glanced up at Zen, my heart breaking at her distress. With a small shake of his head, he answered my unasked question. He was right. There was no way we could keep the little girl with us.

I crouched down and scooped her up, hugging her tightly, eyelashes wet with my own tears.

Gorgonio gave me an apologetic look. With a heavy sigh, I squeezed Imul once more and kissed the top of her head, before gently depositing her into Gorgonio's waiting arms.

There can be no rebirth without death.

The guilt still gnawed at me, but something else burned alongside it now: anger. Li Xul hadn't just killed three people—he'd tried to kill a way of life, to sever connections to the old powers that Rosa had served.

Some fights chose you, whether you wanted them or not.

CHAPTER TWENTY-FOUR

"No." The word came out firm, final.

Zen's jaw muscle jumped as he spoke, each word measured and controlled. "Niki, it is not safe for us to stay here. We need to leave."

I crossed my arms and met his gaze, lifting my chin. "No."

"I am trying to keep you safe," he said through gritted teeth.

"They have guns. They have night vision goggles. Running won't keep us safe." I gestured to Rosa's hut, the lone structure standing in the scorched village. "This is war—a war between Hun-Came and Fire Jaguar, with Li Xul and myself as proxies. What will keep us safe is preparing, and I can do that here."

I reached out, touching Zen's arm. "Running is what they want us to do. It keeps me from focusing on what matters." My voice softened. "I need time to regroup and plan. We'll be as safe here as anywhere else—we're under the protection of Fire Jaguar and..." I hesitated. "Rosa."

Zen flinched at her name, but I pressed on. "Rosa cast a net of spiritual protection around this place."

"The glyphs," Zen murmured, his eyes drawn to the hut.

I nodded.

Zen studied the hut for a long moment before turning back to me. "Fine. A few days, no more. Then we move." He studied me for a long moment. "Are you sure you're ready for this? Once we commit to this fight..."

"I'm not ready at all," I admitted, my voice surprisingly steady despite the fear churning inside me. "But I'm done running from who I am—from what I am." I met his gaze directly. "And you? Are you with me in this? The shapeshifter and the lawyer against a drug lord and a death god?"

Something shifted in his eyes—a flicker of the predator beneath the man. "I've been dealing with this crazy Mayan cosmos since I was sixteen years old, Niki. The question was never if I would stand against Li Xul, but if you would stand with me."

The simple truth of his words hit me like a physical blow. All this time I'd been seeing him as something other, something dangerous, when in reality he'd been fighting this battle alone long before I stumbled into it.

"Then I guess we're in this together," I said, extending my hand to him. "Human, shapeshifter, and whatever I'm becoming."

I felt a spark of something primal pass between us—not just Fire Jaguar's power, but a more human connection. Whatever Zen was, whatever I was becoming, we were bound together now in ways I was only beginning to understand.

I gestured toward the river. "I'm going to bathe and wash my clothes. When I return, you need to tell me everything you know about Li Xul."

"Agreed." His expression softened. "Thank you."

"For what?" I asked.

"For accepting me as I am." He turned away from me, but not before I saw the flicker of something like gratitude in his eyes.

The river glinted harshly in the sunlight as I dragged my

sore, grimy body down to its banks. The villagers had created a bathing area, ringing it with flat stones that slowed the current.

I stripped off my filthy clothes, including the soft bundle of cloth I'd been using as a menstrual pad and cautiously waded in. Zen had promised there were no piranhas in Guatemala. I hoped he was right.

The water felt cool on my skin and while I had no soap or shampoo, rinsing went a long way to restoring my equilibrium. I was slowly coming to terms with the reality of my situation, though it felt like trying to piece together a puzzle with half the pieces missing.

The incident in the cave with Zen haunted me. I'd felt Fire Jaguar's presence then, raw and primal, driving us together with an intensity that still made me shiver. Was that what it meant to be a vessel for an ancient power? To be overwhelmed, possessed, used? I ducked under the water again, trying to wash away the memory of burning hands and golden eyes.

When I surfaced, I stared at my reflection in the calmer water near the stones, half-expecting to see some visible change—some mark that would brand me as Fire Jaguar's chosen one. But the face looking back was just mine—exhausted, frightened, ordinary. How could these people possibly believe I was meant to save them?

My hands shook as I pushed wet hair from my face. I was a lawyer, for God's sake. I analyzed precedents and built arguments—I didn't battle supernatural forces or shape-shifting narcos. My father's stories about Hun-Came suddenly felt less like bedtime tales and more like warnings I'd foolishly ignored—the god of death who corrupted everything he touched, who turned the natural order inside out. Dad's voice would drop to a whisper as he described how Hun-Came could poison minds as easily as Li Xul's illegal gold mines poisoned rivers.

The memory sent a wave of terror through me so intense

I nearly choked. What if I failed? What if more people died because I couldn't figure out how to wield powers I didn't understand? Rosa's lifeless eyes seemed to follow me, an accusation and a warning of what was at stake.

At the thought of my father and Nayla, I felt a flutter in my chest, a reminder that I was now the protector of my sister's wahy. The responsibility pressed down on me like a physical weight. My sister had trusted me with a piece of her spiritual self, but I had no idea how to honor that trust, how to keep it safe when I couldn't even keep myself safe.

The water reflected my face, but for a moment I saw Nayla's features superimposed over mine—softer, more open to the mysteries our father had tried to teach us. My chest tightened as I felt her wahy pulse beneath my breastbone. As twins, we'd always shared a deep connection, but this was different. This was Nayla deliberately entrusting me with a piece of her spiritual self.

"Ny, I wish you were here," I whispered to the river. "You always understood this stuff."

I closed my eyes and breathed deeply, clinging to the hope that Nayla was alive somewhere, that she had sent her wahy to me because she understood I would need her help, not because she was no longer alive. In the darkness behind my eyelids, I could almost feel her presence—that familiar mix of strength and intuition that had always balanced my skepticism.

Nayla should have been the one Fire Jaguar had chosen for this battle, not me. She was the one who had embraced our heritage, who had embraced the old ways, tread the spiritual path. She studied how to interpret omens and read the signs in nature. I was the one who had run away to law school, who had tried to reduce everything to facts and evidence.

"Why me?" I whispered to my rippling reflection. I was a lawyer, not a shaman. I'd spent my life running from this part of my heritage, burying myself in law books instead of learning from my parents. Now that willful ignorance felt like a weakness. How could I fight in a spiritual war when I barely understood the rules of engagement?

Nayla's wahy stirred within me, and for a moment I felt what might have been an echo of my sister's thoughts—a reminder that we were two halves of the same whole. Maybe that was why Fire Jaguar had chosen me. Not because I was the stronger twin or the more spiritual one, but because Nayla and I together possessed everything needed for this fight. Her intuitive connection and understanding of the spiritual world combined with my analytical mind and determination to see justice done.

"We're in this together, aren't we, Ny?" I touched the water's surface, watching the ripples distort my reflection. "Just like always." The wahy pulsed in response, and I felt a surge of something beneath my breastbone that might have been hope. Maybe I didn't need to understand everything right away. Maybe I just needed to trust—in Fire Jaguar, in my sister's wisdom, in my own strength.

The water lapped at my shoulders, and for a moment I imagined I could feel Fire Jaguar's power flowing through it, connecting everything—the river, the trees, the very stones beneath my feet. This wasn't like preparing for a court case. I couldn't just gather evidence and build an argument. I needed to understand how to channel this force that had chosen me, to control it instead of letting it control me.

I thought of Rosa's glyphs, of the protection they'd woven around her hut. She'd understood the old powers, and knew how to work with them. Now she was dead, and I was fumbling in the dark with a power I didn't understand. But I was done running. Done hiding from what I was meant to be.

What I needed was information. About Li Xul, about how he channeled Hun-Came's power, about how Zen connected to all of this. I needed to understand the rules of this supernatural game before I could even think about winning it.

I waded out of the river, wringing water from my hair before braiding it. My clothes were still damp, but I pulled them on anyway. The sun was climbing higher, and I had questions that needed answers.

As I headed back toward the village, I felt Fire Jaguar's presence like a warm shadow in my mind. Not overwhelming me this time, but waiting, watching. Whatever this power was, whatever it wanted from me, I had to find a way to work with it rather than against it whether I was ready or not.

When I returned to the village, Zen was waiting by Rosa's hut, his face unreadable. He gestured to something scratched in the earth. "Do you know what this means?"

I drew in a sharp breath as I stared at the familiar symbol. Two interconnected spirals had been carved into the dirt before Rosa's doorway—one rotating right, one left, drawn with a single continuous line.

"There's another inside," Zen said, leading the way.

My heart rate accelerated with fear at what I might see as I followed him inside. The hut's interior stopped me short—it was untouched, preserved exactly as the day we'd left it. My first reaction was one of relief. I let out a breath I hadn't known I was holding. Given the desecration of the village and her brutal slaying, I'd expected the worst.

Zen glanced over at me as if reading my thoughts. "They never entered her place. They killed her outside," he said flatly, his eyes flickering to the doorway where they had mounted her head. He turned abruptly and pointed to a wall.

There, Rosa had painted the double spiral again, but with a difference. The outer line was transformed into a jaguar, its body curling left while its elongated tail formed the right spiral.

I walked over to the symbol, tracing it with trembling fingers.

Zen's cat-like eyes narrowed as he watched me. "You've seen this before."

It was a statement not a question, but I nodded anyway. "It's called a double spiral. It's a Druid symbol," I explained. I turned back to stare at the spiraling jaguar. "It represents spiritual enlightenment or awakening. The two concentric circles depict the harmony and balance that gets created when two opposing forces interact and coexist—the balance between the physical and the spiritual, between birth and death, creation and destruction."

Zen studied me, his gaze sharp. "And you know this because...?"

"Because it's the logo of my mother's store." The words felt like glass in my throat. "Gaia's Embrace. My mother owns an apothecary shop—herbs, crystals, all that New Age-Druid stuff."

"Your mother is a Druid wise woman?" Zen's voice was carefully neutral, but I caught the tension beneath.

I pressed my palm flat against the wall, feeling the rough texture beneath the paint. "Yes." A bitter laugh escaped me. "I used to think it was all an act. Just marketing for the tourists wanting potions and magical amulets. Funny how the universe has a way of proving you wrong."

The jaguar spiral seemed to writhe under my touch, ancient powers—Maya and Druid—intertwining in Rosa's prophetic art. "She knew. Rosa knew what would happen to the village. She saw it in that vision she had, the night before we left. She sent Imul with us to protect her. She knew we'd come back here. This is a message. For me. For us."

Zen studied the symbol a moment longer. "What kind of message?"

"I'm not sure." I stared at Rosa's artwork, sliding my fingers along the jaguar spiral and following the line to complete the second spiral. I stared at the merged symbols, my mother's double spiral transformed by my father's jaguar. Two traditions, two powers, two truths I'd spent my life denying—now impossible to ignore.

I felt Fire Jaguar's presence stir within me—a deep rumble of approval that vibrated through my chest like distant thunder. The sensation sent a jolt of panic through me even as something deeper responded to it. Part of me wanted to run screaming from this hut, to deny everything I was feeling and experiencing. But Rosa's blood had already been spilled. Villagers had lost their homes. Imul had lost her family. Running wouldn't undo any of that.

My legs trembled so badly I feared they might give out. The painted jaguar on the wall seemed to shimmer in the dim light, its spiraling form rippling with living energy. I wanted to pull my hand away from the wall, but couldn't— or wouldn't. Through my fingertips, I sensed the convergence of worlds I'd spent my life denying—Druid and Maya, physical and spiritual, my mother's mysteries, my sister's wahy, and my father's truths.

Fire Jaguar's energy pulsed through me like a second heartbeat, insistent and ancient. Tears stung my eyes as I finally understood Rosa's message. This wasn't about me being strong enough or knowledgeable enough. It was about bridging worlds—something I'd been doing my entire life, standing between my mysticism and scholarship, between my sister's spirituality and my own rationality.

"I don't know if I can do this," I whispered, my voice breaking. But even as the words left my mouth, I knew I had no choice but to try. For Rosa. For Imul. For my sister. And for myself.

CHAPTER TWENTY-FIVE

I sat cross-legged on the ground, picking the last of the small white bones from the fish we'd cooked. My fingers trembled slightly, betraying the chaos beneath my carefully maintained composure. Zen had returned to the hut before sunset, freshly bathed and carrying fish, onions, potatoes and some large leaves in his string bag. We'd wrapped the food in the leaves and cooked them on a large flat cooking stone over the fire, putting aside the beans for tomorrow's breakfast.

The normalcy of the meal preparation had been almost surreal—as if we were just two people on a camping trip, not fugitives hiding in the burned-out shell of a village with a dead woman's prophecies painted on the walls. I'd watched Zen's hands as he prepared the food, those same hands that could, apparently, transform into deadly jaguar claws. Every movement of his, now seemed loaded with new meaning, new questions.

It was a veritable feast, and we gorged ourselves in tense silence, the weight of unspoken questions hanging between us like smoke.

No longer distracted by hunger, I was finally ready to focus on the problem at hand: How to defeat a narcoshaman, find my sister, and save the world from the ancient Mayan god of death, though not necessarily in that order. The absurdity of it all made me want to laugh and scream simultaneously. Three weeks ago, my biggest concern had been preparing for a deposition.

I fixed my gaze on Zen, chewing the last of my meal thoughtfully as I organized my thoughts. He looked different to me now—every familiar feature overlaid with something wild and unknowable.

He looked up, catching my stare. "What?"

"Are you really working undercover for the D.E.A.?" The question felt almost ridiculous after everything else I'd learned, but I needed something concrete, something from the rational world I understood.

"Yes." His answer was simple, direct.

"It seems unreal. Like something out of a movie or book." I shook my head, a humorless laugh escaping my lips. "That might be the least unbelievable thing about this whole situation."

The corner of his mouth quirked upward. "You're okay with the shapeshifter thing but not the DEA thing?"

I met his eyes, suddenly needing him to understand. "None of this is okay. I'm not okay. I'm a lawyer who can't even keep her own sister safe, let alone an entire village. People are dying, Zen. Rosa is dead because she helped us, and now everyone expects me to channel some ancient jaguar goddess I don't understand and defeat a supernatural narco-trafficker." My voice cracked slightly. "And yes, I'm still trying to process that you can turn into a jaguar. That you've been keeping that from me this whole time while I've been—" I stopped myself, heat rising to my cheeks.

He held my gaze, something unreadable flickering in his eyes. "While you've been what?"

"Trusting you. Depending on you." I looked away unwilling to acknowledge anything more about my complicated feelings for him.

After a moment of heavy silence, I shrugged, forcing

casualness I didn't feel. "Well, given that I'm hallucinating ancient Mayan jaguars with flaming fur, your shape-shifting seems kind of normal by comparison."

He threw back his head and laughed, the sound startling me.

The firelight played across his features, highlighting the sharp angles of his face. I wondered how I hadn't seen the predator in him before. "Is Zen even your real name?"

His expression became serious. "It is. One of them anyway. My baptismal name is, Alejandro Lorenzo Rafael Ignacio Cazares y Mendoza. Zen is my family nickname." He bowed mockingly in my direction. "Pleased to meet you."

"Well, that's a start, I guess." I drew in a deep breath, centering myself. *This was just another deposition*, I told myself. *Just gather the facts*. Facts I could handle. "Okay, Alejandro Lorenzo." I held his gaze as I pronounced his name, watching for his reaction. "I want you to tell me everything you know about Li Xul, Hun-Came, and my sister. And I mean everything," I added for good measure, forcing steadiness into my voice even as fear curled in my stomach.

As Zen began to speak about Li Xul, I wrapped my arms around my knees, trying to steady myself against the mounting terror that threatened to engulf me. Li Xul was what the movies called a bad hombre. According to Zen, the name had popped up on the DEA's radar ten years earlier when illegal migrants began showing up ferrying methamphetamine and other drugs at the border. They'd been recruited as mules by a shaman whom they'd sought to "bless" their journey to El Norte. The authorities' best guess was that Li Xul had broken away from one of the Mexican or El Salvadoran cartels and set up an independent operation in Guatemala. In the past decade, he had expanded his network from smuggling humans and drugs to include wildlife and artifact trafficking as well as illegal gold mining.

Each new detail made my heart sink further. This wasn't

just some local criminal—this was an organized, established operation with tentacles extending across borders. And somehow, I was supposed to stop it.

"I'm probably going to sound naïve, but if you know Li Xul is responsible, why hasn't he been arrested?" My voice came out smaller than I intended, betraying my growing sense of helplessness.

Zen's expression darkened. "Because he exists in the shadows. We don't know his real identity—no photos, no fingerprints, nothing. The migrants we've questioned describe a man of medium height and build who wears an owl mask, but..." He hesitated, and something in his reluctance sent a shiver down my spine.

"But what?" I pressed, though part of me didn't want to know.

"But those are just stories from people who've seen his human form."

My stomach clenched, a cold dread spreading through me. "What do you mean, his human form?"

"The locals say he's a —a shapeshifter."

"Like you?" I whispered, unable to keep the edge of fear from my voice. The fire suddenly seemed too dim, the shadows around us too deep.

The muscle in Zen's jaw flexed. "Not like me," he said firmly, his eyes challenging me with an intensity that made me want to look away. "They claim he travels at night as a jaguar, bat, or owl." Zen's voice dropped lower. "The name Li Xul translates to 'The Beast' or 'Night Predator,' but it's not just about physical predation. They say he can enter dreams, poison minds, and steal souls."

My hands began to tremble in earnest now. I clasped them together tightly, trying to hide my fear. "He's always appeared as a jaguar in my dreams," I said slowly, pieces clicking into horrible place. The words felt heavy on my tongue, an admission that connected me to this monster in ways I didn't want to contemplate. "But there's something else, isn't there? The owl mask connects him to Hun-

Came."

Zen nodded grimly. "The owl mask isn't just a disguise. It's a symbol of Hun-Came's power. According to Maya beliefs, owls are psychopomps—guides between the world of the living and the dead. But Li Xul has twisted that ancient role. Instead of guiding souls, he traps them."

"The drugs." I breathed, a terrible clarity dawning. "For him, it's not just about making money. It's about power."

"Yes. Every addict is a corrupted soul, trapped between life and death. Perfect offerings for Hun-Came." Zen's eyes reflected the firelight, turning them to molten gold. For a moment, I could almost see the jaguar within him, watching me. "The drug trade, the illegal mining, the artifact theft— they're all connected. The mines poison the land, the drugs poison the people, and the stolen artifacts weaken the old protections."

I thought of the glyphs Rosa had painted, of Fire Jaguar's protective presence. "He's systematically destroying everything that could stand against Hun-Came's return."

"Exactly. The DEA think they are dealing with a typical cartel operation. They have no idea that we are up against something supernatural. They sent me here because my anthropology background was supposed to help me understand the 'cultural context.'" He gave a bitter laugh. "They didn't expect the cultural context to involve ancient Mayan gods."

I stared into the dying embers, overwhelmed by the enormity of what we faced. My legal training, my years of education—none of it had prepared me for this. "I don't know how to fight this," I admitted quietly, voicing the fear that had been growing since Rosa's death. "I'm not a shaman or a warrior. I don't know how to use whatever power Fire Jaguar thinks I have."

Zen was silent for a long moment before he surprised me by reaching across the space between us to take my hand. His touch was warm, human, despite everything I now knew.

I reluctantly withdrew my hand from his. "And Jake? How does he fit into this?"

"Jake's been Li Xul's contact at the dig site. Zen's jaw tightened. "But Jake's just a pawn. We're fighting something much more dangerous than drugs or human trafficking and Choja q'eq is the key."

"What do you mean?"

Zen's eyes drifted upward following the tendrils of smoke wafting toward the dried leaves of the thatch roof. "Nayla was convinced that Choja q'eq was a military outpost—used by shamans for spiritual warfare."

"Spiritual warfare?"

"The ancient Maya didn't limit their warfare to this world. The warriors killed people with knives and spears, their priests killed them via dream walking, disease, drought, famine, and flood. Nayla thought that the Maya sealed caves, destroyed temples, burned and buried sacred spaces of their enemies not just because they were symbols of authority but because they needed to protect themselves by severing their enemies' connections with their patron gods.

She was convinced that the Choja q'eq site had been part of a spiritual complex associated with Hun-Came and the underworld. When she found the jade pectoral with the image of Hun-Came, she went to see Kelling. She wanted him to stop the excavation until they had a better sense of what they were dealing with."

The memory of the jade medallion and Hun-Came's malevolent grin flashed in my mind. Even though it was only a digital image of the missing artifact, I had felt the power of it pulsing through me.

The pieces of the puzzle were finally dropping into place. "Kelling didn't agree."

"No."

"That's why you've been looking for Nayla. Why you really don't believe she left the archeology site on her own."

He gave me a curt nod, his expression grim. "Your sister was a threat to Li Xul. She understood both worlds, the spiritual and the physical, in a way that no one else at the site did."

I closed my eyes feeling the flutter of Nayla's wahy under my breastbone. I had no idea what I was supposed to do. How was I supposed to fight something I didn't understand?

Zen's words slipped inside my thoughts. "*Fire Jaguar chose you for a reason, Niki. You can move between realms just like your sister, but in a different way.*"

I opened my eyes to find him studying me. "Your legal training and skepticism—those aren't weaknesses. They're tools. You can use them like your father did to protect the innocent from Li Xul, but you also have something more. You are a dream-walker."

He gestured toward the image of the jaguar and the double spiral on the wall. "You said that symbol represents the harmony and balance that is created when two opposite forces come together. Don't you, see? That is exactly who you are. You embody two opposing belief systems. You have the ability to fight Li Xul in both the physical and the spiritual worlds."

That evening, I lay in my hammock, the spiral jaguar on Rosa's wall swimming in the flickering shadows. My mind refused to quiet, spinning like the endless spiral before me. Zen lying in Rosa's hammock hung just feet away, and I found myself achingly aware of his presence—the rhythm of his breathing, the subtle creak of rope as he shifted. Part of me yearned to cross that small space between us, to feel the safety of his arms and the steady beat of his heart. But I couldn't afford that comfort, not now. Not when every moment of closeness seemed to draw Fire Jaguar's energy to the surface, making me burn with something that was both desire and ancient power.

I closed my eyes, trying to focus. I was fighting Hun-Came—the Mayan god of death and destruction. How does one defeat death? The question felt impossible, yet I could feel the answer hovering just beyond my grasp, like moonlight on water.

Moonlight. The word triggered something in my memory—my mother's voice, soft in the twilight of her shop, telling stories of the Daughter of the Moon, keeper of tides both physical and spiritual. The moon didn't fight the darkness, she'd said. It embraced it, transformed it, and used it to illuminate the path forward.

There can be no rebirth without death.

The phrase that had haunted me suddenly shifted, its meaning transforming like the moon's phases. I'd been thinking of it as a threat, but what if it was a key? My thoughts drifted to the jade pectoral Nayla had discovered—the one that had started all of this. She'd told me jade was associated with the breath of life, the soul's essence. That it could trap a person's spiritual essence.

As my mind circled these thoughts, I felt a familiar warmth spread through my chest. Fire Jaguar's presence rose within me, but this time it felt different. Instead of the raw, overwhelming force I'd experienced before, it was more like moonlight on water—fluid, adaptable, illuminating. My sister's wahy pulsed in response, and suddenly I understood.

I wasn't just caught between two traditions—two worlds. I was the bridge between them. Like the moon pulling at the tides, I could learn to work with these forces rather than against them. The jade pectoral wasn't just a vessel for trapping spirits; it was a tool for transformation. If Li Xul had used it to bind himself to Hun-Came, perhaps it could be used to unbind them—to transform death's power rather than simply trying to defeat it and by doing so, restore harmony and balance between opposing sacred powers.

Fire Jaguar's energy surged through me, and in my mind's eye, I saw the double spiral beginning to make sense. One spiral represented the cycle of physical power—life, death, rebirth. The other was spiritual power—waxing, waning, transforming. Where they met, on the one continuous line, that was where true power lay.

I sat up in my hammock, suddenly alert. "Zen," I whispered into the darkness.

He stirred immediately, as if he hadn't been fully asleep. "What is it?"

"The jade pectoral—it's not just an artifact. It's a nexus point, like the spirals in Rosa's painting. Li Xul isn't just using it to channel Hun-Came's power. He's using it to bind their essences together, to create a bridge between the world of the living and the dead."

Zen sat up, his eyes catching the moonlight filtering through the thatch. "And?"

"And if I can understand how he did it, I might be able to undo it. Not by fighting death, but by transforming it— like the moon transforms darkness into light." I touched my chest where Nayla's wahy rested. "That's what Rosa was trying to tell us with the spiral jaguar. It's not about balancing different kinds of power. It's about weaving them together into something new."

Fire Jaguar's approving rumble echoed through my bones, and I felt my sister's wahy pulse in harmony with it. For the first time since this began, I felt something like hope. I didn't have all the answers yet, but I had a direction. Like the moon pulling at the tides, I would learn to work with these forces rather than against them. And maybe, just maybe, that would be enough to save us all.

"Zen, what can you tell me about Hun-Came?"

Zen lay into his hammock, pillowing his head with his hands. He blew out a breath, his eyes straying to the thatch roof overhead. "Hun-Came, the god of death and destruction. He's usually depicted as a skeleton, sometimes wearing bells, sometimes rattling bones. He is associated with owls—who are considered his messengers and omens of death. Though he's also associated with dogs, vultures, maggots, and flies. He's a bad dude, so it usually doesn't end well for people who hang out with him."

I stared at him. "Tell me something else. Something

that might help me fight him."

Zen turned his head to look at me. "Sorry. That's all I've got."

I gritted my teeth in frustration, my thoughts tumbling over each. The jaguar that Rosa had painted on the wall seemed to shift and move in the flickering light of our fire. I needed to find out more about Hun-Came. I'd been blocking Li Xul from my dreams, but now I needed to find him and see through his eyes to better learn about his connection with the Mayan god of death. I was tired of playing defense, I wanted to go into this fight swinging, but I was worried about protecting myself and Nayla's wahy.

I glanced over at Zen. His eyes were closed and he looked relaxed as if he were already sliding back to sleep. When the time came to confront Li Xul, I'd need Zen, but right now what I needed was a lesson on the Mayan spirit world.

I slipped out of my hammock.

Zen cracked open one eye. "You going out?"

"Just for a minute."

Satisfied with my answer, he closed his eyes and settled back into his hammock.

I stepped outside into the cold and dark. An almost full moon gleamed like a polished bone in a sky pinpricked with millions of stars. Its light carved the world into stark contrasts of silver and shadow. The air was thick with the scent of damp earth and something more elusive— something that shimmered at the edges of reality pouring over the jungle like the breath of forgotten gods—waiting for the right soul to see beyond the veil. I closed my eyes, felt the earth beneath my bare feet, and asked Fire Jaguar to show me what I needed to know.

For a moment, nothing happened. Then warmth bloomed in my chest, spreading outward until my skin tingled. The world around me began to blur, physical reality giving way to something else entirely.

Fire Jaguar appears before me, glowing like a torch. The heat of her flaming fur warms my skin as we fly through the jungle—branches, trees, and rivers skim past my vision, the images blurring like watery paint until dark and the colors merge. We stop in front of a cave hidden among a dense shadowy tangle of trees and vines.

Fire Jaguar steps back, her eyes lock onto the cave entrance. I can feel a dark ancient energy emanating from within, pulsing like a heartbeat, its gaping maw opens as if to swallow me.

I know this cave. I've seen it countless times in my nightmares. My breath quickens and I cast my eyes upward at the moon, barely discernible through the tree canopy. I inhale, drawing her cold energy into my lungs, letting it settle deep into my bones.

Shafts of moonlight follow me as I enter the cave, lighting the way as I creep toward the cenote. Tiny puffs of dust and dirt rise like small clouds with each step I take. I know who awaits me: Death.

The smell of decay and putrification grows stronger as I approach the sacred sinkhole. I walk past piles of disarticulated bones scattered along the walls, the faint echo of their owners' souls fading out to infinity like a thousand plucked harp strings.

My heart hammers against my rib cage, my mouth feels like it is filled with ashes. I stop at the cenote's edge and I force myself to stare into the black water. Something glows with a bioluminescent quality from its depths of the sinkhole, I creep closer and the grinning skull of Hun-Came, the Mayan god of death looks up at me.

His voice whispers in my mind like dry leaves rustling across stone. "Daughter of Moon and Jaguar, at last we meet."

The moonlight streaming through the cave opening seems to dim, as if retreating from his presence. Yet, I force myself to stand my ground, drawing on Fire Jaguar's warmth at my back.

"Where is my sister?" I demand.

A sound like bells jangling and bones clicking together might have been his laugh. "Ah, but that's not the real question you came to ask, is it? You want to understand." His skull face emerges further from the water, owl feathers adorning his headdress. "You want to know why."

"Why what?"

"Why I must exist. Why death must exist." His hollow eyes fix on me. "Your Druid mother taught you about cycles, did she not?

209

About balance? I exist because without me there is only disorder and chaos—the world would cease to exist. Balance must be maintained. There is no rebirth without death. There is no creation without destruction."

Images flash through my mind: green shoots pushing through scorched earth, mushrooms sprouting from a rotting log, maggots writhing on decaying flesh, flowers blooming atop a grave.

"Death nourishes life." Hun-Came's voice is a whisper against my skin. "That is how balance is maintained. You cannot have one without the other."

"Li Xul is corrupting people's souls," I counter. "That's not balance."

"Is it not?" Hun-Came's voice grows stronger. "Humans have forgotten the old ways, forgotten their place in the great cycle. They poison the earth, destroy the sacred places, sever their connections to the spirit world. Perhaps corruption is necessary to remind them of what they've lost. I seek only to restore balance."

I feel the truth in his words like a physical ache, remembering my own rejection of my heritage, my dismissal of the old ways as superstition. But I also feel the wrongness in his methods. "You speak of balance while demanding submission." My voice grows stronger. "True balance doesn't require one force to be subjugated to another. It requires harmony between opposing forces—like the double spiral."

Fire Jaguar's approving growl reverberates through the cave as I continue: "I am Daughter of Moon and Jaguar. I understand cycles, understand transformation. But I also understand justice." I step closer to the water's edge, feeling moonlight and Fire Jaguar's power merge within me. "You want to teach humans about balance? Then help me show them a better way. Work with me to transform their understanding, not destroy their souls."

Hun-Came's skull face tilts, considering. "And if I refuse?"

"Then I will stop you." I lift my chin. "Not by trying to destroy death—that would be impossible. But by showing people how to embrace both sides of the cycle, how to live in balance with both worlds. Every soul Li Xul corrupts; I will work to heal. Every sacred place he defiles, I will work to restore."

The god of death regards me silently for a long moment. When he speaks again, his voice carries a note of something almost like respect. "Bold words, Daughter of Moon and Jaguar. But words are only wind. I suggest you choose your path wisely."

He lunges from the water, bone fingers reaching for my throat— but I'm ready. I call upon the moon's power of transformation and Fire Jaguar's protective strength. The energies merge within me, creating something entirely new. My skin tingles as moonlight slides through my veins, touching the glowing flames within me. Where they meet, they don't extinguish each other but transform into something I've never felt before—not cold, not hot, but fierce and dazzling illumination.

Light blazes from my hands, catching Hun-Came mid-lunge. He hisses, skeletal fingers curling away from the light—not in pain, but in reluctant recognition. For an instant, I see something like respect in those hollow eye sockets.

"Remember." his voice whispers as the vision begins to dissolve. "In the end, all come to me."

The vision shattered. I gasped, stumbling slightly as I found myself back outside Rosa's hut. The moon still hung overhead, unchanged, though I felt irrevocably altered. Fire Jaguar's presence remained warm within me.

From his hammock inside, Zen stirred. "Niki? You okay out there?"

"Yes," I replied, touching the spot where Nayla's wahy pulsed beneath my breastbone, weaving together my sister's wahy and Fire Jaguar's energy. "I think I finally understand."

LISA DIETRICH

CHAPTER TWENTY-SIX

When I woke the next morning, Zen's hammock was empty. I had fallen into a deep dreamless sleep after my visit with Hun-Came, my mind and body heavy with exhaustion. It turned out that spending time with Mayan deities took a lot out of a girl.

Hun-Came had called me Daughter of Moon and Jaguar. The title echoed in my head as I rolled out of my hammock, my muscles protesting. I flexed my fingers, remembering the way I had channeled Fire Jaguar and the moonlight to transform death's shadow into light. Light was how I was going to fight Li Xul.

Li Xul's power emanated from the dark. He was the night predator, stalking his victims from the shadows as he crept into people's dreams and stole their futures. I had the ability to stop him because I was the Daughter of the Moon and Jaguar. I had the power to cast light into the darkness and the power to hunt in the shadows.

Though I couldn't deny the fear and that doubt slithered through my mind like a serpent. A small voice in the back of my mind whispered that I might not be worthy. Who was I to carry such a title? Someone who'd spent years denying her heritage, dismissing it all as superstition. And yet here I was, with no other option but to put my faith in visions and spirits.

It was time to strategize with Zen.

I stepped outside into bright sunshine, the heat pressing against my skin. The heavy scent of charred wood and ash still hung in the air as I scanned the scorched remains of the village. Insects buzzed incessantly in the surrounding jungle, a constant soundtrack to the tragedy that had unfolded here. Zen was nowhere to be seen, but some large animal had visited us last night, its paw prints clearly visible in the blackened soil. The prints appeared to circle our hut once before disappearing into the jungle.

I crouched down to study them, running my fingers along the edge of one print. The soil was still slightly damp, the impression deep and precise. Something about it made the hair on my arms stand up. Not fear exactly, but awareness of something ancient and powerful having circled our temporary sanctuary. Fire Jaguar's presence stirred within me, a warm pulse of recognition. Had she manifested physically to guard us while we slept? Or was this something else—Zen in his jaguar form? Li Xul? Or another player in this game of gods and spirits I was still learning to understand?

The old me would have looked for a logical explanation—a curious jungle cat, perhaps a local species I wasn't familiar with. But after last night's vision, I was done pretending this was anything but what it was: supernatural magic, ancient and wild.

I straightened, deciding to head to the river for a much needed cleansing embrace of cool water. The air was already heavy with heat and humidity as I made my way down the path to the bathing area, sweat beading on my skin. The calls of tropical birds echoed through the trees, punctuated by the occasional rustling of unseen creatures in the underbrush. When I rounded the final bend, I stopped short.

Zen stood waist-deep in the river, his back to me. Water

droplets caught the sun as they traced paths down the smooth planes of his shoulders causing his tawny skin to glow. My eyes followed the graceful lines of muscle along his back, lingering on the scars of pink new flesh where the jaguar had marked him. They made him look dangerous, untamed—a reminder of who he was and of our wild tryst in Fire Jaguar's cave.

I should have turned around. Should have given him privacy. Instead, I stood frozen, heat rising to my face as desire pooled in my belly. Fire Jaguar stirred within me, responding to my attraction with a warm pulse that only intensified the feeling.

There was something different about this desire—it wasn't just physical attraction, but something deeper, as if our spirits recognized each other. Was this what my mother had meant when she spoke of souls that had known each other across lifetimes, explaining how the moon's energy connected all living things across time and space. I had always nodded politely, while internally rolling my eyes at her New Age nonsense. But I couldn't help but wonder if this was what Zen meant when he said our shadow spirits were linked through my dreams.

"Enjoying the view," Zen asked without turning around, his voice carrying a hint of amusement over the gentle burbling of the river.

My face blazed hotter. "I just got here. I—I wasn't watching." The words tumbled out too quickly to be convincing.

Now he did turn, just enough that I could see his profile and the ghost of a smile playing at his lips. "Of course not." Water rippled around his waist as he shifted. "Would you like me to leave so you can have your turn?"

"No! I mean, yes. I mean—" I took a steadying breath, inhaling the fresh scent of water and river stones. "I'll come back later."

His soft chuckle followed me as I retreated up the path, my skin still tingling with awareness. It wasn't until I was halfway back to the hut, the dense foliage closing around me like a green tunnel, that I realized I was smiling despite my embarrassment. In the midst of all this darkness and danger, there was something oddly comforting about feeling such a normal, human attraction.

Then I remembered the paw prints circling our hut, and my smile faded. Nothing about this situation was normal, and I couldn't afford to allow myself to get distracted—no matter how appealing that distraction might be.

When I returned to the hut, I busied myself organizing our meager supplies, trying not to think about what I'd seen at the river—or more accurately, what I'd felt seeing him there. The sound of footsteps eventually drew my attention to the path. Zen returned, freshly washed, damp tendrils of dark hair curling at the base of his neck. He was carrying something—a large dead bird.

I stared at the limp carcass dangling from his hand, its black and white feathers striking against the blood that tipped some of them. "What is that?"

"Lunch. I thought it might go well with the beans." His tone was casual, as if hunting wild birds with his bare hands was perfectly normal.

"How did you...where did you...I mean... did you catch it?" I stuttered, my eyes glued to the dead bird.

The question that really burned in my mind remained unspoken: had it been human-Zen or jaguar-Zen who had hunted the bird? I pictured him shifting forms in the jungle undergrowth, powerful spotted limbs replacing human ones, amber eyes tracking the bird's movements before pouncing with deadly precision. The image both fascinated and unsettled me.

I resolutely pushed the thought aside. I still hadn't fully processed what it meant that Zen could transform into a jaguar at will. It was easier to compartmentalize—to think of him simply as Zen, the man standing before me, rather than Zen the shapeshifter who blurred the boundaries between human and animal.

"Yes," he replied with a look of smug satisfaction that was decidedly feline. "It was either this or a couple of frogs and a salamander. I figured the bird was the better option."

I wondered how much of the jaguar remained when he was in human form—the heightened senses, the predatory instincts, the connection to his jaguar soul that seemed to run deeper than my own. Part of me wanted to ask, to understand this fundamental aspect of who he was. But another part feared the answers might make it impossible to see him as simply human ever again.

My eyes dropped to the dead bird. He was right. I was hungry, but I wasn't sure I was hungry enough to eat frogs. Not yet anyway. "Do you know how to cook it?"

He shrugged. "I'm sure I can figure it out. Why don't you jump in the river? I'll have this thing roasting by the time you finish up."

With a quick nod, I hurried to the river to bathe, the prospect of clean skin and cool water momentarily overriding my concerns about supernatural beings and upcoming confrontations.

The river's embrace was a balm to my aching muscles and troubled mind. As I submerged myself in the clear water, watching sunlight filter through the canopy above to dance on the rippling surface, I thought about my mother. She had always been drawn to water—rivers, lakes, oceans—saying they were places where the veil between worlds thinned, where the moon's influence could be felt even in daylight. I'd dismissed it as poetic fancy, but now I wondered if she had been sensing something real all along.

My fingers traced the spot on my chest where Nayla's wahy pulsed beneath my skin. What would my sister make of all this? I hoped she'd be proud of me for embracing the very aspects of our heritage she had devoted her career to studying.

I finished bathing, slipping my still damp clothes over my body and made my way back to Rosa's hut.

True to Zen's word, the aroma of roasting food filled my

nostrils as I drew closer to the village clearing, causing my mouth to water. The rich, gamey scent mingled with the smoky smell of the fire.

Zen crouched next to an outdoor firepit. The bird, plucked of its finery, sizzled over glowing embers. He'd spatchcocked the bird and skewered it with two green branches balanced atop the rocks enclosing the firepit. Fat dripped from the cooking meat, hitting the coals with a satisfying hiss.

He looked up as I approached, his golden eyes dancing. "Gourmet dining at its finest. The beans are warm, but the bird needs a few more minutes. Why don't you get a couple of bowls from the hut."

My empty stomach rumbled in anticipation, the smell making me suddenly aware of how little I'd eaten in the past few days. "I can't believe you did all of this. You are so amazing I could kiss you!"

He cocked his head to one side, his amber-colored eyes locking onto mine. "I wouldn't object to that."

Heat rushed to my face as I remembered our last intimate encounter, when Fire Jaguar's power had surged through us both. I turned quickly toward the hut. "Let me get those bowls."

Inside, I took a moment to collect myself, pressing my cool palms against my warm cheeks. *Focus, Niki.* I needed to keep my head clear, especially now that I was beginning to understand what we were up against. The small voice of doubt whispered again: what if I was wrong about all of this? What if I was leading us into danger based on nothing more than hallucinations and coincidences?

But then I felt Fire Jaguar's warmth pulse within me, and Nayla's wahy responded with a flutter of energy that couldn't be dismissed as imagination. Whatever was happening, it was real. Different from anything I'd ever known, but real nonetheless.

When I returned, Zen had pulled the bird from the fire and was carefully dividing it between our bowls. The aroma made my mouth water, but I had more pressing matters to discuss.

"I had a vision last night," I said, accepting my portion. Steam rose from the bowl, carrying the rich scent of roasted meat. "Hun-Came, he was in it. He spoke to me."

Zen's hands stilled. "What do you mean you had a vision."

"Maybe vision isn't the right word. It was more like dream-walking only I wasn't asleep. I think it had something to do with Fire Jaguar. I'm...I'm not sure." I poked at the meat with my fingers, the heat still too intense to eat.

"You went dream-walking with Hun-Came?" His voice was carefully controlled, but I caught the undertone of concern—or was it anger?

"It wasn't exactly dream-walking. It was more like daydream-walking." I laughed weakly at my poor attempt at a joke.

Zen's eyebrows rose. He was not smiling. The brief moment of lightness between us dissolved, replaced by the gravity of what we were facing.

"Now that I think about it. I'm fairly certain that Fire Jaguar put the images in my head. I needed answers. I think she—um—facilitated my meeting with Hun-Came."

He set his bowl down with more force than necessary, a few beans spilling over the edge. His tightly controlled expression unable to mask the fury simmering within him. "How could you not realize how stupid and dangerous that was?"

"I...I was with Fire Jaguar. Under her protection."

I watched fascinated as he fought to master his emotions. The muscle in his jaw flexed as he ground his teeth together. "You need to find a way to bring me into these dreams," he continued, his voice carefully controlled, though I could hear the tension beneath the words. "Whatever you need to do to pull me into these daydreams of yours, you need to do it."

I felt my face flush again, remembering our last shared

dream. "Yeah, because that worked out so well last time."

His eyes darkened. "That was different. You weren't in control because you were tripping."

"I know that," I said, tearing off a piece of meat and putting it in my mouth to avoid his gaze. "And I know what I'm doing."

"No. I don't think you do."

I looked up at him. His eyes pinned me in place with their ferocity. "Niki, dream-walkers have souls that travel where they aren't supposed to. If you're not careful your wahy could become untethered from your body. Permanently!"

The meat I was chewing seemed to lodge in my throat. I managed to choke it down. He was right. I had no idea what I was doing, but that didn't change the fact that I couldn't fight an enemy I didn't know or understand. I'd had no choice but to do what I did.

"I needed to understand Hun-Came, to see what I'm really up against. I was safe. Fire Jaguar was with me. She was protecting me," I insisted stubbornly.

"You're never safe when you dream-walk…" His voice softened as he reached for my hand. "I know you're scared. I know you want to do everything you can to even the odds in our favor. I'm just asking you to find a way to bring me into those dreams. I can help." His eyes caught the sun's light, turning them into pure gold. "Promise me, you won't try this again without me."

I nodded.

"Good." He released my hand. "Now, tell me about your vision."

I related everything I could remember about my encounter with the Mayan god of death.

"He tried to manipulate you," he said when I finished. "To make you question yourself."

"Yes, but I also learned something." I leaned forward, the bowl warming my hands. "I can harness the moon's energy. The full moon is in a few days. That's when my connection to lunar energy will be strongest. If we're going to confront Li Xul, that's when we should do it."

"We'll need to find him first."

"Or let him find us," I countered.

"How do you propose we do that?"

"We go back to Choja q'eq." The words came out firm, certain. "Nayla was right about that place being an outpost for spiritual warfare. The jade pectoral she found—we need to get our hands on it. It's the key to Li Xul's power."

"You're thinking if we find the pectoral, we might be able to break the connection between Li Xul and Hun-Came," Zen stated, nodding slowly. "There's only one problem, we don't know where it is."

"Actually, I do know where it is. Li Xul. He has it. I'm sure of it. If we can get Li Xul to come to us, he'll bring the pectoral. I know he will."

Zen regarded me silently, his expression darkening as he realized what I was suggesting.

"Li Xul wants us. Wants me," I amended. "We need him to bring it to us. It's the only way."

"No." Zen's voice was low but firm, his hands clenching into fists at his sides. "Setting yourself up as bait is not a plan."

"It's the only way. You know it is." I leaned closer to him, my eyes pleading with him to understand. "There will be two of us at Choja q'eq. He won't expect that."

For a moment, neither of us spoke. I could see the conflict in his eyes—the protectiveness warring with the knowledge that I was right. The only sounds were the crackling of the dying fire and the distant calls of birds from the jungle.

After a long moment, Zen nodded, though the tension didn't leave his shoulders. "Fine. But you don't go anywhere or do anything without me. Understood?" His eyes held mine, intense and unwavering. "No more solo dream-walking. Whatever we face, we face together."

The image of the dark energy pulsing from Hun-Came's

cave, the way death itself had reached for my throat floated before my eyes. Zen was right, there was wisdom in not facing that alone. I nodded.

He studied me for a long moment, his expression unreadable. Finally, he sighed. "Good. Now eat your lunch before it gets cold. We've got a lot of planning to do."

We spent the rest of the afternoon preparing supplies for our trek back to Choja q'eq. Zen estimated that it would take two days of hard walking which wouldn't leave us much time to make the necessary arrangements if we were going to confront Li Xul during the full moon.

That night as we climbed into our respective hammocks, the day's heat finally giving way to a cooler breeze that rustled through the thatch overhead, Zen paused and turned to face me. "I've been thinking about how Hun-Came called you 'Daughter of Moon and Jaguar.' You said your father called you his hija de la luna. Could he have been referring to Ix Chel the Mayan goddess of the moon?"

I knew about Ix Chel from my father's stories. The Mayan goddess was both a nurturing mother and a destroyer of worlds. Sometimes she was depicted as a young woman carrying a rabbit representing the crescent moon, other times as an old woman wearing a skirt with crossed bones and a snake on top of her head.

I glanced over at the double spiral painted on the wall, its lines seeming to shift in the flickering light of our small fire. "I think my connection to the moon comes from my mother, not my father."

Nayla and I had grown up with a mother who constantly arranged collections of crystals in patterns according to the moon's phases. She'd wake Nayla and me during lunar eclipses, bundling us in blankets to sit outside and watch the shadow creep across the moon's face. When we were older, she'd taught us to track my own cycles with the waxing and waning of the moon, explaining that women's bodies were naturally attuned to lunar rhythms. All those years, I'd humored her while secretly thinking it was mystical nonsense.

"I know, but what if Ix Chel and the druid moon goddess are one and the same," Zen suggested.

"That doesn't make any sense. How would that even be possible? The Maya and the druids were two very different cultures, living in two different parts of the world at two different time periods. How would the druids even know about Ix Chel?" I couldn't help poking holes in his theory.

"Maybe they didn't have to." Zen's expression was thoughtful. "If you think about it—time and geography mean nothing to supernatural beings."

"What are you talking about?"

"I'm not sure, I'm just trying to piece something together—to understand what we're dealing with. We know that Mayan gods were shapeshifters, so why couldn't they take different forms, different names in different cultures? Ix Chel is known as Cihuacoatl among the Aztecs. Why couldn't she also be the Roman goddess Diana, the Greek Artemis, or Cerridwen of Celtic mythology—all goddesses associated with the moon?"

A chill snaked down my backbone as I pondered Zen's words. My mother had once shown me ancient symbols of the moon goddess from cultures around the world—crescents and spirals that appeared in cave paintings from Europe to the Americas, thousands of years apart. "These are the footprints of the goddess," she'd told me, her eyes bright with conviction. "She has walked with women since the beginning of time."

I let my eyes stray once again to the jaguar and double spiral as I settled deeper into my hammock. The ropes creaked softly with my movement.

I didn't know much about druid religion and what little I did know I'd learned from my mother. She used to tell me that the moon was a powerful symbol of change and the feminine aspect of the divine—not so very different from the Mayan goddess Ix Chel.

"It kind of makes sense," I said slowly, shifting in my

hammock to face him better. The cords swayed with my movement, and I caught a trace of his familiar scent—earthy and something wild I couldn't name. "Gods wouldn't exist without humans to recognize them and worship them. When civilizations fall, gods disappear and become myths. Maybe the myths get transmitted over time to different cultures."

Zen leaned forward, his hammock dipping closer to mine. His amber eyes seemed to catch every bit of light in the room. "Not myths. The gods themselves. History turns gods into myths, but what if these beings simply transform, adapt? Think about it—the Mayan god of the underworld goes by many different names: Hun-Came, Cizin, Kisin, Yum Cimil. Why couldn't he also be Hades, Pluto, Anubis, Satan—all rulers of the underworld in their respective religions? What if the gods of death are all the same supernatural being?"

The double spiral on the wall seemed to pulse in my peripheral vision. My mother's voice echoed in my memory: Balance exists in all things. Light and dark. Life and death. Beginning and end.

The air between us felt charged, heavy with unspoken words. I forced myself to look away from his intense gaze. "Even if you are right, it doesn't change anything. I know what I have to do. I have to stop him. To stop Hun-Came." I took a deep breath, the scent of ash and jungle filling my lungs. "I've been blocking Li Xul from my dreams, but now... now I have to let him in. He needs to know we're going to Choja q'eq."

Zen's hand shot out, catching my wrist. His touch sent electricity racing up my arm. "That's dangerous."

"Everything about this is dangerous," I countered, though I didn't pull away from his grip. "But at least this way, we control when and where we face him."

The concern in his eyes warmed something deep in my chest. He slowly released my wrist, his fingers trailing across my skin. "Then we'll dream-walk together."

CHAPTER TWENTY-SEVEN

I built my dream slowly, deliberately. The ruins of Choja q'eq materialized—first the trenches, the weathered stelae, then the tents, their canvas walls rippling in a cool breeze. Zen padded beside me, his dark fur gleaming like polished obsidian in the sun. At the temple ruins, I called to Fire Jaguar, inviting her ancient power to flood my veins. Heat radiated through me, my eyes closed, and I pictured Li Xul in my mind.

Tongues of flame to twist and coil around Li Xul.

His red-rimmed eyes blaze as he shakes his massive head in snarling fury, flinging ropy strands of saliva that seemed to sizzle where they hit the ground. Beside me, Zen's muscles bunch, as a low threatening growl vibrates through his body. I rest my hand on his back, as much to steady myself as to reassure him.

I stare at the shaman's wary snapping and snarling with rage, and the rush of power is intoxicating. Li Xul is here against his will. I am in control of this dream.

Before I can complete the thought, my dream shatters and I am yanked off my feet, twisting and tumbling as I fall backward into a black void, my stomach lurching with each disorienting spin.

My dizzying plunge ceases with a violent snap that whiplashes my head back. My eyes fly open to absolute stillness as a bone-deep cold creeps up my spine, raising every hair on my body.

Hun-Came's sacred cave.

The glyphs on the rock walls pulse with sickly phosphorescence, casting writhing shadows. A dry clacking fills the cavern, like thousands of teeth chattering in the dark. I turn slowly, horror crawling up my throat as the disarticulated bones lining the cave walls began to move, skittering across the ground like pale spiders before knitting themselves into skeletons.

Hun-Came's laugh scrapes through the air like brittle leaves shaking in a winter wind.

I spin around to face the cenote, anger flaring hot enough to burn away my fear. "What the hell are you doing!"

His skull face splits into a terrible grin. "Tsk tsk. I merely wish to show you... possibilities. What could be yours, if you choose wisely." His skeletal arm rises from the water; a bony finger extends behind me. "Look."

I hesitate, every instinct screaming not to turn my back on him. But something compels me to look. The skeletons have transformed into ghostly figures, translucent flesh hangs loose on their bones, their eyes dark hollows in haunted faces. They stream past me in two silent columns, like a river of lost souls as they march toward the dark waters of the sinkhole.

When I turned back to the cenote, Hun-Came's reflection has vanished. In its place, the blue jade pectoral hangs suspended in the dark water, pulsing with an inner light that makes it seem alive, aware. Hungry. It consumes the strange ghosts slowly disappearing into the water.

"You walk in shadow as well as light." Hun-Came's voice slithers through my mind. "Join with me. I can give you what you seek. I can give you power over life and death."

I feel my sister's wahy beating against my heart like a bird trapped in a cage and my breath catches in my throat.

They appear before me—my father and sister, so real I could almost touch them, floating above the glowing jade pectoral. A deep aching need rises within me. I press a fist against my chest to keep my heart from rupturing.

"Join with me," Hun-Came whispers, his voice honey-sweet poison.

"I can give you everything you desire."

I step toward the jade amulet, unable to tear my eyes from the ghosts of my family. One more step and maybe—

My sister's body suddenly bursts into white flames. I watch, transfixed, as her bones melt and reconfigure themselves into the flaming shape of Fire Jaguar, neck arched, teeth bared. Her roar shatters the darkness, blinding me with a fierce explosion of white light.

I blink. My retinas feel like they've been fried and there is a dull thudding inside of my skull as I try to focus.

I am back in my own dream. The temple ruins of Choja q'eq appear in front of me as Zen presses against my legs, forcing me to step back. He crouches protectively between me and Li Xul, his snarls echoing off the temple walls.

I know he will fight to protect me, but this is not a battle he can win. Zen is no match for Li Xul and the Mayan god of death. This is my fight.

Li Xul bares his teeth, his muscles bunch and he gathers himself to spring—

I ripped us out of the dream, surfacing into consciousness with a gasp, my body shaking with residual terror and something else. Sorrow. Grief. Regret. The vision of my father and my sister have left a terrible aching sense of loss simmering deep within me, as if someone had taken a carving knife to my heart and hollowed out my chest.

I tipped out of my hammock and curled into a fetal position by the fire, a dull thudding ache at the back of my skull. My throat constricted with raw, jagged pain that threatened to tear me apart from the inside. The guilt crashed over me in waves—I had almost given in to Hun-Came. For one sickening moment, I had been willing to betray everything, everyone, for the hollow promise of seeing my dead family again.

Zen gently wrapped his arms around me and pulled me close, cradling me like a cherished child. The tenderness in his touch only made the guilt bite deeper. I didn't deserve comfort. Not after what I'd almost done.

I curled into him nevertheless, hungry for any warmth

that might ease the cold aching emptiness inside me. His heat seeped into me. It undulated outward, warming my torso, my limbs, my fingers, my toes, smoothing away the pain in my head, slowly filling the empty void within me with something else, causing my skin to buzz with awareness.

"Hun-Came pulled me from my dream into his cave," I whispered against his shirt, my voice fractured and thin. "I saw them. My father, my sister—they seemed so real. For a moment I thought..." My voice cracked. "I wanted so badly to reach out and touch them. I almost..." *Betrayed you. Betrayed everyone. Betrayed myself.* The unspoken confession hung in the air between us.

His hand moved to cradle the back of my head, fingers threading gently through my hair. "Hun-Came knew exactly how to tempt you."

I nodded, feeling the steady thump of his heartbeat against my cheek. The rhythm anchored me, gave me something to focus on besides the heart ache that threatened to swallow me whole. "But then my sister...she transformed into Fire Jaguar. How is that possible? What does it mean?"

"I don't know," Zen said softly. His other hand traced slow circles on my back, and I felt some of the tension begin to drain from my muscles. "But whatever connection exists between them, your father and sister found a way to reach you when you needed them most."

I pulled back just enough to look up at him. The light from the fire seemed to dance across his skin and catch in his dark hair. The tenderness in his eyes threatened to break me completely. I needed something else—something to obliterate thought, to drive away the memories of what I'd almost done, to silence the voice inside whispering that I might still fail when it mattered most.

I realized that I wanted this man. Not Fire Jaguar this time. Me. I wanted to be comforted. I wanted to feel safe. I wanted to be cherished and loved. But more than that, I needed to forget—to drown in sensation until there was no room left for grief or guilt or terror.

I leaned in, softly brushing my lips against the base of his throat, feeling his pulse quicken as he gazed down at me, eyes glowing like burnished gold in the firelight.

"Niki," he groaned, the sound vibrating against my lips.

"Any chance you have a condom?" I whispered, desperation edging my voice.

His eyes held mine, his expression turning somber, serious. "Are you sure you want this?"

I nodded, not trusting myself to speak. If I opened my mouth, I might confess everything—my weakness, my fear, my need to use him as a shield against my own thoughts.

He kissed the top of my head and rose to his feet with a slow, feline grace to search through his backpack.

A surprised laugh escaped me. "You keep condoms in the First Aid kit?"

"I bought them in Santilq'ol."

"Feeling sure of yourself, were you?" I asked, one eyebrow raised, grateful for this moment of normalcy.

A slow grin spread across his face. "A guy can hope, can't he?"

I shook my head, a smile on my lips. Normal. That's what this was. A man. A woman. A mutual attraction. No gods or shamans or ghosts. I wanted him to chase away the lingering images from my dream, to help me forget. I wanted normal. I wanted him. I held out my arms. "Yes, he can."

His gaze skittered across the hard-packed dirt floor, a doubtful expression on his face. "Should we try one of the hammocks?"

Now it was my turn to look doubtful. I cast a quick look at the string hammocks hanging from the ceiling. "How would that work exactly?"

His eyes sparked with heat as they raked me from head-to-toe. "I'm not sure, but I'm willing to try."

I patted the ground next to me. "I say we stick with the

floor."

"Your wish is my command." He grabbed the thin blankets from my hammock and with the flair of a Spanish torero, twirled and spread it on the ground.

Fizzing with anticipation, I stood and walked into his open arms. I lifted my free hand to his face, tracing the line of his jaw. His eyes darkened as I surged up on my tiptoes, eliminating the last space between us.

When our lips met, it was soft at first—a whisper of contact that slowly deepened into something more. His arms tightened around me as I wound my fingers into his hair, pulling him closer, harder, desperately seeking to lose myself in him. His hands cupped my buttocks, propelling me with firm but gentle pressure against his hips as he buried his face in my hair. We slowly swayed back and forth, our tongues dancing.

He caught my lower lip between his teeth, then released it, leaving a trail of kisses along my jaw and neck. Liquid heat pooled in my belly, burning away the icy grip of grief and fear. I moaned softly as he slid his hands under my shirt and along my rib cage, his warm breath tickling my neck.

"I think we should take off our clothes," I murmured breathlessly. "Now." My voice was urgent, almost pleading.

He stepped back, a feral glint sparking in his eyes, and in one fluid motion pulled my shirt over my head, before removing his own. I quickly unbuttoned my pants and slid out of them, waiting impatiently for him to do the same.

Firelight danced on his skin, highlighting hard smooth muscles. His amber eyes raked my naked body, simmering with fierce need and the promise of something wild and untamed. He quickly rolled on the condom, and we lay down on the blankets.

I rolled on top of him, groaning with pleasure at the feel of him inside of me, the fullness driving away the hollow emptiness that had threatened to consume me moments before. His hands gripped my hips as I slowly rocked, enjoying the delicious friction. His mouth found my breast, his tongue teasing and sucking, as I groaned with pleasure.

I rode him with increasing urgency, as if trying to outrun the shadows in my mind. Each thrust was both forgetting and remembering—forgetting the nightmare, remembering what it meant to be alive. I ground my hips against his, chasing sensation like salvation, my nails digging into the hard planes of his chest.

"Look at me," he commanded, his voice raw with desire.

I opened my eyes to find his burning into mine, seeing too much. For a moment, I wanted to look away, afraid he would glimpse the desperate need driving me—not just desire, but the frantic attempt to escape from my own thoughts. But the intensity in his gaze held me captive.

"I'm here," he whispered, lifting his hips to meet me, his hands sliding up to cup my face. "I'm not going anywhere."

Something broke open inside me then—not just pleasure, but a dam holding back emotions I couldn't name. I squeezed my thighs and ground myself against him, driving him deeper inside of me, oblivious to everything but my need for release. Each thrust drew us closer to the brink, our bodies slick and hot.

I threw my head back climaxing with a shudder, every nerve in my body sparking like a live wire as I collapsed on top of him. One final juddering thrust, a low rumbling groan of pleasure, and Zen's body quivered beneath me. Eyes closed, we lay together, panting.

After a moment, Zen gently extracted himself from underneath me, cleaning himself up before curling his body around mine and draping a blanket over us. The momentary escape faded, leaving me exposed once more to the reality of what awaited us. I was terrified that I wouldn't be able to resist Hun-Came. I'd come close, too close, to giving in to him.

"When we reach Choja q'eq..." I couldn't finish the sentence. "I'm not sure..." *I'm not sure I'm strong enough. I'm not sure I won't fail.*

"I know." His thumb brushed my cheek, wiping away

tears I hadn't realized were falling. "But you're not alone, Niki. We'll stop him."

"I can't let you fight Li Xul," I interrupted, pressing my palm against his chest. "I'm the one who has to do this. I have to stop Hun-Came."

"You will. We will. You aren't fighting him alone." Zen caught my hand in his, bringing it to his lips. The gentle press of his kiss against my knuckles sent shivers down my spine. The wave of emotion that crashed over me then was overwhelming—fear and gratitude and something deeper I wasn't ready to name. Zen's arms wrapped around me, bare skin against bare skin.

From the corner of my vision, I sensed Fire Jaguar's protective presence, standing like a sentinel at the entrance of the hut. A gentle weight caressed my eyelids and they closed of their own accord as I drifted into sleep, a small part of me still afraid of what dreams might come.

CHAPTER TWENTY-EIGHT

The jungle pressed in around us, no longer merely dense vegetation but something sentient and malevolent. Today the air felt thick, almost viscous, as if the very atmosphere conspired to slow our progress—each breath like breathing through wet cotton. We'd added to our supplies by taking what we needed from Rosa's hut. I shifted the string bag to my other shoulder, grateful for the cloth padding Zen had added, though it did little to ease the deepening ache burrowing into my back.

"Here." Zen lowered his machete, pointing to a fallen log that appeared unnaturally black against the jungle floor. "Let's take a water break." His voice sounded hollow in the dense air, as if the jungle swallowed the edges of his words.

I nodded, happy for the respite. I sat on the log—suppressing a shudder at its damp, yielding texture beneath me—and pulled out one of the leaf-wrapped packages of masa we'd prepared for our hike, handing it to Zen.

A sound like a distant roar ricocheted through the trees, distorting as it bounced between trunks until it resembled something other worldly. We both tensed, scanning the dense foliage.

"It's just a howler monkey," Zen said, but he couldn't

quite mask the wariness in his eyes. A muscle in his jaw twitched. I knew what he was really thinking as he glanced around us—something felt off.

I took a bite of the baked masa, chewing slowly, tasting ash instead of corn. "Are you worried about Li Xul's men finding us?" The name felt dangerous to speak aloud, as if it might summon him.

His amber eyes met mine, flickering with something primal and tense. In that moment, I saw the jaguar beneath his human skin—cornered and ready to fight. "I don't think he'd send someone after us. He knows we're headed to Choja q'eq. But something *is* following us."

Zen gestured to the surrounding vegetation. "Notice how we haven't seen any animals for the past hour? No birds, no monkeys. Even the insects are quiet."

He was right. The jungle had grown uncharacteristically still, save for the way the leaves seemed to whisper even without wind—like a sibilant conversation just below the threshold of comprehension. A vine near my foot twitched, curling toward my ankle with deliberate purpose. I quickly pulled my legs up onto the log, heart skipping as the vine paused, then slowly retreated like a disappointed predator.

The memory of my father and sister's ghostly forms invaded my thoughts. My chest constricted as if bound by invisible ropes, each heartbeat a painful struggle. I looked down at my half-eaten gordita, no longer hungry, the masa now spotted with dark patches that hadn't been there moments before. "If Li Xul is channeling Hun-Came, I don't know how I'm..."

A sudden rustling overhead interrupted me—not the gentle stirring of leaves but violent, intentional movement. We looked up to see the canopy writhing, branches twisting like serpents. Dark shapes slithered through the leaves, occasionally catching the filtered sunlight to reveal matted fur and glinting teeth.

"Time to move," Zen said quietly, his voice tight with controlled fear.

I quickly stuffed the remaining gorditas into my net bag as the nearby trees filled with a dozen red and black beasts, larger than any howler monkeys I'd ever seen—their bodies bloated and misshapen, limbs too long, eyes bulging with an intelligence that was distinctly unmonkey-like. They perched among the branches like a strange flock of vultures, their eyes fixed with unnerving intensity on us, tracking every small movement with synchronized precision.

One of the monkeys—the largest—shook his head, ruffling the heavy fur around his thick neck so that he resembled a lion with a rotting mane. He pulled back his lips to reveal canines that gleamed like yellowed daggers, too large for his mouth. The grimace he offered wasn't just threatening—it was knowing.

Keeping his eyes fixed on the monkeys, Zen slowly slipped on his daypack and reached for the machete. I noticed his hand trembling slightly before his fingers closed around the handle. "Let's back up carefully and edge over to the left. We don't want to scare them, no sudden movements. We do everything slowly. Very slowly."

I acknowledged him with a slight nod of my head, afraid even that small motion might trigger an attack. Heart thundering against my ribs like it wanted to escape my body entirely, I stood and began inching away from the monkeys, my eyes never leaving the tree canopy. The air between us seemed to vibrate with malice.

Several of the monkeys made deep grunting noises. They began to rattle and shake branches at us, creating a cacophony that formed a rhythm that made my skin crawl.

"Keep moving," Zen said softly as the sound of rustling leaves grew louder and more aggressive, the monkeys turning to face us as we passed like tracking sensors. "We'll head that way," he indicated the direction by shifting his eyes to the left. "Don't stop," Zen cautioned. "Just keep moving."

A large red howler monkey suddenly leaped from his perch to another tree directly in front of me—but the movement wasn't quite right. It didn't arc naturally but jerked through the air as if pulled by invisible strings. I clutched my machete with sweaty palms and locked eyes with him. In their depths, I saw something else looking back—something ancient and hungry.

The monkey rocked back and forth in agitation, its movements mechanical, puppeted. It let out a short warning bark that sounded more like the blare of a foghorn than a monkey.

The low guttural roar sent shivers up my spine, ice spreading through my veins despite the tropical heat. "Zen?" My voice shook, barely audible even to myself.

The red howler thrust out his thick neck and bellowed a second warning, setting off a chain reaction among the monkeys until the jungle was filled with the harsh grating bellows, pummeling us with noise—but beneath that sound, I heard words: *"Death walks."*

My eyes darted back and forth as I warily watched the agitated monkeys, now certain they were vessels for something else—Hun-Came's eyes in the jungle, his voice in their unnatural calls.

The loud roaring reached a crescendo as the emboldened animals began to drop from the trees onto the ground surrounding us. Their fur rippled like liquid, bodies reforming as they landed—larger, more dangerous, less monkey and more nightmare.

Zen whirled around to face me, his face pale beneath his tan. "*Run!*"

He raised his machete and charged, slashing at everything in our path. The blade caught the light strangely, leaving phosphorescent trails that glowed in the air with each swing.

The jungle floor buckled and heaved beneath our feet like the skin of some enormous beast. Vines lashed out with deliberate intent, trying to snag our clothes and packs, leaving burning welts where they touched bare skin. The very trees seemed to shift, closing ranks to block our path, trunks grinding against each other with sounds like breaking bones. Roots erupted from the ground, whipping through the air like tentacles, each one tipped with something resembling a mouth.

My lungs burned as we ducked and wove through the vegetative assault. Behind us, something roared—not a howler monkey. This was an unnatural sound that made my bones vibrate with ancient recognition, a sound that existed before humans had words to name their fears.

"This way!" I pulled Zen left, following an instinct that flared hot and urgent in my chest. Fire Jaguar's energy thrummed through my blood, awakening fully now, warming me despite the unnatural chill that had descended. Where my feet touched the ground, tiny flames flickered and died, leaving scorched footprints that made the animated roots recoil with silent screams I could feel in my teeth.

We burst into a small clearing where the assault suddenly ceased, as if we'd crossed an invisible boundary. The jungle went still again, but now the silence felt expectant, watchful—the quiet of an ambush predator moments before it strikes. I doubled over, chest heaving as I gasped for breath, while Zen scanned the tree line, his knuckles white around the machete handle.

I straightened on shaking legs, meeting Zen's gaze. His eyes had changed—gold flecks burning brighter, pupils contracted to slits. "Hun-Came is testing us," I said, my voice stronger than I expected, resonating with Fire Jaguar's power.

A dry rattling sound followed by the echo of jangling bells reminiscent of the death god's laughter rippled through the trees, as if confirming my words. The vegetation at the edges of the clearing withered visibly, leaves blackening and curling as the sound passed through them. Fire Jaguar stirred within me, her presence expanding until I felt my skin might split to contain her fury. I understood now that I wasn't just her chosen proxy—I was a battlefield. A conduit for an ancient conflict that predated human understanding.

Zen's expression was grim, a trickle of blood running from his temple where a branch had caught him. "We need to keep moving." His voice carried the growl of his own wahy now, the jaguar rising closer to the surface.

I readjusted my string bag, wincing as the strap pressed against what felt like bruises blooming across my shoulder. I took a step, muscles protesting. "How much farther to Choja q'eq?"

"If we can maintain this pace and the jungle doesn't try to kill us again?" Zen's attempt at a smile didn't reach his eyes, which remained wary and vigilant. "We should make it by tomorrow afternoon."

I nodded, trying not to think about my stiff aching legs, the gnawing hunger in my belly that felt too sharp to be natural, or what waited for us at Choja q'eq. I focused on putting one foot in front of the other, drawing strength from Zen's solid presence beside me, the warm pulse of Nayla's wahy in my chest and Fire Jaguar's power coursing through my veins, her ancient rage lending me courage.

The jungle watched us go, its malevolent attention prickling against my skin like static before a storm. Tomorrow, we would reach Choja q'eq. Tomorrow, I would face Li Xul and the Mayan god of death.

We set up camp in the quiet clearing, the tree canopy thinning just enough to reveal the sky above. A faint wind stirred the air, rustling the branches, but it did little to shake the strange, creeping feeling that had settled in my bones.

Zen had found a relatively flat area, and we built a small fire that cast flickering shadows against the surrounding vegetation. The flames seemed to dance nervously, as if they too sensed that something was lurking in the trees, watching us.

After we'd eaten, Zen tossed a few leafy green branches onto the flames. "The smoke should help with the bugs. I'll take the first watch."

I nodded; the events of the day etched into my tired muscles and lay down atop the rain poncho. He pulled the blanket over me and I closed my eyes, falling asleep to the buzzing and chirring of millions of insects.

After what seemed like only minutes, Zen gently shook me awake. "You good with keeping watch for a few hours."

I roused myself, nodding groggily. As I slipped out from under the blanket, Zen slid under it, taking my place.

The night air was cool, raising goosebumps on my skin. I poked a stick at our meager fire and edged closer to the heat, a sudden prick of unease setting my sense on alert— the sharp call of an owl. There was a rustling in one of the trees nearby drawing my gaze to the bird. The owl's head swiveled toward me, its eyes reflecting the dying firelight with an unnatural crimson glow. He let out another hoot, sharp and unnatural—Hun-Came's messenger, making sure I'd received his warning.

My heart pounded with dread, and I clenched my fists, willing the fear to subside, my eyes fixed on the bird of prey in the tree. I could feel the whisper from Hun-Came himself, his dark presence lingering on the edges of my awareness. A chill ran down my spine, but I pushed it aside. I would not be cowed by the Mayan god of death.

If Hun-Came thought he could intimidate me, he was in for a surprise. I slid out from under the blanket, grabbed a stick near the fire and threw it at the bird. With one last mocking hoot, Hun-Came's messenger stretched its wings and flew away. I watched it disappear into the darkness.

Law school had taught me more than legal statutes and precedents—it had taught me strategy. The courtroom was its own battlefield where preparation meant survival. Now, facing a far deadlier adversary than any opposing counsel, those lessons seemed even more vital.

Sun Tzu's wisdom echoed in my mind: "If you know the enemy and know yourself, you need not fear the result of a hundred battles." Walking into Choja q'eq blind would be suicide. Li Xul had Hun-Came's power, ancient knowledge, and home field advantage. I needed more than courage and Fire Jaguar's protection—I needed insight into his mind, his weaknesses, his intentions.

The solution crystallized with dangerous clarity. Rosa's words to me echoed inside my head. *"You will wrap yourself in moonlight. You will hide in the trees and slip unseen into the rivers of time. You are the jaguar!"* It was time for me to hunt.

I stood and carefully slipped from our campsite.

Zen's soft breathing was steady, uninterrupted. The moon hung heavy and almost full—perfect for what my mother called Night-knowing, and what my Irish grandmother had named *Taisteal Anam*—soul traveling. I told myself that I wasn't betraying my promise to Zen, that this wasn't dream-walking, it was something else.

My father's Mayan ancestors and my mother's Celtic forebears had both known this truth: the boundaries between minds were thinnest under the light of the full moon. I just needed a moment. One small peek into Li Xul's mind. I needed to know my enemy.

I reached up, pulling the tight braid from my hair, letting the strands fall loose around my shoulders—a ritual as old as time, releasing constraints to free the spirit for wandering. I stood and stepped barefoot into the cool grass, feeling the pulse of the earth beneath me. This connection to soil and stone was the druidic way—drawing power from the land itself.

The air wrapped itself around me, a cold chill rolled down my spine as moonlight caressed my skin. I let the chill of the night air ripple across my skin, sending a wave of energy coursing through my veins. I wasn't sure I had the strength to do this. I wasn't even sure if I could do this. But desperation gnawed at me. The connection had to be made.

The world blurred as I focused all my energy on the moonlight—on its pulse, its rhythm—and I let it wrap around me like a cloak. I called on Ix Chel, the Mayan goddess of the moon, weaver of fates and guardian of childbirth, to guide my path. I invoked Fire Jaguar, asking her strength to protect my shadow soul on its journey.

In my mind's eye, I saw the spiral patterns my grandmother had carved into stones—that matched so strangely with the Mayan glyphs Rosa had drawn in sand. Both spoke of pathways between worlds, of connections across vast distances, of the thinness of the veil between minds.

The air hummed with anticipation, vibrating at the frequency between waking and dreaming, and before I knew it, the earth beneath me had vanished, replaced by a swirling vortex of silver and shadow. The sensation was familiar yet alien—like diving into dark water, feeling it press against every inch of skin, but still being able to breathe.

I was no longer in the clearing.

I was inside Li Xul's mind.

I saw through his eyes. His vision was sharp, intense, the limestone walls around him bathed in a cold, blue jade glow. He stood atop the temple ruins of Choja q'eq, the jade pectoral in his hands. It pulsed with energy, and as my eyes traced its every curve, I felt the heat of it, the power that radiated from it like a drug—strong, intoxicating. It flowed through me, and I could feel it altering me, seeping into my blood like fire.

For a moment, I was him.

I could feel his thoughts, his ambition, the hunger that clawed at his insides. It was more than a desire for power. He wanted to be more. He wanted to be a god. Unstoppable. Invincible.

I felt the rush of it—how it called to every part of me, how it wanted to consume me, too. His feverish craving clung to the edges of my mind. Focus. I had to focus.

The Mayan part of me understood this hunger—the ancient rituals of blood and sacrifice designed to elevate mortals closer to godhood. But the Celtic wisdom in my blood warned of balance, of natural laws that could not be broken without terrible consequence.

The connection began to shift, becoming unstable. Li

Xul was beginning to sense an intruder. I could feel him probing, testing as if he were aware of my presence pushing through the haze of his addiction.

Our connection suddenly shattered like glass. Pain exploded behind my eyes as Li Xul violently ejected me from his consciousness. The silver threads of moonlight that had guided me snapped like guitar strings, each break reverberating through my body with shocking force. I stumbled backward, moonlight still clinging to my skin like spider webs, and crashed into something solid and warm.

"Niki!" Zen's arms caught me before I hit the ground.

My head throbbed. The world tilted and spun as fragments of Li Xul's thoughts clung to my mind—the blue jade pectoral pulsing with promised power, the intoxicating rush of near-godhood, and underneath it all, a desperate hunger that felt uncomfortably familiar. It was the same hunger that had driven Mayan kings to pull still-beating hearts from sacrificial victims, the same hunger that had led Celtic druids to preserve heads of the vanquished in cedar oil—the eternal human desire to transcend death.

"I had to know," I mumbled, trying to focus on Zen's face. "Had to see what we're up against."

His amber eyes blazed with anger and something else—fear maybe.

"I had to see...Li Xul...his thoughts," I stuttered, the words slurring as my consciousness struggled to fully return to my body.

"You promised me you wouldn't go dream-walking alone!"

His anger slammed into me with an almost physical impact as if the residual pain hammering through my skull wasn't enough. I forced air into my lungs; each breath was like inhaling shards of glass. My body was paying the price for what I'd done, but that didn't change what I knew, what I'd seen, what I'd felt. Li Xul wasn't just Hun-Came's chosen vessel anymore. He was becoming something else entirely, and the thought sent ice through my veins despite the humid jungle air.

"He's going to try to use the pectoral to become a god," I said, my voice hoarse as the pain eased. "Not just channel Hun-Came's power—actually transform himself." The words tasted like ash in my mouth. "He thinks he can become a god."

Both sides of my heritage warned against such hubris— the Mayan created myths where gods destroyed imperfect humans and the Celtic tales of mortals struck down for reaching beyond their station. The balance between worlds wasn't meant to be broken this way.

Zen's arms tightened around me. I stood barefoot, shivering in the cold, the surrounding trees silvered by moonlight, the essence of Hun-Came's medallion lingering like smoke in my lungs.

In the distance, an owl called again—three sharp notes that felt like a warning. Or maybe a countdown.

CHAPTER TWENTY-NINE

Li Xul stood motionless in the shadowed chamber, his fingers tracing the images that adorned the cold stone walls. The flickering candlelight cast erratic shadows, as if the very walls themselves whispered forgotten secrets, their echoes tangled with the promise of something ancient—and something deadly.

He could feel it in the air. Her approach.

Niki.

A disturbance in the spiritual current, like a ripple on the surface of a still pond. He'd sensed it for days, an itch at the edges of his awareness—something lurking, growing. At first, he had dismissed it as a phantom sensation, a trick of the mind. But now, with her presence drawing nearer, the truth was undeniable. She was no mere nuisance. No simple intruder. She was a rival.

A girl. A mortal. Yet somehow, she had the audacity to challenge him. To challenge his devotion.

His devotion to Hun-Came was his very blood, a sacred flame that had burned within him for years. Every ritual, every incantation, every drop of blood spilled in the name of the god of death had brought him closer to the divine power he sought. And now—now this girl, this foolish child, threatened everything he had worked for.

She had no place here.

Li Xul's gaze swept across the room, the dim light catching on the dried human skulls hanging from the ceiling. Their empty eye sockets seemed to follow his every movement, judging him, silent witnesses to the sacrifices that had brought him to this point. Obsidian blades lay meticulously arranged on the stone altar, their edges gleaming like dark promises, sharp enough to slice through both flesh and spirit.

The air was thick with the scent of rare pigments—powdered minerals, crushed bone, organic substances mixed into ritual pastes. Some for sacred symbols. Others for... more visceral purposes. The symbols would mark the ritual, bind it, and the blood would feed the god of death himself. It was a ceremony as old as the Mayan civilization, and it would be her blood that would complete it.

Her blood.

He had known from the moment he had first felt her presence that this would be inevitable. She had the power, but her power would be his—consumed, absorbed, transformed into something more. He would prove his worth to Hun-Came. He would show his devotion by offering her as a sacrifice—a living offering, her death sealing his place as the god's chosen vessel.

Li Xul's lips curled into a thin, predatory smile. She was coming. Let her.

He was ready.

CHAPTER THIRTY

The jungle pressed in around us, its dense canopy blotting out the sky as if the earth itself sought to reclaim us. Every step I took felt like an affront to the ancient land, its pulse vibrating beneath my feet, alive with eyes watching. The vines writhed like serpents, the air thick with the scent of decay, wet earth, and something... else. Something older, darker.

My legs ached, my body felt stiff—sore from two nights on the hard ground and yesterday's frantic sprint through the undergrowth. The net bag's string handle dug painfully into the back of my neck, and I rubbed at the spot absentmindedly, feeling the slick perspiration drenching my skin, the oppressive humidity making it seem as if I were breathing under water.

Zen moved ahead, his anger visible in the tense set of his shoulders, his machete cutting through the dense vines with a steady rhythm. The crack and swish of his blade seemed to stir something in the air, the jungle momentarily parting for him, as if acknowledging his presence. It was Fire Jaguar's doing. The spirit god moved with us, a force of nature that cloaked us in protection. Still, there was something about the jungle that made it feel like the trees were watching us, their twisted limbs reaching toward us, the echo of Hun-Came's voice in the rustle of their leaves.

I couldn't shake the feeling that the god of death was here, too—his cold, malevolent gaze following us from the shadows of the jungle, playing with us, like a cat toying with its prey. I could almost feel the weight of his gaze—heavy and suffocating, as if he were savoring every step we took closer to our destination.

I forced my mind to focus on something else. On Zen. On placing one foot in front of the other. Anything that wasn't the oppressive weight of death looming over us. My thoughts circled back to Nayla and my parents.

"You know what you said before—about gods being interchangeable?" I said, breaking the silence between us.

Zen didn't slow his stride, the machete flashing through the air in a practiced arc. "Not interchangeable—the same entity, assuming different forms for different people. They vanish in one time, one place, only to reappear in another."

"Right," I muttered, pushing through the fatigue that made every step a little harder. "Well, I've been thinking about that. I keep hearing this phrase in my head: *There can be no rebirth without death…*"

Zen paused, just for a moment, his eyes flicking to me from over his shoulder. Sweat glistened on the back of his neck, and I could see the taut muscles in his back as he shifted his weight. "I think that's from the *Popol Vuh*—a sacred text of the K'iche' Maya. It's all about duality and the interconnection between life and death and how one can't exist without the other. Creation is fueled by destruction, over and over again. No rebirth without death."

He turned back to his machete work, the blade gleaming like an extension of his own will. "In the silence of darkness lived the gods whose names hold the secrets of creation, of existence and of death." He looked over his shoulder at me. "I read that somewhere. It's not an exact translation, but you get the idea. Death and rebirth. We are the playthings of the gods."

I smiled tentatively at him, unsure whether his angry mood was the result of my dream-walking last night or his concern about what we were going to find at Choja q'eq. "You're right. I can't believe I didn't make the connection with the Popol Vuh."

My father had often shared stories from the Popol Vuh with my sister and I, especially the stories of Hunahpu and Xbalanque, the hero twins. The images of the twins locked inside caves with giant bats and flying knives had populated my nightmares as a child.

The jungle seemed to grow darker, the shadows deepening as if the very earth itself was holding its breath. The vision of Hun-Came and Fire Jaguar locked in their eternal battle filled my mind, the two gods' conflict playing out in endless cycles of the earth and among the beings who inhabit it. Each god fighting for dominion over the other. This war was ancient, born of primordial forces that stretched across centuries, destruction giving rise to creation. If that was what my sister meant by *rebirth*, then what role did I play in it?

Was I just another pawn? Or was there something greater I could do? And Li Xul—his ambition to become a god—what did that mean for me?

"Do you think…" I hesitated, my throat tightening as the weight of the question loomed over me. "Do you think you have to actually die—*literally* die—to be reborn, or is it more like a metaphorical death?"

Zen stopped, his machete pausing mid-swing. He wiped sweat from his brow with the back of his hand, his eyes thoughtful. "Water break?" His voice was steady, but I could sense the fatigue in him, too.

I nodded gratefully, the net bag bumping against my hip as I found a patch of ground to sit on. Zen handed me the water bottle, and I took a long drink, the lukewarm water soothing my parched throat. I passed it back to him, watching as he took his own long pull.

"I don't think it's metaphorical," he said after a beat,

lowering the bottle. "The ancient Maya weren't about symbolism when it came to life and death. For them, genuine human blood nourished the gods. To ensure their survival, to make sure the gods continued to protect them, they made the ultimate sacrifice—real, literal death. Sacrificing humans." He paused, and there was a certain hardness to his gaze as he met my eyes. "If I had to bet, I'd say it's the real thing. Actual death."

A cold shiver rolled down my spine despite the stifling heat. My fingers tingled, and I felt the weight of the jungle's oppressive presence pressing closer, the air growing thick with an invisible threat. Li Xul, with his obsession for power, practiced the old ways. There could be no rebirth without death—but whose death?

I swallowed hard, the sympathetic flutter beneath my ribs tightening painfully. My sister's wahy, a soft but insistent pulse that had always been there, confirmed what I wasn't ready to admit. The answer was written, hidden in the bloodline that connected us. And the jungle seemed to murmur in agreement, the leaves rustling like dark whispers, a reminder that the gods were always listening.

Li Xul's ambition, Hun-Came's game…and me. Caught in the middle, trying to survive a battle between gods. We had less than a few hours journey left to Choja q'eq, and I still had no idea how we were supposed to fight Li Xul.

***

My steps slowed as we neared the archaeological site, dread settling in the pit of my stomach like a heavy stone. The jungle seemed to close in around us, the shadows darker now, as if even the trees were holding their breath.

"We're almost there," Zen murmured, lowering his machete. His voice was low, tight with the same unease I felt. "How do you want to play this?"

I shook my head, the knot in my chest tightening. "I have no idea."

A low murmur of voices reached us through the dense underbrush punctuated by laughter and the metallic scrape of tools against stone. My pulse quickened.

Zen and I exchanged a glance—surprised, uncertain.

He lifted a finger to his lips, motioning for quiet. His eyes narrowed, scanning the jungle ahead. Slowly, deliberately, we began to backtrack, retreating into the thick undergrowth.

"What the hell?" I hissed, keeping my voice as quiet as possible.

"Could be looters," Zen muttered, his expression grim. "Or maybe Li Xul beat us to the site."

The weight of his words pressed down on me. My shoulders sagged, a lump forming in my throat as fear churned inside me. "I don't know what we should do."

Zen's eyes flicked back toward the site, calculating. "First, we need to figure out who's there, how many, and what they're doing. No point in rushing in blind."

He slipped his pack from his shoulders with practiced ease. "I'll take a quick look."

I hesitated for only a moment before replying, "I'll come with you." I didn't want to be left alone.

Zen's eyes held mine for a second, like he was about to protest. But instead, he gave a slight nod. He knew as well as I did that staying apart wasn't an option.

We crept toward the edge of the site, each movement deliberate, silent. The thick foliage offered some cover, but it also made every step feel like we were inches from being discovered. Zen pulled back a branch, just enough to give us a clear view.

My heart skipped a beat when I saw him.

Jake.

There was no mistaking the blue bandana and blonde ponytail. He stood over a trench, leaning on a shovel, laughing with a small group of men. His face still bore the traces of his fight with Zen, swelling and bruising under his eyes and a nose that was no longer perfectly straight.

I scanned the others working at the site. At least a dozen men, some with shovels in hand, others using picks, all moving with practiced efficiency. They were systematically filling in the trenches and excavation pits.

I turned to Zen, eyebrows raised in silent question.

He nodded slightly, his expression unreadable, and motioned for us to retreat.

We withdrew into the thick jungle, careful to stay out of sight. My mind raced, processing what I'd just seen.

"What's going on?" I whispered when we were out of earshot.

"Looks like they're closing up the site for the season," Zen said, his voice low but steady.

"Do you think everyone's here? David, Roman, Alma? Kelling?" I asked the weight of the unknown settling over me.

Zen shrugged, his gaze distant, but he didn't answer right away.

I felt a cold knot form in my stomach. "Shit. That kind of screws up my plan."

Zen's lips twitched, the faintest ghost of a smile. "You have a plan?"

"No," I admitted, a bitter laugh escaping me. "But if I had one, it wouldn't have involved all of these people. I kind of assumed it would be a showdown between Li Xul and me."

"And me," Zen added, his tone dry.

"And you," I agreed, a rueful smile tugging at the corners of my lips despite the tension.

"So now what?" I asked, my voice growing serious again.

"Now we show up," Zen said, a reluctant determination setting in. "If Jake is here, then there's a high probability that Li Xul is close. But first, we need to get our story straight. The less we say, the better." He rolled his shoulders, then hefted his pack, slipping his arms through the straps. "Okay. We'll tell them that after we got stranded on the beach, we found our way back to Imul's village. Left her with her family, then hiked back here. Nothing more."

I nodded. "Agreed." I hesitated, my stomach tightening. "And what about Jake?"

Zen's amber eyes were piercing, serious. "You can't let him know we suspect him." Zen's gaze didn't waver. "And you can't go anywhere with him alone."

"Agreed," I said quietly, swallowing my unease.

I slipped the string handle of my net bag back over my head, so it crossed my chest, the weight of it resting against my hip.

"Ready?" Zen asked, looking down at me, his expression guarded.

I blew out a breath, trying to steady my nerves. "Let's go."

LISA DIETRICH

CHAPTER THIRTY-ONE

"I can't believe it! Pastor Miguel had his entire church scouring the jungle looking for you. How did you manage to find your way back?"

I patted Jake awkwardly on the back before extricating myself from his hug. My eyes flicked to Zen standing stiffly next to me, his expression carefully blank. "We...um went back to the village. With Imul. Then came here. Zen had a compass."

Jake's smile hardened at the mention of Zen's name, his hand instinctively touching the bridge of his nose where a purple-yellow bruise still bloomed. He deliberately positioned himself between us, turning his back to Zen as he draped his arm around my shoulders. "You look wiped out. Let's get you something to drink and eat, then I'll tell the others the good news. It's almost quitting time anyway."

His voice dropped to a near-whisper. "You don't have to stick with him anymore. You're safe now."

I let him shepherd me through the site, watching as he pointedly widened the distance between us and Zen, who trailed silently behind us like a shadow.

"How did you get here?" I asked Jake.

"Pastor Miguel." His eyes flicked toward Zen with

undisguised loathing. "If you two hadn't run off—or if he hadn't dragged you off—you would have saved yourself a trek through the jungle." The emphasis made it clear who Jake blamed.

I shot a quick glance over my shoulder at Zen. His expression was carefully neutral, but the tension between the two men crackled like an electrical current.

Careful to avoid igniting any sparks, I faced forward again. The site was bustling with activity. I counted maybe twenty men of all ages. Several stopped to stare at us as we walked past, most continued working doggedly at their tasks.

"What's going on? Who are all these people?" I asked, my head swiveling from side to side as we wound our way past the piles of dirt and half-filled trenches.

Jake smiled. "Isn't it great? Pastor Miguel brought his congregation here to help us secure the site. Alma, Roman, and David are here too. Kelling isn't able to travel, but we're in contact with him."

I eyed the mounds of loose dirt being systematically dumped into the excavation pits. "Secure the site?"

"The government pulled the excavation permits for the project. This is the last season for us," he said with a casual shrug of his shoulders. "We're making hay while the sun shines and closing up shop as we go."

"Oh." I shot another quick look Zen's way before asking, "When do the permits run out?"

"They've given us ten days." Jake ducked under the thatch roof of the Dining Hall, tugging me along with him. "What can I get you? Gatorade? Water?"

Doña Juana, Maria, and Josefina were busy cooking and preparing plates and bowls of food in the cooking area. My stomach growled at the savory smells wafting from their makeshift kitchen. I offered a friendly wave in their direction. Josefina acknowledged me with a shy smile. Doña Juana raised her dark eyes in my direction and quickly made the sign of the cross as if she were warding off an evil presence.

I dropped my hand and turned away. "Anything would be great," I told Jake before sinking gratefully onto the hard wooden bench. My eyes followed him as he strode toward the coolers. Zen dropped his pack on the ground and settled next to me.

I turned to face him. "He's not here," I whispered. I sounded defeated even to my own ears. "Li Xul isn't here. I was so sure we needed to come back here to face him, but now…" I gestured vaguely. "I think I was wrong," I whispered.

Zen shook his head. "He knows where we are. He'll come."

"Here? The entire village of Santilq'ol is here, not Li Xul."

"He'll come."

Jake returned with one bottle of water and one bottle of Gatorade. He deliberately placed them both in front of me, positioning himself so his back partially blocked Zen from the conversation. "I wasn't sure what you wanted so I brought both."

He glanced over at Zen, his eyes cold. "Sorry, dude. I guess I should have brought one for you." His tone made it clear it was anything but an apology.

"Really, Jake," I said, arching a reproving eyebrow in his direction. I slid the bottle of Gatorade to Zen, before uncapping the bottle of water for myself and guzzling it thirstily.

Jake's jaw tightened as he watched the exchange. He plopped down on the other side of me, sitting close enough that our shoulders touched. "I still can't believe that you're here. Walking out of the jungle like that. It's a friggin miracle." His eyes darted to Zen. "Almost makes me wonder how you managed it."

I rolled my eyes. "Like I said, Zen had a compass."

"Yeah. Whatever." Jake's fingers drummed against the table, his bruised face tense.

The air between the three of us crackled with unspoken hostility. Zen remained impassive, but I could feel the tension radiating from him like heat off sun-baked stone.

"Oh my, god! It's true!"

I was almost bowled over by Alma's fierce hug as she wrapped her arms around me from behind causing me to choke on my water.

"When I heard the men talking about a girl coming out of the jungle, I didn't believe it." Her eyes filled with tears. "I thought that..."

"You thought I might be Nayla," I said, finishing her sentence for her.

She nodded. "Have you found out anything about where she..." Her voice faltered.

"No." The word lodged in my throat like a dry bone. I'd seen my sister's ghost. I carried her wahy in my heart, but I couldn't tell Alma that.

She rested a consoling hand on my shoulder. "Well, I'm glad you're safe." Her eyes flickered between Zen and me. "We were worried about you two. I'm so glad you're safe."

Jake covered his hand with mine. "Ditto."

Alma settled herself on the bench across from me as other people began trickling into the dining area and claiming spaces at the plywood tables.

Roman and David appeared and sat next to Alma. "We heard about what happened out there." Roman sent a quick look in Jake's direction. "We packaged up Enrique's belongings and Jake let the university know the approximate location of his..." he trailed off.

For a brief moment, everyone retreated to a place inside themselves. Each of us paying silent homage to Enrique. Alma looked down at her hands. David cleared his throat. Jake, Roman, and Zen stared unseeing into the distance.

Doña Juana banged a metal spoon on a pan, startling us. With a scraping of chairs and shuffling of feet, the Santiq'ol men lined up, paper plates in hand, as Doña Juana, joined by Maria and Josefina fed the multitudes. The men chatted among themselves as the women filled their plates. I felt like I was taking part in a parish potluck instead of an archaeological excavation.

Pastor Miguel stood to bless the meal. I dutifully folded my hands and bowed my head, though my thoughts and stomach churned with anxiety and dread. My eyes darted around the Dining Hall beneath half-lowered lids, searching desperately for any sign of Li Xul. Though I had no idea what he looked like, something in me—some primal instinct—believed I would know him if I saw him.

The prayer washed over me unheard, drowned by the thundering of my heart. Something was wrong here. Terribly wrong. The cheerful atmosphere, the bustling crowd, the facade of normalcy—it all felt like a thin veneer stretched over something darker. My sister's wahy stirred violently beneath my ribs, a frantic fluttering that made it hard to breathe.

"Are all these people staying at the site?" I asked, my voice tight as I scanned the crowd again, cataloging each unfamiliar face.

Roman and Jake exchanged a loaded glance that made my skin prickle. "Most do, but not all," Roman answered, his tone casual—too casual. "A few of the men leave after this meal and make the hike back to Santilq'ol, but quite a few stay. We've had to shuffle the—uh—sleeping arrangements to accommodate everyone. Not enough tents and cots."

"Exactly how have you 'shuffled' the sleeping arrangements?" Zen asked, his face carefully blank but his voice carrying a dangerous edge.

David, Roman, Jake, and Alma exchanged nervous looks. No one spoke.

With a sigh of exasperation, David rolled his eyes then looked over at Zen. "Josefina and Abram are staying in your tent."

Zen's jaw tightened with an audible click, a muscle jumping beneath his skin. His voice, when it came, was too calm—the inhuman stillness of a dangerous predator before he pounces. "Really. And where are my belongings?"

"We boxed them up and stored them in the field lab," Alma said quickly, her expression apologetic, fingers fidgeting with her napkin. "We weren't sure if...I mean..." She looked down at her hands, leaving the unspoken words hanging in the air: *We weren't sure if you were coming back alive.*

Zen inhaled deeply, his nostrils flaring. I could feel the tension radiating from him, could see the rigid control it took for him to keep his voice cool and calm. "Fine. After we eat, I'll collect my things and move into Alma and Niki's tent."

Alma's head snapped up, eyes widening. "Um...I'm not sure that's..."

"Perfect," I interjected, cutting through the building tension as I stood abruptly, my chair scraping loudly against the floor. "I'm starving. Is anyone else ready to eat?"

The meal passed in a nightmarish blur of faces and voices. Despite my hunger, the food turned to ash in my mouth, each bite a struggle to swallow past the knot of fear in my throat. I mechanically shoveled it in, as Zen sat beside me like a coiled spring, his shoulder pressed against mine.

Li Xul was coming. Or worse—he was already here, hiding behind one of these familiar faces, watching me, waiting. Every laugh sounded hollow, every casual conversation a possible mask for something sinister.

"Niki? Zen?" Pastor Miguel's voice cut through my spiraling thoughts. I flinched, looking up to find him standing beside our table, his smile not quite reaching his eyes. "Could I speak with you for a moment?"

I hesitated, feeling Zen tense beside me. "Sure," I said with a weak smile.

Pastor Miguel's expression was tinged with embarrassment, but something else lurked beneath—something I couldn't quite place. "I wish to apologize to both of you about the confusion with José and Abram. They truly meant no harm."

"Your men stranded us in the middle of the jungle. At gun point," Zen said, his words clipped, his expression hard. "How exactly does that translate into meaning us no harm?"

Pastor Miguel looked at Zen with a gentle smile on his face. "I know it must be hard to understand, and you have every right to be upset. But I hope that you will appreciate that while the members of my flock are good people, hard-working people, they are not sophisticated people. When they saw the helicopters, they became frightened for their families and for me."

"Why?" I asked. "I mean why were they frightened?"

The pastor's gaze shifted back to me. "We've had some difficulties with a local drug trafficker. He is unhappy with my presence in the area. Abram and José wanted only to lighten the boat so they could return to Santilq'ol quickly. Of course, I was upset when I'd heard what they had done. They returned before nightfall to rescue you, but of course you..." His eyes drifted back to Zen. "Both of you had disappeared by then."

"Pastor Miguel was worried sick about you. He organized most of the search parties himself," Jake added, his tone carrying a desperate edge, as if willing me to believe.

"I do hope the both of you forgive Abram and Jose and accept my apology."

Jake, sitting across from me, nodded encouragingly.

I felt cornered by their expectant looks. "Of course," I replied graciously, beside me Zen remained silent.

After our meal, I helped Zen collect his belongings and carry them to my sister's tent. The tension between us and everyone else had created an invisible barrier, isolating us from the others. I could tell that Alma was less than thrilled with the arrangement.

"Wouldn't you be more comfortable sharing with Roman and David?" she suggested, her voice pitched slightly too high as she watched Zen push the cooler to the back of the tent with more force than necessary.

He dropped his sleeping bag on the canvas floor next to

my cot with a heavy thud. "No."

The word was final, brooking no argument.

"It's just that it might get awkward. You know with changing clothes and...um...you know." Her eyes darted between us, fingers twisting the hem of her shirt.

Zen rolled out his sleeping bag. "I'll close my eyes if that makes you feel better but I'm not leaving."

Alma glanced over at me for support. I gave her an apologetic shrug. There was no way Zen was going to leave my side, especially not tonight.

She sighed, shoulders slumping with resignation. "Okay, I guess we're roommates for the night." She looked over at me, forcing brightness into her tone. "I'm going to make a quick run down to the shower before the sun sets. Niki, do you want to come while Zen is setting up his space?"

I grinned, the expression feeling strange on my face after so much tension. "You don't have to ask me twice! Let me grab some clean clothes."

Zen stood abruptly, his expression darkening. "I can finish later."

I rolled my eyes at him. "I think Alma and I can manage to take showers without an escort."

I dug through my sister's clothes before grabbing her shower caddy and a towel while Alma waited patiently for me. When we left, I could feel Zen's eyes boring into my back like twin lasers.

The sun had burned low on the horizon, staining the sky in hues of orange and indigo as Alma and I made our way to the showers. The air was thick with the pungent scent of warm soil, decaying vegetation and wood smoke. The cicadas had already begun their evening symphony, their chirring sound rising and falling in rhythmic waves.

"You go first," Alma had offered graciously, leaning against the wooden post, arms crossed.

I didn't argue. Sweat and dirt clung to my skin like a second layer, and I relished the thought of washing it away. I poured the first bucket over my head, gasping at the chill before lathering my hair and body with quick efficiency. The sensation of clean water sluicing down my back was heavenly.

By the time I stepped out, I felt lighter, refreshed. Alma was waiting, her face unreadable in the fading light.

"Sorry if I took too long," I said, wringing the dampness from my hair.

She shook her head. "You didn't." She paused, gazing at me appraisingly. "I asked you to come to the showers because I wanted to talk to you about something privately."

I frowned, noting the odd tension in her voice. "Talk to me? About what?"

She opened her fist and extended her hand toward me. A delicate pendant lay in her palm, catching the last, dying rays of sunlight. My breath hitched, my heart stuttering inside my chest. A gold triskele, the druid symbol of protection. Nayla's.

My fingers instinctively flew to my own neck. "Where did you get that?" I asked, my throat suddenly dry.

Alma's gaze never wavered. "I found it after you left with Enrique and Jake."

My heart pounded so hard I felt dizzy. "Where? Where did you find it?"

A smile flitted across Alma's face. "I can show you if you like. It's not far."

Doubt gnawed at my gut, but I couldn't say no. I needed to see. I needed to understand what had happened to my sister. I nodded stiffly, feeling as though I were agreeing to something far more significant than a simple walk.

She gave me a small, almost reassuring smile. "Do you mind if I take a quick rinse first?"

I did mind. But what could I say? I forced a nod, watching as she disappeared behind the screen, the sound of water splashing against the ground filling the silence. The pendant burned in my palm, and Nayla's wahy stirred restlessly beneath my ribs.

The sun dipped fully below the horizon, plunging the

jungle into that brief, eerie twilight where shadows lose definition and familiar shapes become alien. The darkness pressed in closer, the air shifting with something unseen, something wrong. The jungle sounds—birds, insects, the rustle of leaves—fell silent one by one, like instruments in an orchestra dropping out until only an uneasy silence remained.

A twig snapped in the underbrush.

I turned sharply, the pendant still clutched in my palm, its edges digging into my skin. My eyes strained against the gathering darkness, searching for movement, for a face, for anything that might explain the mounting sense of dread.

The jungle had gone silent. Completely, utterly silent, as if all living things were holding their breath.

Nayla's wahy fluttered wildly in my chest, like a trapped bird beating its wings against my ribcage. Was it trying to warn me? Or was I just paranoid, seeing threats in every shadow? I pressed my hand against my sternum, feeling the frantic pulsing beneath.

My breath hitched in my throat as Alma stepped out from behind the screen, braiding her still wet hair with practiced movements. Her silhouette was outlined against the deepening blue-black of the sky, her face half in shadow.

I smiled weakly at her, unwilling to admit even to myself how nervous I felt, how every nerve ending seemed to be screaming a warning I couldn't quite understand.

"We can leave our things here and pick them up on the way back," she said, her voice oddly flat, lacking the warmth it had held just minutes before.

I nodded, my fist closing tightly around my sister's necklace. The sharp edges of the pendant bit into the soft flesh of my palm, but I welcomed the pain—it anchored me, kept me present when everything else seemed to be spiraling into unreality. I opened my hand and squeezed it closed again and again. The sharp staccato bursts of pain mimicked the rhythm of Nayla's wahy now beating fiercely beneath my breastbone.

Alma walked a step ahead, leading me toward the ruins with unhurried ease that seemed at odds with the urgency of our mission. I forced myself to focus on the pendant she had given me, the weight of it pressing against my palm, the connection it represented to my lost sister.

"You said you found it after I left with Enrique and Jake," I said, my voice tight with the effort of sounding normal.

She glanced back, her expression unreadable in the fading light. "That's right. Near the pyramid. I knew you'd want to come. I knew you'd want to find out the truth about what happened to Nayla."

We crossed the excavation site, past the half-filled trenches that now looked like open graves in the twilight, and my breath caught in my throat. The ruins loomed before us, bathed in the deep blue of twilight, their ancient stone faces watching us with the patience of millennia. In that moment, they looked less like abandoned buildings and more like sentinels, guardians of secrets that were never meant to be disturbed.

"It's on the far side of the pyramid. This way." Alma skirted the ancient limestone walls only to be instantly swallowed by the trees, the darkness beneath the canopy nearly complete now.

I stopped short, my heart hammering against my ribs.

"I found the necklace right here," Alma's voice called encouragingly from somewhere hidden among the trees. "Oh my, gosh. You need to see this, Niki. This is amazing!"

Thrusting my fear aside, I plunged into the vegetation following the sound of Alma's voice. Branches and vines snapped and twined around each other as if the jungle were folding closed behind me.

"Alma! Where are you?" I called out, my voice tinged with panic.

"Right here." She stood next to the crumbling limestone wall of the pyramid and turned to face me fully, her posture relaxed, almost amused.

My pulse thundered in my ears. "What's going on?"

Alma tilted her head, a slow smile spreading across her face, making her look like a stranger. She took a step closer. "You never suspected, did you?"

Ice slid through my veins freezing me in place. "Suspected? Suspected what?"

She laughed softly. "Poor, Niki. So blind. Just like your sister."

I took a step back, my mind racing. "What are you talking about?"

Her smile deepened. "Li Xul."

"I don't understand?" But even as I said it, understanding was dawning, bitter and horrifying.

"No. I suppose you don't." She regarded me with amusement. "It's been so easy. A comment here. A suggestion there. Asking just the right question. People see and hear what they want to see and hear. I started a rumor about military operations. Mentioned it to one of the men and suddenly everyone knew that the helicopters we were hearing at night were part of a military operation. No one gave it a second thought when one landed at night on our landing field to pick up special cargo."

I stared at her incredulously. "You? You're the one who's been working with Li Xul? But...but Jake had the satellite phone. He was using it to contact Li Xul."

She threw back her head and laughed. "No. I was. After all that ranting and raving, he did about the lost phone, I bet Jake was surprised when he found it in his backpack. I slipped it in before you three left Choja q'eq."

My heart began thumping wildly in my chest. "My sister? That was you?"

A small crease formed between her eyebrows. "Yeah. I made a mistake of suggesting she see Pastor Miguel. When she returned, I could tell that she had become a problem. I drugged her. One of the helicopters arrived at night and took her with them."

My mind was spinning as it tried to make sense of what

Alma was telling me. Any of the graduate students could have stolen the phone, but only Alma shared a tent with my sister. It suddenly became so clear. Alma had access to Nayla and her things. No one would have questioned her version of events. It had been Alma all along, hinting to the others that Nayla had left the site to do research among the villages. Alma insinuating that Nayla had a relationship with both Jake and Zen and cultivating rivalry between them to keep everyone off balance. Alma always quietly making suggestions, playing everyone like a master puppeteer pulling strings.

"Why?" The word came out as barely more than a whisper torn from my throat.

Her eyes glittered with something dark and hungry. "Power. Knowledge. Everything your sister stumbled upon, everything you are too afraid to embrace." She gestured to the cave. "Li Xul promised me what no one else could. A place among the great shamans. The chance to wield real power, not just study it from the sidelines."

For an instant, her mask slipped, and I saw beneath it— not evil, exactly, but a bottomless hunger, a need that could never be satisfied. "You don't understand what it's like," she continued, her voice dropping to an intimate whisper. "To always be the observer, never the participant. To document other people's power while having none of your own. I was tired of watching, Niki. Tired of being nothing."

A rustling sound behind me made my breath hitch. I turned to see a figure emerge from the jungle. Pastor Miguel. I turned to him, relief flooding through me. "Pastor Miguel!"

Then everything suddenly clicked into place with crushing force. Pastor Miguel was Li Xul. He stepped forward, his presence as suffocating as the heat pressing down on my skin. His black eyes fixed on me with something like triumph, but beneath that, something else, something ancient and terrible.

Dread coiled in my gut. I had been so wrong. About

everything. And now, I was trapped.

"You've done well, Alma," he said, voice smooth as silk.

Alma's shoulders squared, pride flickering across her face. "As always." But there was something else there too—a flicker of uncertainty, perhaps even fear.

"You may leave," he ordered Alma, his eyes never leaving my face.

For a moment, I thought Alma might argue, yearning for recognition visible in her expression, but after a moment's hesitation, she acquiesced. Before turning to go, she met my eyes one last time, before disappearing into the darkness and leaving me alone with a monster wearing a man's face.

The jungle darkness pressed in around us. The setting sun cast long shadows through the canopy, turning familiar shapes into looming specters. Nayla's wahy fluttered wildly in my chest. My legs felt weak, unsteady.

Li Xul glanced up at the canopy, peering through the leaves at the quickly darkening sky. "The moon is particularly powerful tonight," he said. "The Maya believe the full moon is when the veil between worlds is at its thinnest—when gods can walk among men."

My blood turned to ice. In that moment, I knew—this was what we'd come back for. This was the confrontation I'd been dreading. But I was alone, separated from Zen, from anyone who might help me. The temple loomed before us, its stepped facade reaching toward the moon like an altar to ancient powers hungry for blood.

The wahy's frantic beating told me everything I needed to know. There would be no escape, no delay. Whatever was meant to happen would happen tonight, beneath this moon, in this sacred, terrible place.

He tilted his head, observing me in the moonlight filtering through the canopy. "I see that you understand." He held out a hand toward me. "Shall we?"

My feet seemed rooted to the ancient stones, every muscle locked in terror. Every instinct screamed at me to run, but where? There was nowhere on earth I could hide from what he represented. My sister's wahy thrummed against my ribs, her warning now a constant pulse of danger.

"This way," he parted the foliage surrounding the base of the pyramid with a gesture that seemed to command the plants themselves, which bent away as if eager to please him.

We skirted the crumbling limestone blocks, pushing our way through the underbrush. His hand pressed against the small of my back, the touch burning through my clothes like dry ice, as he urged me forward. Each step felt like moving deeper into a nightmare from which there would be no waking.

"Stop here."

The pyramid formed a screen, concealing us from view, from any hope of rescue. He pointed to a narrow fissure at the temple's base, choked with vines and hidden in shadow. The opening seemed to breathe, exhaling air that smelled of damp stone, ancient incense, and something metallic that I recognized with instinctive horror—old blood.

"We have your sister to thank for finding this. Hun-Came's sacred chamber. It's where the ancient ones made their offerings to the god of death." His smile didn't reach his eyes, which had grown darker, deeper, like wells into nothingness. "Fitting, don't you think?"

I knew what he meant by offerings. Human sacrifices. My sister's words echoed in my mind: *There can be no rebirth without death.*

"After you," he said, his gentle Pastor Miguel facade cracking further with each passing moment, ancient malice bleeding through. When I didn't move, frozen by terror, he added, "You will soon be reunited with your sister."

The mention of Nayla sent a jolt through me, electric and clarifying. The wahy responded with a surge of fierce protectiveness, and suddenly I knew—this was where I needed to go, despite my terror. This was where answers waited in the darkness. Where my sister's final message would become clear.

I squeezed myself into the passage, the temperature

dropping immediately. The limestone walls pressed close, slick with condensation that felt like cold sweat against my palms. Li Xul followed, his presence at my back making my skin crawl, the hairs on my neck standing on end. The sound of dripping water echoed from somewhere ahead, growing louder as we descended, punctuated by what sounded almost like whispers—countless voices speaking just below the threshold of hearing.

The ancient Maya had built the pyramid of Choja q'eq above a cave, a gateway to the underworld. Each step downward felt like passing through layers of time, descending not just into the earth but into the past, into myth. I followed the path, the same one I'd walked in my dreams—realized now that they hadn't been dreams at all, but visions, messages—until its narrow twisting passageway opened into the chamber.

Li Xul's flashlight created shifting patterns on the dark water of the cenote. The surface was like black glass, reflecting the light like an eye staring up from the underworld. Ancient carvings covered the walls—symbols and glyphs that seemed to writhe in the wavering light, telling stories of gods and death and rebirth. In one, a figure had its heart torn from its chest; in another, a deity rose from the body of a sacrifice, newborn and terrible.

This was Hun-Came's domain. Nayla's wahy trembled beneath my heart, no longer fluttering in panic but pulsing with purpose, with power. This was where the god of death held court in the world of the living, where blood had been spilled for centuries to feed his hunger.

And now Li Xul had brought me here, to complete whatever ritual he'd begun with my sister.

"Beautiful, isn't it?" Li Xul moved past me to stand at the cenote's edge. "The Maya believed these waters were portals to Xibalba—the underworld. They were right, of course." He turned to face me, and in the ghostly light, his features seemed to shift, becoming something ageless and otherworldly. "This is where the boundaries between worlds are thinnest."

I tried to steady my breathing, to think past my terror. "Is this where you killed my sister?"

"Killed her?" He frowned. "Oh, Niki. How very disappointing. You really don't understand, do you?" He actually laughed—a sound that echoed off the chamber walls like breaking glass. "Your sister's death was necessary, yes, but it wasn't the end. It was a beginning." He gestured to the dark water, which rippled though there was no breeze. "Her sacrifice opened the door. Your sacrifice will complete the transformation."

As he spoke, the surface of the cenote began to glow with a sickly greenish light, illuminating the chamber from below. Shadows danced across the carved walls, bringing the ancient scenes of sacrifice and godhood to life. The temperature dropped further, my breath fogging in the air despite the jungle heat just above us.

My sister's wahy pulsed strongly within me. "You're trying to become a god."

"Not trying." His eyes gleamed with an unnatural light, reflecting the glow from the cenote. "Becoming. The old gods are weakening, Niki. They need human belief, human sacrifice, to maintain their power. But I've found a better way. Your sister's death began my ascension. Your death—" He smiled, showing too many teeth, sharp and wrong in a human mouth. "Your death will complete it."

"Why us?" My voice echoed across the water, across time itself. "Why my sister and me?"

"Because of your bloodline. You carry the power of wayob in your blood. Your sister's wahy was the key to opening the portal. Yours—" He took a step toward me, his movements fluid yet somehow wrong, like a puppet with too many joints. "Yours will give me the strength to step through it. To merge with Hun-Came."

The water in the cenote began to churn, the light beneath it pulsing like a heartbeat. My sister's wahy fluttered frantically, and I felt a surge of something—not fear this time, but power. My sister's final gift, perhaps. Or something older, something that lived in my blood, in my lineage, passed down through generations uncounted.

From the water, a mist began to rise, coalescing into shapes—shadowy figures that might have been human once, their eyes hollow pits of darkness. The dead, watching. Waiting.

"There can be no rebirth without death," I whispered, understanding at last what my sister had been trying to tell me. This wasn't about death at all. It was about rebirth—but not Li Xul's. Something else was meant to be reborn here tonight.

Li Xul's expression changed, confidence giving way to uncertainty as the wahy's power began to radiate from my skin, casting its own light in the darkness. "What are you doing?" For the first time, there was fear in his voice.

"My sister didn't die to help you become a god." I took a step forward, feeling the ancient power of the cenote resonating with the wahy's energy, feeling the presence of those who had come before me—not just Nayla, but countless others, a lineage of guardians stretching back to the beginning. "She died to show me how to stop you."

The chamber trembled, water rippling in the cenote as something stirred in its depths. Li Xul's eyes widened as shadows began to coalesce around us—something darker and ancient.

"You can't—" Li Xul started to say, but his words were drowned out by a sound like thunder from below. The war between gods was about to begin again, but this time, I knew my role in it.

I was never meant to be the sacrifice. I was meant to be the weapon.

CHAPTER THIRTY-TWO

The battle erupted on two planes of existence at once. Above the cenote, Fire Jaguar and Hun-Came clashed in a maelstrom of flame and shadow—ancient enemies locked in their eternal dance of destruction and resurrection. The air itself seemed to scream as it tore apart, reality bending at the seams where divinity bled into the mortal world. Armies of shadow warriors attacked, their cries echoing through the chamber like the wails of tortured souls, their obsidian weapons smashing, spearing, and stabbing. Their blood— black as night—splattered across ancient stone, nourishing the warring gods with each crimson droplet.

Below, Li Xul lunged toward me, his fingers digging into my arms like iron talons, breaking skin. Pain lanced through me as he dragged me toward the stone altar, its surface still stained dark with centuries of sacrifice. The stone seemed to pulse beneath the flickering light, hungry for its next offering.

"Your sister fought too," he grunted, his human mask slipping further with each step, skin rippling unnaturally over shifting bone. His eyes blazed with unholy fire. "But in the end, she understood her purpose. As will you."

I struggled against his grip. But he was inhumanly strong,

each finger a vise clamped around my flesh. Terror and rage warred within me, neither winning, both feeding a desperate need to survive. Above us, Fire Jaguar's roar shook the chamber, dust and small stones cascading from the ceiling as Hun-Came manifested fully—a being of smoke and bone, his jade ornaments glowing with sickly green light that cast ghastly shadows across his death-mask face. Their battle cast wild shadows across the cave walls, making the ancient glyphs seem to dance and writhe, telling their own stories of ancient sacrifice and godly appetites.

A different roar echoed through the chamber—closer, more immediate. The sound vibrated through my bones, speaking to something primal in my blood.

Zen burst through the passage, silhouetted for one heart-stopping moment against the darkness beyond. One moment he was human—beautiful, fierce, eyes like burning fire—the next a jaguar darker than shadow, muscle rippling beneath midnight fur. He launched himself at Li Xul with a sound that was part battle cry, part promise of vengeance. The impact tore me free from Li Xul's grasp, sending me sprawling across the slick stone floor, my palms scraping raw against rough stone.

Li Xul's snarl raised the hair on my neck. His body elongated with a series of sickening cracks, bones reforming beneath stretching skin. Fur erupted from his flesh like living darkness taking form. Where the pastor had stood, a jaguar now crouched, its red-rimmed eyes burning with supernatural hatred and ancient hunger.

The two big cats circled each other on the cave floor, muscles coiled tight as springs, while their godly counterparts waged war overhead. Fire Jaguar's flames illuminated the chamber in strobing bursts of gold and crimson, each flash revealing a different aspect of the battle—Zen's teeth snapping at Li Xul's throat, saliva flying in glittering arcs; Hun-Came's skeletal hands grasping for Fire Jaguar's burning heart, the air between them shimmering with heat and power.

I scrambled backward, lungs burning with each ragged breath, searching for anything I could use as a weapon. My hand brushed something cold and sharp—an obsidian blade, ancient but still deadly. My fingers closed around it, and a jolt like electricity shot up my arm. Nayla's wahy surged beneath my ribs, cresting like an ocean wave, drawing my eyes upward to where Hun-Came and Fire Jaguar grappled in a storm of shadow and flame.

The jade pectoral around Li Xul's neck pulsed with the same sickly light that emanated from Hun-Came's spectral form, casting the death god's skeletal face in eerie relief. With each pulse, both god and mortal grew stronger, the connection between them feeding power back and forth like a circuit of malevolence. Zen was being driven back, his midnight fur singed by the dark energy rolling off Li Xul in waves. Above, Fire Jaguar's flames dimmed as Hun-Came's power grew, the fire god's roars becoming desperate, weakening.

Nayla's wahy hammered frantically inside my chest, loud and hard like it might smash open my heart, each beat a desperate plea. Understanding of what I needed to do crashed over me like ice water, clearing the fog of terror.

The obsidian blade felt heavier in my hand, the weight of centuries of ritual sacrifice pressing into my palm. I realized with crystal clarity that I didn't need to break Li Xul.

I needed to break the connection.

I needed to destroy the pectoral—the conduit—the physical link between mortal and divine. Li Xul wasn't trying to replace Hun-Came. They were merging, becoming a hybrid of god and man, each feeding the other's power in an unholy communion.

"Zen!" My voice tore from my throat, raw with desperation. "I need the pectoral!"

Zen's eyes locked with mine for one electric moment. Understanding passed between us without words. He launched himself at Li Xul with renewed fury, his claws ripping across his opponent's chest. Li Xul howled in pain and rage as Zen's teeth closed around the jade amulet, tearing it from his neck with a snap of ancient cord. Li Xul's primal roar of fury bounced off the cavern walls.

My eyes frantically sought the jade pectoral, panic rising in my throat as I scrabbled on my hands and knees desperately searching. Somewhere, it had to be somewhere. Bursts of light and dark filled my vision as I slipped between the physical world and the spirit realm, reality becoming fluid around me. The edges of existence blurred, stone and shadow and light converging and separating like oil on water. I had to find it! Where was it?

A touch like moonlight beneath my skin skittered along my veins, freezing me in place as the chaos swirled around me. Zen's snarls and Li Xul's roars faded, replaced by an odd swaying sensation filling my chest. For a moment, I was both deaf and blind, suspended in the space between heartbeats. I stood perfectly still in the soundless dark, the eye of the storm raging around me, my sister's wahy a guiding star within my chest.

Then I saw it.

It lay on the ground below the stone altar, pulsing with soft blue light like a living thing, each beat in perfect counterpoint to the rhythm of my heart. The same altar where I now knew my sister had died. But where Nayla's death had been taken, mine would be given. I walked toward it with slow, measured steps.

I reached out, brushing my fingers along the smooth stone altar. A prick of something tiptoed along my spine, an ancient awareness taking notice of my presence. My head began to pulse in perfect time with the jade amulet. Short flashes of light fanned across my vision, and I felt him— Hun-Came, ancient and terrible, his presence seeping into my bones like ice water. Our hearts beating to the same rhythm, a drum song of death and rebirth that had played since before the first mortal drew breath.

I placed my hand, palm facing up, across the jade stone. Its cold surface burned against my skin, hungry for what I was about to offer. I lifted the pectoral with reverent fingers and placed it on the altar, its weight far greater than its size should allow.

There can be no rebirth without death.

The truth of it resonated in my blood, in my bones, in the very substance of my soul. But this death would be my choice, not Li Xul's. Where my sister's sacrifice had been stolen, forging Li Xul's connection to Hun-Came through violence, mine would be freely given to sever it. I unlocked the protective wall I'd built around Nayla's wahy and felt her presence surge within me like a tidal wave, understanding at last why she had left this final gift. In death, she had become my guardian; in my sacrifice, I would become her vengeance.

I could not let Li Xul sacrifice me. I could not let Li Xul die. This was about transformation, not destruction—a circle completing itself.

I raised the obsidian knife, its edge catching the pulsing blue light in a dance of shadow and revelation. The blade felt alive in my hand, humming with centuries of sacred purpose, every sacrifice it had ever tasted singing in its volcanic glass. The cut was swift and clean, barely painful at all as I drew it across my wrist. A moment of pressure, then release.

My blood welled up dark and thick, spilling across my skin and onto the stone—carrying the essence of my life force, my intention, my will. Each drop seemed to pulse with its own inner light as it met the jade surface, tiny explosions of power that sent shockwaves through both physical and spiritual planes. The pectoral's blue light flickered like a candle in a storm, then flared brilliantly as the connection between mortal and divine began to unravel.

A deafening crack split the air as reality itself protested what I was doing. Li Xul's howl of rage echoed off the stone walls as he realized his bond with Hun-Came was beginning to dissolve. The cave trembled around us, stone groaning against stone.

With a fierce explosion of light that burned shadows into my vision, the pectoral shattered. Sharp splinters of glowing stone erupted outward like deadly stars, carried on a shockwave that smelled of decay, blood, and the peculiar scent of death itself. The world wobbled and slipped from me as darkness crept in at the edges of my sight.

My sister's wahy, her wings now tinted with golden sunlight, burst from my heart with the force of a thunderclap, taking with it the last of my strength. She spiraled upward through the chaos, trailing light like stardust, her essence merging with my freely given blood.

Behind me, Li Xul's roar of rage turned to one of despair as his power—born of stolen sacrifice—met the stronger force of a gift freely given. My vision blurred, colors fading, but I smiled as my sister's wahy disappeared into the darkness above, carrying with it my final act of defiance. Not an ending, but a transformation. Not a death, but a rebirth of my own choosing.

CHAPTER THIRTY-THREE

Darkness wrapped around me like the primordial waters before creation. No light, no sound—just the void that had existed before the gods spoke the world into being. The ancient texts of the Popol Vuh called this the silent darkness, where consciousness floated untethered before form took shape.

Yet within this nothingness, I existed. A paradox.

Time held no meaning here. I drifted, formless yet aware, in the space between heartbeats. The sacrifice that had severed Li Xul from Hun-Came's grasp should have ended me—completely and utterly. Instead, I lingered in this liminal space, neither among the living nor counted among the dead.

The first sensation to return was touch—the rough texture of hospital sheets beneath my fingertips. Then came smell—antiseptic and the faint scent of roses someone had placed nearby. Sound followed—the steady, rhythmic beeping of monitors, whispered conversations just beyond my reach.

But something else whispered too, something deeper, something that resonated not in my ears but in the hollow of my chest where my heart struggled to remember its purpose.

"You paid the price of passage," the voice murmured, ancient and terrible in its beauty. *"But prices can become investments, little one."*

I knew the voice. Hun-Came. Not as an adversary now, but as something... connected. Intimate in a way that made my skin prickle with both dread and wonder.

My eyelids felt impossibly heavy, as though weighted with obsidian discs like those placed on the eyes of the honored dead. When I finally forced them open, the world appeared different—colors more vibrant, shadows deeper, as though I could now perceive layers of reality previously hidden.

Zen sat beside my bed, his head bowed. Exhaustion had carved new lines into his face, and several days' worth of stubble darkened his jaw. His fingers were intertwined with mine, his thumb absently tracing circles on my palm. He hadn't noticed my awakening.

"The darkness," I whispered, my voice rough from disuse, "it's inside me."

Zen's head snapped up, his eyes wide with disbelief and something close to reverence. "Niki?" he said, my name on his lips was half question, half prayer.

I tried to smile, though it felt strange on my face, as if my muscles had forgotten their purpose.

Relief and wariness battled across his features as he studied me. "There was so much blood. I didn't think...I thought you were going to die."

"I did."

Zen leaned closer, his gaze searching.

I reached up, my movements slow and deliberate, to touch his face. My fingertips left the faintest shimmer on his skin, like frost that vanishes in sunlight. "There can be no rebirth without death."

The voice inside my mind chuckled, sending ripples of cold fire down my spine. Deep within, in the place where my soul had once resided alone, Hun-Came stirred with anticipation.

LISA DIETRICH

A Note to My Readers,

Thank you for joining Niki on her journey through the Guatemalan jungle. When I first set out to write this story, I thought I was simply crafting a romantasy that would blend my love of fantasy and romance with my background in anthropology.

But somewhere along the way, this book surprised me. What emerged wasn't just a story about ancient gods and dangerous love—it became a story about sisters. About the bonds that transcend logic, the fierce protectiveness that drives us into dark jungles both literal and metaphorical, and the lengths we'll go to for the people we love most.

I wrote much of this book thinking about my own sister, who had a wicked sense of humor and would have absolutely roasted me for some of the steamier scenes while secretly loving every page. She won't be able to read this story—cancer took her from us before I could finish it—but I like to think she would have gotten a kick out of seeing our shared love of sarcasm and stubborn determination reflected in these characters.

If this story moved you, made you laugh, or kept you turning pages late into the night, I would be incredibly grateful if you could take a moment to leave a review. Reviews help other readers discover books, and they mean the world to authors like me who are still pinching themselves that people actually want to read the stories we've dreamed up.

Thank you for reading, for believing in the magic of a good story, and for understanding that sometimes the most powerful forces in any world—supernatural or otherwise—are the bonds between the people we love.

With all my gratitude,
Lisa Dietrich

ACKNOWLEDGEMENTS

I owe immense gratitude to my stalwart readers Amy Strommer and Kathy Burke, who have willingly waded through countless drafts of my works-in-progress. Their attention to detail and invaluable input have shaped this story in ways I never could have achieved alone. They are both wonderful writers, and I eagerly await the day when I can read their published novels.

My heartfelt thanks to Charlotte Merryman, whose love of fantasy started me on this writing journey and who genuinely worried about Imul's fate. Sara Kelly deserves recognition for ensuring that the archaeological dig at Choja q'eq was authentically portrayed.

I also must acknowledge Dr. David K. Jordan and my former dissertation committee. My academic training has proven surprisingly useful for writing characters who make questionable life choices in the name of love. I hope they are not too horrified that I have tried to make Pre-Columbian archaeology both educational and inappropriately steamy.

Special thanks to Toni Kelley, my editor, who helped polish my prose and kept my characters from getting hopelessly lost in the jungle. To InkSpell Publishing for taking a chance on an unknown author—thank you for believing in this story.

Finally, I wish to thank my husband, who has supported me through every endeavor, including years of schooling so I could spend my time explaining to people that I was not, in fact, Indiana Jones. Your unwavering belief in my dreams made this book possible.

Sneak Peek at the Stunning Sequel to In the Silence of Darkness

In the Midst of Light

The god of death inside me craved blood.

Blood was the price of life for the ancient Maya. The gods had sacrificed their own blood to shape humanity, and in return, humanity fed them with its blood . Life—Death—Life. A cycle sustained by sacrifice.

The scent of blood coiled through the air, a single drop igniting something primal in my veins. Heat slithered beneath my skin, pooling in my throat, in my fingertips. My tongue pressed against the roof of my mouth as I forced my body to remain still. The feverish compulsion clawed at me—to drink, to drown in the warm, coppery rush of it.

I closed my eyes. Breathed. Fought for control.

"There's a first aid kit in the staff break room," I said, my voice taut.

Stella, our new administrative assistant, frowned at the papercut on her finger. "Thanks." She turned and strode out, still nursing the tiny wound.

A dry, rustling laugh slithered through my skull.

"Weak," Hun-Came murmured. *"You deny what you are, but your body knows the truth."*

I exhaled slowly through my nose. Hun-Came, the Mayan god of death who had haunted me since I'd awoken in a hospital in Guatemala, continued to snicker merrily. I exhaled slowly, pressing the manila folder in front of me as if I could crush his voice beneath legal paperwork. I could not give in to my possession-induced blood cravings. I had to focus.

This was my first real court case.

For two months, I had been working as an attorney for the Global Indigenous Advocacy Alliance, a nonprofit dedicated to defending Indigenous land rights. It had taken everything—student loans, years of study, my own relentless drive—to get here. I should have felt proud. Instead, I was barely holding myself together.

My clients were fighting to enforce a Restrictive Covenant—a legal agreement meant to protect their land from development. The current owners had violated it, blocking access to sacred grounds. The case was a battle between preservation and profit, between those who saw the land as a living entity and those who saw it as real estate.

"They do not understand the weight of the dead," Hun-Came whispered. *"Their ancestors sleep beneath that soil, their bones woven into the roots. They cry for justice."*

I squeezed my eyes shut. "This is about land rights, not death," I muttered.

"Everything is about death, little vessel. All law, all civilization— it exists in defiance of mortality. You cannot escape me by hiding in legal documents."

I returned to my notes, but my hand trembled as I wrote.

My phone buzzed. A text from my boss, Elena: *Telephone conference with clients moved up to 3 PM. Developer's lawyers pushing for early settlement.*

I checked my watch—barely an hour to prepare. The developer had been making aggressive moves to force a low settlement, hoping the Tribal council would take quick cash rather than fight a prolonged legal battle. They didn't know how stubborn I could be.

"How stubborn WE can be," corrected Hun-Came.

ABOUT THE AUTHOR

Lisa Dietrich holds a Ph.D. in Anthropology, which means she's professionally qualified to explain why ancient civilizations are infinitely more interesting than whatever is currently trending on social media. When she's not busy debating the finer points of Pre-Columbian mythology with her extremely patient husband, she writes steamy romance novels.